CURSE OF AL CAPONE'S GOLD

CURSE OF
AL CAPONE'S GOLD

MIKE THOMPSON

FIVE STAR

An imprint of Thomson Gale, a part of The Thomson Corporation

Detroit • New York • San Francisco • New Haven, Conn. • Waterville, Maine • London

THOMSON
＊ ™
GALE

LIBRARY OF CONGRESS CATALOGING-IN-PUBLICATION DATA

Thompson, Mike, ca. 1942–
    Curse of Al Capone's gold / Mike Thompson. — 1st ed.
    p. cm.
    ISBN-13: 978-1-59414-634-3 (alk. paper)
    ISBN-10: 1-59414-634-9 (alk. paper)
    1. Smuggling—North Dakota—Fiction. 2. Prohibition—North Dakota—Fiction. 3. Capone, Al, 1899–1947—Fiction. I. Title.
PS3620.H6839C87 2007
813'.6—dc22   2007035960

First Edition. First Printing: January 2008.

Published in 2008 in conjunction with Tekno Books and Ed Gorman.

Printed in the United States of America on permanent paper
10 9 8 7 6 5 4 3 2 1

"I ask you now, could I, with good conscience, let a man starve? No. Could I, with good conscience, let a man die of thirst? No. Therefore, I consider what I do, a moral service to mankind."

—Guido Salvatore

This book is dedicated to:

My mother, Wanda Thompson, who gave me my first pencil and signed all my rotten report cards.

My good writer friend, Ken Hodgson, who showed me where the door knobs are.

Most of all to my editor, toughest critic, best friend, patient and understanding wife, Ruthie Thompson.

AUTHOR'S NOTES

During prohibition North Dakota was a main traffic artery for illegal liquor being brought into the United States from Canada. North Dakota enacted prohibition in 1889, and it remained in effect until the national repeal of 1933. The three-hundred-plus miles of open border along the Canadian provinces of Manitoba and Saskatchewan were perfect for the development of numerous bootlegging operations. The area where the borders of the two Canadian provinces and North Dakota meet became known as the "three corners." This area was where the American bootlegging contacts met their Canadian counterparts for the delivery of contraband liquor. The border crossing north of Minot, North Dakota, became known as "Whiskey Gap," and the city itself was known as the "gangster capital of the western United States."

The liquor was easily moved from North Dakota to the Twin Cities of Minneapolis and Saint Paul, Minnesota, where it came under the control of people like Isadore Blumfeld, also known as Kidd Cann. The Kidd Cann gang was an extension of the Meyer Lansky crime syndicate out of Miami. It has never been determined if Lansky was working with Capone.

The tighter Manitoba laws caused the liquor industry to blossom along the Saskatchewan border in the city of Yorkton and eventually the liquor company operating out of there became known as *Seagram's*. Saskatchewan had loopholes in their liquor laws which allowed distillers to easily produce products for marketing to the south and it soon became known as the "rum-running capital of the world."

The Bronfman Brothers, in setting up their distillery in York-ton, purchased ten one-thousand-gallon redwood vats for mixing their liquor, a bottling machine capable of filling a thousand bottles an hour, and a labeling machine that would affix two labels on the sides of each bottle and a third label over the cork. They negotiated deals for railroad carloads of sixty-five over-proof ethyl alcohol from Kentucky and Ontario distillers which they used to make Scotch, rye, and bourbon whiskey.

Into one of the one-thousand-gallon vats was poured one hundred gallons of aged rye whiskey, three hundred eighteen gallons of sixty-five overproof alcohol, and three hundred eighty-two gallons of water. This mixture would produce eight hundred gallons of whiskey. After several days of aging it would sell at wholesale, in bulk or bottled, to exporters. Caramel was often added to rye whiskey to bring it to the proper color. A base of dark-colored Scotch was used to give the Scotch whiskey a trace of its peat smoke taste. Rum caramel and blackstrap molasses were added to straight alcohol, and then thinned with water to make passable imitation rum.

The bootleg culture had a great effect on the corruption of local citizens and governments. "Under-the-table" money became normal operating procedure in several communities.

Bootleg whiskey, like income taxes, made criminals of many honest men.

CHAPTER ONE

May 1923

"Do you boys have any ideas about how much money those damned wops are making running this booze into and through North Dakota?" Andy Larson asked, waving a partial bottle of whiskey above the bonfire. Yellow lights danced on his dark eyes, and his grim face was aged beyond his twenty-three years. He was tall and thin, and his short black hair and thick mustache were flecked with gray. The light reflected off the bottle as he looked around at the others and shook his head. "You don't have a clue, do you?" He took a long drink and passed the nearly empty bottle to Billy Nestoss.

"Well, I know it's a whole damned lot more cash than I'm making at the lumberyard," Nestoss answered before taking a drink and passing the bottle on to Bert Garske.

"What are you making at the lumberyard, Billy?" Larson asked. "Twenty, twenty-five bucks a week?"

Nestoss nodded. "If I work a full sixty hours." Billy was short and stocky, with piercing blue eyes and long brown hair.

"My cousin, Rod, was making more'n that driving a truck down to Bismarck and back up to the three corners," Larson said. "He was paid a nickel a mile to drive a truck loaded with some damned wop's illegal booze. They even paid him the same to drive it back empty."

"How come he ain't doin' that anymore?" Nestoss asked.

"About three weeks ago he dropped a case of whiskey on his

11

foot and broke a couple of bones in it. He can't work the pedals to drive. Now he just sits around and bitches about the price of whiskey and how life ain't fair."

Bert Garske shook his head after he held the bottle up toward the fire to judge how much whiskey was still in it. "This bottle ain't gonna last too much longer at the rate you boys're suckin' it down," he muttered, took a drink, and passed it to his identical twin brother, Mike. The Garske brothers were tall and thin with sad blue eyes, cropped blond hair, and short, fuzzy mustaches.

Mike took a long swallow and passed the bottle to the last man in the circle, Louie Bergavin, who tipped it up, drained it, laughed, and passed it on to Larson.

Bergavin, who worked in his father's blacksmith shop, was tall and powerfully built. His face was lined and had the darkness that comes from working long hours in a hot, smoky, sooty atmosphere. His hair was dark, and a large walrus mustache covered most of his mouth. His squinty brown eyes had a know-it-all twinkle.

"I told ya it wouldn't last very long," Bert Garske said as he pulled out his tobacco bag and began to roll a cigarette. "Hell, it barely made it around the circle five times."

"Those wops are taking millions running their whiskey through here," Andy Larson said, in answer to his own question as he swung the empty bottle in the air. "We're paying three dollars a bottle for this stuff, and it's coming across the Canadian border, two hundred miles north of here where they're making it. There's one hell of a profit in whiskey. I'm told it costs them less than seventy-five cents to distill, bottle, and ship a single quart bottle. They wholesale it to the speakeasies and blind pigs for anywhere from two to three bucks a bottle. We have to buy it for three to four and a half bucks. There's about thirty shots to a bottle, and in a bar we pay two bits for one measly shot. That's making at least five and a half bucks a bottle before they add water and tobacco juice or who knows what else they do to water it down."

"So what's yer point?" Bert Garske asked, as he used a branch from the fire to light his cigarette. "If we want the booze, we gotta pay for it, don't we?"

"There's a damned big difference between paying a fair price and getting screwed," Larson declared. "I got a plan to steal some of this stuff." He emphasized his point as he swung the empty bottle again and then tossed it back over his head into the darkness. "We're gonna cut out the middle man for our drinking and make a profit of our own."

"Stealing from the guineas ain't the smartest thing a man can do. It's hard on your health," Louie Bergavin said. "Those bastards are meaner than cops when it comes to handing out their own justice. You just don't mess with those people. Look at what happened to the three guys from Minot when they tried to hijack that truckload of booze."

"Yeah, they left the shot-up car and bodies on the street to show what would happen to anyone else who tried it," Billy Nestoss said.

"You try to steal a truckload of whiskey, Andy, I'll be sure to send a nice bouquet of flowers to yer grieving mother," Mike Garske said and the others all laughed.

"From what I read in the papers, those guys were stupid," Larson said. "They tried to force the truck off the road without checking out how many men were in it, if there was a backup car, and what they had for guns. When the guard in the truck opened up with that Tommy gun, those poor bastards didn't have a chance."

"Those Tommy guns can chew up a car," Mike Garske added. "Then there was them boys what stole a couple of barrels of whiskey and tried to sell it to the wrong bar owner. He told the wop they'd stole it from, and then they got paid in lead instead of cash. Those guys running the blind pigs and speakeasies are all watching out for each other."

"I ain't wonderin', but just out of curiosity, Andy, what's your plan?" Nestoss asked.

Larson slowly rose to his feet and looked around at the four other men. "We ain't gonna be stupid like those guys that're dead. This is gonna be planned out like a military operation. We're gonna study it all real careful before we make our move. Those of you that're afraid can leave now. Those who want to get a little free whiskey and possibly make some big money can stay."

"Andy," Mike Garske said, looking up at Larson. "Me and Bert are farmers; Billy works in a lumberyard, and Louie's a damned blacksmith. We ain't geared up to go after these professional . . . ah . . . gunners. You maybe, but not us. You know what I mean?"

"And we ain't crooks," Louie Bergavin added. "We've never done anything against the law. I mean really against the law. We've stolen some small stuff. All kids do. We got drunk when we were underage, but we never stole anything big as a truck of whiskey."

Andy Larson raised his hands and laced his fingers behind his head as he thought.

"I've never thought stealing from crooks made me a crook," he said slowly. "Granted, it is dangerous because those people think they're God and we've seen they can be pretty damned mean. Maybe you're right and I shouldn't involve you boys in this. Forget it." He turned and walked off into the darkness.

"Hey, Andy, come back!" Billy Nestoss shouted. "We ain't against makin' some money an' gettin' free whiskey. Come on back an' tell us what you've got in mind. We can't get shot for listenin'."

Andy Larson returned to the ring of firelight, carrying a brown paper bag. "Okay, I told you this was going to be carefully planned. Anybody who doesn't want to get in on it can walk away. None of you are obligated to go along with me," Larson answered. "If I get it all planned out and it doesn't look like it'll work, we're not gonna to do it. Getting killed isn't in the plan."

The men sitting around the fire looked questioningly at each other, then one by one rose to their feet.

"I'd say we're all in on this, Andy," Bill Nestoss said, and stuck out his hand. "I figure since you're a veteran with military experience, you'll be good at the military kinda planning you were talkin' about."

"What with them medals you brought back from the war," Bert Garske said, "I agree. You're the man to lead us. We're all just sorry we weren't old enough to go in the army during the war like you did."

Larson looked at the small circle of his friends. "War isn't anything a man should have to go through. I'm glad that none of you were there." He shook Nestoss' hand and smiled. "But now I'm glad to have you with me," he said as he opened the bag and brought out a new bottle of whiskey. "Let's drink to it."

CHAPTER TWO

The raspy sound of his secretary's voice from the wooden intercom box on his desk startled William Werner. "Mister Salvatore is here to see you." He reached up, pushed a button, and leaned toward the box. "Send him in."

Werner stood up, wiped a hand across his slicked down hair, straightened his tie, and pulled his gray silk vest into place. He was a wealthy man who enjoyed the best of things his hard work had brought him. He adjusted his pince-nez glasses, worn in honor of the past president Theodore Roosevelt, as he walked around his desk and put a smile on his face just as the door opened.

A short, swarthy man dressed in a natty black pin-striped double-breasted suit entered. The corners of his eyes crinkled and a row of perfect white teeth appeared under his pencil-thin mustache as he smiled. "It's good to see you, William," he said, sticking out his hand.

"Guido, the pleasure is indeed all mine," Werner answered, pumping the man's hand. "It's been a long time since we've done any shipping for you."

Salvatore nodded. "Yes, William, I'm sorry to admit we haven't been giving you any business lately because we've been using the northern route from Minot to Minneapolis. That is about to change. People I know in Minneapolis report rumors of Kidd Cann possibly planning to hit my trucks on those routes. He buys from me in good quantities in the city, but I don't trust him. If he steals liquor from me, it makes his profit margin that much higher. It cuts out a middle man and he makes better deals with his sales."

"Are the northern routes the only ones that might be dangerous?" Werner asked. "I'm not willing to put my trucks into some sort of a shooting gallery. Those vehicles cost a lot of money these days, whereas I can replace men for next to nothing."

"Not to worry. He won't take a chance on hitting vehicles on the main highways, and he won't venture into Dakota to try anything on the trucks coming down out of Canada."

"I'm going to trust you on that, Guido."

"It's good that you see I'm a man of my word, William. I can get your trucks into the city and keep moving my drop-off and pick-up locations. Kidd Cann won't know how my whiskey is getting in, and he won't mess with me in the city because he knows about my connections in New York and Chicago. The bastard's too smart to take any chances on irritating Uncle Alphonse."

"I'm glad to know that we'll be doing business again."

Salvatore nodded and smiled. "I'll have one truckload of whiskey coming down here from three corners every Monday, Wednesday, and Friday. I've paid off all the necessary people between the border and here. It's surprising what you can get for a case of whiskey these days. We'll be bringing the whiskey down in three hay trucks. The one in the middle has the whiskey. The other two are decoys. We'll switch the cargo to your distinctive company trucks for the trip to Minneapolis. I'd like you to stack something in the back of the truck so if anybody gets nosey they'll see it's just a load of legitimate merchandise."

"My old horse barns are a perfect place to switch the loads. I only use them for storage these days. Trucks of hay going into the horse barns, what the hell? I'm bringing a large order of doors in from Montana tomorrow. They'll make a perfect shield," Werner said and smiled. "As a matter of fact, I'll make a deal to buy part of this order for myself, and we can leave them on the trucks and use them over and over between here and Minneapolis. We'll be using my drivers and your guards?"

"Of course. My men are loyal. I trust them, and they're not afraid to shoot anyone who interferes with us. I'm not taking any chances of being hijacked. I have a guard, with a rifle or a Tommy gun, riding on the whiskey truck. I've put shotguns in the other two trucks, and I'll see your drivers get automatic pistols. So far, there's nothing to be worried about over here in Dakota. Just between you and me, these loads will average about three hundred and eighty cases. Twelve bottles to a case. The distillery up in Yorkton is working twenty-four hours a day, seven days a week. That much whiskey, depending on the label, can be worth over thirteen thousand dollars a load by the time it hits the streets."

Werner's eyes widened, and he whistled. "I understand about the guards. I'll make sure the drivers can handle a gun if necessary. When should I expect the first of your trucks?"

"I'll have the first of them here by tomorrow evening," Salvatore answered. "I'm willing to pay two hundred dollars a load, and I know that's more than double the going freight rate. Besides that, I'll throw in a case of whiskey for each truck."

"That sounds like one hell of a sweet deal to me, Guido," Werner said, smiling and proffering his hand.

Salvatore shook Werner's hand, put his hat on his head and smoothed the brim. "Like I said, it's a pleasure to be doing business with you again, William."

CHAPTER THREE

June 1923

Andy Larson leaned against the hood of his truck, lowered his binoculars, and smiled.

"That middle hay truck is loaded with whiskey," he said.

"What makes you so sure?" Billy Nestoss asked, as he slowly lowered his binoculars. "It looks just like the one in front an' in back."

"It rides lower and doesn't bounce as much. It's got a heavier load. It's either whiskey or a damned fat driver."

"How do you know it's not beer?"

"There's not enough profit on a keg of beer to haul it that far. A keg of beer has about seventy-two bottles in it. A bottle sells for thirty-five cents or three for a dollar. The saloonkeeper makes about six cents a bottle. With waste, he's clearing about four bucks a keg. You start whittling things like hauling off the profit end, and he's gonna have to start raising the price of the beer. People are bitching now about three for a dollar."

"I understand," Billy said. "We been watching all day and you're sure that's the first truck of whiskey today?"

"We saw those three trucks going north just after sunup. Nobody's gonna take whiskey up north. It's about two and a half hours up to three corners from here. The weather's been good, so the roads are packed and they make good time. It starts to rain, and those roads north of Minot turn into pig shit. Some of the farmers up there make damned good money hooking their horses onto trucks or cars full of whiskey and yanking them out of the mud. Figure it takes an hour or so to load the trucks, pile on the hay, tie it down, and drive back past here." Larson pulled a watch from his pocket and looked at it. "That'd mean about six to seven hours. It's two-thirty right now. Those trucks are right on schedule."

"You're sure those are the same three trucks?" Nestoss asked.

Larson gave a snort of derision as he dropped the watch back into his pocket. "I've been watching the same thing for over a month now. They bring a truck of whiskey down here in the middle of a convoy every Monday, Wednesday, and Friday. Get in the truck, and we'll follow them to Bismarck."

Billy Nestoss smiled and quickly climbed into the truck. "I've heard the feds watch these highways pretty close."

"They're watching up between Minot and the border. These are state highways, and the feds don't want to go through all the bullshit to patrol these. It's up to the local law and I'm told there's a lot of money passed under the table to keep the booze moving."

Larson started the engine, put the vehicle in gear, and drove out of the trees down to the main highway. "One more thing. The middle truck was the only one with two men in it. The passenger is the guard. He's probably got a Tommy gun and knows how to use it. I've started bringing each of you along on different days so you can see how this whole whiskey delivery thing goes. You need to understand their operation," Larson explained. "I can tell you they're going to the old Werner horse barns on the south side of town. As a matter of fact, we'll pass them and go to the barns to wait. This'll be a good day to get inside and see what they do with the whiskey once they have it there. I know which barn they're going to and I found a way to get into the loft from the outside."

Two hours later Billy Nestoss tapped the bottom of Larson's

shoe. "Hey Andy, they're here," he whispered.

Larson sat up, yawned and stretched. "I heard 'em."

The barn, almost a block long, was one of two left over from the days when Werner Transportation was a horse-drawn freight wagon business. Two large double doors opened on the center of the building for easy movement of wagons and horses. One end of the ground floor had a line of stalls down each side and the other end was a large open area for storage and working on wagons. For fire safety reasons, the blacksmith shop was in an adjacent building. The hayloft where the two men waited was one big room full of old hay and great dusty gray spider webs stretching across openings. Pigeons cooed, and sparrows and other small birds fluttered and glided between the rafters. Small beams of light shone down through holes in the roof, and the slightest movement raised dust from the hay that magnified the light beams.

Larson moved quickly to the edge of the loft to snuggle down in the hay to watch the activity below.

The three trucks loaded with hay drove up to the front of the building and stopped. The man in the lead truck honked the horn, and a man came out of the office in the corner of the barn. He waved and the lead truck drove through the barn and parked, blocking the rear door. The middle truck drove into the barn and stopped. A blue truck embellished with *Werner Transportation* painted in large yellow letters backed into the barn and stopped immediately behind the middle truck. The two men in the cab got out of the vehicle and joined the man from the office. The rear hay truck drove through the open front door and stopped. The drivers of the two outside trucks pulled short-barreled pump shotguns from under their seats and positioned themselves in the doorways of the barn. The passenger from the middle truck stepped out carrying a lever action rifle.

"I guess I was wrong about the Tommy gun," Larson whispered.

"They sure as hell had them up in Minot," Nestoss noted.

The two men from the middle vehicle joined the other two men and listened as the man from the office talked, pointing at the vehicles.

Billy Nestoss suddenly put his hands to his face to cover a sneeze.

The man with the rifle pointed it up at the loft and said something.

"Get down and stay down," Larson whispered as he rolled over onto his back and brought a large automatic pistol from under his shirt.

Billy Nestoss' eyes grew wide with the surprise of seeing the pistol in Larson's hand.

Larson put his finger to his lips and threw dusty hay over Nestoss as he burrowed down. Satisfied Billy was well covered, he rolled over, slowly brought his head up, and glanced down into the barn.

The man who had pointed up at the loft was walking to the ladder that reached up to it.

Larson ducked his head and moved so the pistol was pointed at the top of the ladder. "Billy," he whispered. "If any shooting starts, you make a run for the back way we got in here. I'll shoot two shots. One over his head and the other one close into the hay. That should start a fire and that'll keep them busy. The men at the doors will come running in and you can dive into the hay down in the yard and watch for a chance to get away. They'll come after me. Got that?"

"I'm okay, Andy," Billy whispered. "Do what you've gotta do." He put his hands over his face and pushed down into the hay, stifling another sneeze.

The man from the office shouted, "Damnit, Chuck, I told

you there's nothing up there! This old place is full of strange noises. The damned birds can be loud as hell. You're just looking for an excuse to do something besides load whiskey. Now get over here and help us get this stuff moved."

The man muttered a string of curses as he climbed down the ladder and walked across the barn to join the others.

Larson flopped down on his back in the hay and let out a long breath. "Damn, that was close."

"I'm sorry, Andy," Billy whispered as he crawled back up to join Larson.

Larson nodded and pointed to the action below.

The men untied the ropes over the top and the sides of the hay and began to roll back a large canvas with hay tied and sewn onto it.

"Pretty damned clever," Larson whispered.

The man who had attempted to go up into the loft kept looking up at it and scowling.

"Let's get out of here," Larson whispered. "We've seen enough for today."

"You didn't tell me you had a gun," Nestoss said as Larson drove out onto the street.

"So? I've always got one."

"Well, I might have needed one."

"Were you gonna shoot the guy coming up the ladder?"

"I don't know. Maybe . . ."

"That's why I didn't give you a gun. Hell, you mighta shot me."

Nestoss nodded and glanced down at his hands. "Yeah, I guess you're right."

"C'mon, let's get outta here," Larson said, giving Nestoss a light punch on the shoulder. "I gotta get cleaned up and go to work tonight."

CHAPTER FOUR

July 1923

Billy Nestoss, Bert and Mike Garske, and Louie Bergavin looked down at the map spread on the table before them.

Andy Larson ran his finger along the red line that was the main highway from the Canadian border to Bismarck, North Dakota. "Okay, here's my plan. Any time anyone wants to add something or has a question, feel free to jump in. We've studied this whiskey run from the border to Bismarck on this road for three months now. We know for sure there's more than twelve thousand dollars' worth of whiskey on a truck that passes through here three days a week. We also know we can't sell any of that whiskey right away. They'll be looking hard and have a reward out for both the whiskey and us. I figure if we wait about six months, we can take it down into South Dakota and get a good price for it."

"Where are we gonna hide a truckload of whiskey for six months?" Louie Bergavin asked.

"We're not gonna hide the truck," Larson answered. "We're gonna unload it and run the truck into the Missouri River."

"Okay," Bergavin said. "Where are we gonna hide all that whiskey then?"

"I'll get to that later," Larson answered. "We know there's one armed guard in the middle truck with the whiskey. All three of the drivers have sawed-off pump shotguns under or behind the seat but they can't get to them unless they open the door.

The guard carries a lever action rifle. Everybody agree?"

All of the men nodded and murmured an agreement.

"All right." Larson looked down and tapped the map. "There's a series of curves and a long hill here between Washburn and Wilton. That's where we're gonna take the truck."

"You make it seem pretty damned easy," Mike Garske said.

"I'm not done yet," Larson answered. "We know they'll be suspicious and on guard the minute they see anything unusual along the highway. We're gonna start having a work gang along that section of highway three days a week when they pass. We give 'em a wave when they go by, and after about the third or fourth time they pass they won't pay a bit of attention to us or what we're doing. A couple weeks of that, we'll take 'em."

"What kinda work party you talkin' about?" Billy Nestoss asked.

"Filling holes, making road repairs," Larson answered. "They come back through there at about the same time every trip. Somewhere between two and three o'clock in the afternoon. We'll only have to be there at that time. We'll have a truck, wheelbarrows, shovels, and stuff like that. We'll start our road work at the bottom of the hill and work our way up so we'll be at the top of the hill when we take them."

"What about other cars?" Bert Garske asked. "What if somebody drives up when we're heisting the truck?"

"So far I haven't seen much traffic that time of day. But I'm thinking about putting up a roadblock saying the road is temporarily closed for repair at the bottom of the hill after they pass. I'll decide," Larson answered.

"What if the highway patrol or the sheriff comes along and wants to know what we're doin'?" Mike Garske asked.

"I've noticed there's no sign of any lawmen during the time they're making that whiskey drive," Larson answered, with a smile.

"They've all been paid off," Bert Garske exclaimed.

Andy Larson smiled and nodded. "Exactly."

"Okay, they'll be used to us being there. Then what?" Billy Nestoss asked.

"The trucks don't have much speed when they get to the top of that hill," Larson continued. "Two of you'll be standing in the ditch and shoot out a front tire on the first and third truck. Then you raise the shotgun and cover the driver."

"They'll see our faces," Mike Garske argued.

"You'll have a bandana around your neck. Pull it up just before you turn and shoot out the tires. They won't be able to see your face. In the meantime, whenever they pass don't let them get a good look at your face. Everyone will wear floppy hats or caps and plain worker-type clothes that'll all go in the fire after the hit's done."

"You sure got this figured down to a gnat's ass," Louie Bergavin said. "What about the guard with the rifle?"

"He's mine," Larson answered. "I'll be in position to cover the middle truck when you've stopped the other two. That rifle ain't gonna be all that easy for him to get it up to where he can get a shot at me. If I have to, I'll shoot him."

The other men looked at each other to see if any one of them had another question.

"You're really gonna shoot him?" Mike Garske asked.

"I don't want to, but I killed in the war, so I know I can do it. I guess it's up to him."

They all studied Larson's face for a minute, trying to decide if he was telling the truth.

"Okay, what're we gonna do with them guys in the trucks?" Nestoss asked.

"We get 'em out of the trucks on the ground and tie 'em up," Larson answered. "We set fire to the hay on the other two trucks and drive away."

"You're makin' this sound too easy," Billy Nestoss said.

"If we follow the plan, it *will* be easy. Hell, how'd a bunch of good old country boys ever hatch up a plan like this?" Larson asked and grinned.

"Okay, now we got the whiskey," Mike Garske said. "What next?"

"We drive down through Wilton and take the river road to Bismarck. Then we cross to the Mandan side and head north to the edge of the Blackstead ranch. My grandpa left me a little slice of land up there along the river. There's a sandstone dug-out cabin he built into the side of a hill when he homesteaded back in the late 1800s. We used to camp in there all the time when we were kids, but nobody else knows about it.

"Grandpa abandoned it when he got married and moved to town. It's a ways off the Blackstead Ranch road. There're no roads into it anymore, but I know how to find it. We'll unload the whiskey into that place. We'll take the truck farther north and dump it off a high bluff into the river. For six months or so we just go about our business. We don't go into the dugout because we don't want to take a chance on anybody seeing the tire tracks. At the right time, we take the whiskey to South Dakota and sell it. Of course we'll keep a few cases for ourselves."

The others all laughed and applauded.

"Tomorrow is the first day of the road crew," Larson said.

"I can't take the day off," Billy Nestoss said. "Old man Herman has to know a week in advance. He's a real asshole about things like that. I won't be able to make it."

"That's all right," Larson answered. "They won't be taking a head count when they drive by. Four of us are enough. Maybe a couple of days we'll cut it to three and then back up to four. No real pattern of workers then."

"Thanks, Andy. I'm really sorry I can't be there."

Larson patted him on the shoulder. "It's okay. We'll drive my truck and park it off in the distance so they can't get a good look at it. I've got a wheelbarrow. The rest of you bring rakes and shovels and the kind of stuff a work gang would be using. Be at my place at noon. Wear old clothes like I told you. We'll drive up there and get to work. While we work, we'll figure out where each of us is gonna be when we go for the booze."

"How long'll it be before we make the hit?" Mike Garske asked.

"I figure two to three weeks. That'll give 'em plenty of time to get used to us. There's plenty of potholes to fill and the hill's a long one. None of those whiskey runners'll suspect a thing until we hit 'em just when they're moving their slowest at the very top of the grade."

CHAPTER FIVE

Andy Larson leaned on his shovel, raised his hand and gave a friendly wave at the three hay trucks as they passed. He was always careful to put his hand in front of his face when he waved. As the last truck disappeared, he signaled for the other four to join him in the center of the road. "We'll take them next Friday," he said and wiped his sleeve across his forehead. "The drivers all smiled and waved back. They're used to us now, almost like old friends. Everybody go to their assigned positions and we'll practice a few more times. Then it'll be for real."

Billy Nestoss motioned with a shovel. "Here they come." He started walking down the hill to where he had hidden the roadblock he was to put in the middle of the road after they'd passed. He waved and made a production of coughing into his bandana as they passed him.

"Get ready!" Andy Larson shouted.

Bert and Mike Garske lifted their shotguns, held them next to the handles of their shovels, stepped up to the side of the road, and turned their backs as they pulled up their bandanas. Spaced between them, Louie Bergavin knelt with his shotgun in the grass and pulled the bandana up over his nose.

Andy Larson pulled his hat down, thumbed the hanky up onto his nose, patted the automatic pistol stuck in the back of his pants, and checked his lever action rifle a final time. He turned, holding the rifle against his back, and watched the lead truck. "This is it," he muttered to himself. "Now we'll see if all that practice works."

As the lead truck came abreast of Bert Garske, he dropped the shovel, swung up his shotgun, fired a load of buckshot through the front tire of the lead truck, and swung the barrel of the gun up to point at the driver.

At the same time Mike Garske tossed his shovel aside, raised his shotgun to his shoulder, and blew out the front tire of the rear truck.

The drivers screamed curses and fought to keep control of their vehicles as the flattened tires pulled them toward the side of the road.

Andy Larson raised his rifle to cover the guard in the middle vehicle while on the opposite side of the vehicle Louie Bergavin raised his shotgun to cover the driver.

The guard jerked a Thompson machine gun up over the top of his door and fired a staccato burst of flame, smoke, and lead at Larson.

Larson saw the movement, dived toward the rear of the truck, and dropped to his knees. He fired a shot at the guard who was desperately trying to get his door open for a free range of fire. The bullet slammed into the guard's head above his ear. As he bounced back against the door, the machine gun dropped to the ground with a thud.

The driver of the lead vehicle raised his hands and shouted out the window, "Don't shoot!"

Bert Garske lowered the barrel of his shotgun only slightly, but it was enough. The driver suddenly swung a large automatic pistol up level with the window and fired a shot into the center of Bert's chest. Garske's eyes were large with pain and surprise as he flopped backward into the grass of the ditch and muttered a single word, "Mama." He grasped a hand to the bloody spot on his shirt, twitched, and died.

Louie Bergavin ran toward the lead vehicle. Cursing, he fired both barrels of his shotgun at the driver's arm holding out the pistol. The load of heavy buckshot blew away most of the man's hand and arm, and they flew along with the pistol off into the tall grass.

The driver screamed and managed to open his door and fall out into the road.

"Bastard," Bergavin muttered as he broke open the shotgun, thumbed out the shells, and reloaded. As he walked toward him, he fired both barrels into the downed driver. "You bastard," he muttered as he broke open the shotgun again. "Bert was my friend."

Andy Larson leaped forward and grabbed the machine gun from the ground. He raised it, spun, and fired a short burst through the windshield of the rear vehicle, killing the driver. "Set fire to that son-of-a-bitch!" Larson shouted to Mike Garske, who was standing frozen a short distance away, looking at his brother's body in the ditch.

The driver of the middle vehicle, seeing that no one was paying any attention to him, shoved his door open and fired an automatic pistol three times at Mike Garske, who, untouched, turned and looked at him blankly.

Larson stepped up onto the running board of the truck and fired a short burst from the machine gun across the cab. The spray of slugs tore a chunk from the steering wheel and punched holes in the door before lifting the driver from the seat and dropping his bloody body into the ditch.

Billy Nestoss ran up from behind the rear truck, pulled a box of matches out of a pocket, and tried to open it. The matches spilled to his feet and he dropped to his knees, fumbling his trembling fingers among them. He finally managed to lift two, scratched them to a flame, and held them to the hay. Fingers of fire immediately began to claw up the pile of hay. "I got it,

Andy!" he screamed as he rose to his feet.

Everything had happened in less than two minutes.

Larson walked up to Mike Garske and took the shotgun from his shaking hands. "Let's go, Mike." It was a look he had seen many times in combat.

"Billy, help Mike into my truck. Put Bert's body in the back and cover it with a tarp. You drive my truck; I'll drive the hay truck with the booze."

"Louie, switch the license plates between my truck and the hay truck. Fire up the front truck and you'll ride with me. Let's go!"

Billy walked over to Mike, who was kneeling beside his brother's body, and helped him to his feet. "Get in the truck, Mike. Louie and I'll put Bert in the back."

Mike Garske looked blankly at Billy. "Ma and Pa died last year. Now Bert's dead. I'll have to run the farm by myself," he said weakly.

"You can do it, Mike," Billy answered. "You can do it. Now get up in the front of the truck."

"We'll have to bury Bert up on the hill with Ma and Pa," Mike said, tears coursing down his cheeks.

Billy patted him on the shoulder and repeated. "Get in the truck, Mike."

"The license plates are switched," Louie announced. "I'll set fire to the other truck."

"I'll do that, Louie," Andy called. "I changed my mind. You ride with them and keep an eye on Mike. Make sure we've picked up all our guns and any of theirs you can find." He clapped his hands. "Let's go, we gotta be moving. Remember when you get to Wilton be sure to stay in the speed limit. The sheriff there likes to give tickets. The story goes he keeps most of the fines for himself. You boys sure as hell don't want him snooping around that truck while he's writing you up. When you're through town, pull off along the river road someplace and wait for me. I won't be far behind. Okay, get rolling."

Billy swung the truck into the ditch around the lead vehicle and waved as they drove away.

Andy walked over to the first truck, pulled a box of matches from his pocket, and set fire to the hay. He returned to the whiskey truck, started it, and drove around the burning vehicle. He stopped a short distance in front of it, turned his truck across the road, swung up the machine gun, and fired it back at the burning truck until the magazine was empty.

"There's always something you don't plan on," he muttered to himself. He managed to slide the hot machine gun under the seat, turned the truck back onto the road, and drove toward Wilton.

CHAPTER SIX

Andy Larson's mind was racing as he approached the tiny town of Wilton. He slowed down as he drove into the sleepy farming community. *I sure as hell don't want a speeding ticket now.*

A man suddenly stepped out into the street ahead and began to wave his arms above his head. Andy could see the glint of the man's glasses and the star on his shirt. *Shit,* he thought as he quickly glanced down at the speedometer, took the truck out of gear, and pumped the brakes.

The sheriff looked the vehicle over carefully as he approached.

Andy leaned forward, pulled the pistol out of his pants, stuck it under his leg, and leaned his arms on the window sill. He pulled his hat down to put his face in a shadow and began to aimlessly rub his chin with one hand. *This'll make it harder for him to see my whole face.* "Something wrong, Sheriff?" he asked, with a smile.

The sheriff crossed his arms, put a foot up on the running board and shook his head. "No, not really. Didja see all that smoke back up the road?"

Andy reached out with one hand and adjusted the mirror so he could see the two columns of black smoke rising in the distance behind him. "Damn, something sure as hell's burning back there, ain't it?" he said, wiggling the mirror again. "Do you know what it is, Sheriff?"

The sheriff stepped back and spit a brown gob on the front

tire of the truck. "No, 'at's why I'm stoppin' ya," he answered. "Ya see anything burnin' back there?"

"Nope, but there were some men standing around a couple of trucks arguing about something back there a few miles. I started to slow down, but they waved me to keep on going. There wasn't anything burning then and that's the only thing I've seen between here and Washburn, where I picked up this load of hay."

"Ya got some stock to feed?" the sheriff asked, studying Andy's shaded face over the tops of his glasses.

I met him about six years ago before I went into the army. He doesn't recognize me now with this mustache, but he'll sure as hell know me the next time he sees me. "No, I'm just hauling this for the Blackstead ranch."

The sheriff took off his glasses, pulled out a red hanky, and began to polish them as he turned and made a slow walk around the truck.

Andy reached down and brought the pistol up next to the door. *I don't want to do this.*

The sheriff returned to the side of the truck, shoved the hanky back in his pocket, and held the glasses up to carefully examine the lenses. "Blackstead ranch, huh?" he said, hooking his glasses back over his ears and pushing them up his nose with his thumb. "Ya'd think a ranch that big'd be able to grow enough of their own hay."

Andy nodded his agreement. "Hard to tell why rich folks spend their money the way they do."

The sheriff dug a block of tobacco out of his pocket, gnawed a chunk off the corner, and stuck it back in his pocket.

C'mon, quit stalling, Andy mentally told the sheriff. "Well, Sheriff, I 'spose I'd best be getting this load over to the ranch. I'm sure they'll have more for me to do when I get back."

The sheriff turned his head and spit another brown gob onto

the tire. "Yah, I reckon ya should. It sure is a puzzlement to me what could be burnin' back there. Ya said ya didn't see anything suspicious lookin', huh?" he asked, pointing to spiraling twin columns of black smoke.

"Just those men who appeared to be arguing over something," Andy answered, continuing to rub and scratch at his chin.

"Did ya tell me what was on those trucks?" the sheriff asked.

"As a matter of fact it was hay."

"Like ya got here?" the sheriff asked, reaching up next to the cab and grabbing a handful of hay.

Andy nodded. *If he pulls that and finds it's sewed onto a tarp, all hell's gonna break loose.* He coughed loudly to cover the sound of his cocking the pistol.

The sheriff pulled loose a small bunch of hay, brought it up close to his face, looked at it, and smelled it. "Don't look like a real good crop," he commented, dropping the hay and watching it blow down the street. "Ya'd think, what with all their money, them Blackstead brothers could buy a better grade a hay."

Andy let out a long breath of relief. "Maybe it's for bedding."

"Yah, ya could be right. Well, I 'spose I'd best be gettin' in my car an' goin' back there to see what all that smoke's about." The sheriff stepped back and gave a casual shrug. "Drive careful."

Andy coughed again as he eased down the hammer on the pistol in his hand. "Yes, sir, Sheriff, I will."

CHAPTER SEVEN

Louie Bergavin stepped out from behind a large cottonwood tree, waved at Andy Larson, and walked up to the truck when he stopped. "We were beginnin' to wonder where you were," he said, looking back up the road.

"I had a little run-in with the sheriff back in Wilton."

"No shit? What happened?"

"Nothing. He stopped me and asked if I knew what the smoke was from back up the road."

"What'd you tell him?"

"Told him I didn't know, just saw some men arguing about something back that way when I passed," Larson answered. "He was snooping around the truck enough to make me nervous."

"Well at least nothing happened."

"Yeah, but he sure as hell knows what I look like now. How's things here?"

"Billy and I are okay, but I ain't so sure about Mike."

"Why's that?"

"He's sitting in the back of the truck talking to Bert."

"Bert's dead."

"Yep, dead as last year's corn crop. Mike went and pulled the tarp off him, and he's just sitting there talking. Telling his brother how hard it's gonna be running the farm all by himself and things like that. I think he's slipped a cog or two."

"Get the truck and follow me. We have to get this stuff to the dugout and unloaded damn fast. Then we get rid of the truck in the river."

"We'll be right behind you."

An hour later Andy Larson pulled the whiskey truck over to the side of the road, stepped out, and waited for the others to join him.

Louie Bergavin stopped the second truck, climbed out, and stood beside him in the road.

"That's the gate over there," Larson said, pointing. "There's a road that runs along the other side of the fence. We'll follow it for about a quarter mile to the draw where the dugout is. I was out here a couple of weeks ago and walked it. Everything's just like I remembered. We'll leave my truck on top and I'll lead the whiskey truck down on foot." He gave a nod to Louie. "You'll drive."

"Let's go," Bergavin said.

Larson walked carefully down the rutted hillside to the stone cabin, followed by the creaking truck loaded with whiskey. Mike Garske and Billy Nestoss followed on foot.

"Think it's okay to leave Bert up there in that truck?" Mike asked when they arrived at the dugout cabin.

"The truck's hidden from the road in the trees," Billy assured him. "He'll be okay."

Larson used his pocketknife to cut the ropes holding the hay-covered tarp in place. He shook it loose and pulled it off to reveal the neat stacks of wooden whiskey boxes held securely in place by a heavy rope net.

"There it is, boys," Larson announced, waving his hand at the precious cargo. "Here." He handed Louie Bergavin the knife. "You cut the net off and we'll get to work. I need to know how many cases we have here." He stepped back and began to count. "Six cases to a stack, eight rows to a side. That's forty-eight cases to a row." He moved to the back of the truck and counted again. "Eight rows across the back." He knelt down, smoothed a patch of dirt with his hand, picked up a stick and began to scratch numbers. "Let me see now . . . Forty-eight times eight is . . ." He finished scratching numbers then whistled low as he stood up. "Three hundred and eighty-four cases of whiskey!"

The others were silent as they tried to run over numbers in their heads.

"It's time to start writing some of this down," Larson said as he patted a shirt pocket and brought out a pencil and a small pad of paper. "The dealer's price on a case of whiskey is twenty-four dollars." He muttered and scratched numbers on the pad. "Damn! That comes out to nine thousand, two hundred and sixteen dollars."

"What's that worth on the street at three bucks a bottle?" Billy Nestoss asked, gleefully rubbing his hands together.

Larson returned to his figuring. "Let's see. We've got . . ." He hesitated and double-checked his numbers. "That'd be almost fourteen thousand dollars," he said.

The other three men whistled.

"We're rich!" Billy Nestoss shouted. "We're rich!"

"Let's get this done," Louie said as he finished cutting the ropes on one side and tossed the net up onto the top of the stacked boxes. "We can do it now," he said as he climbed up onto the truck, grabbed the top box on the first stack, and held it above his head. "This is it, boys."

"Hand that one case down to me, carefully," Larson ordered, pulling a tire iron from under the seat of the truck. "We'll pry it open and have a drink to our success."

When the case was open Larson looked at the label on the bottle he pulled out of the wooden box. "Damn, this is *Superior.* This is the top of the line rye whiskey. This stuff sells for four and a half to five dollars a bottle. That jacks up the value of this shipment by a considerable amount, boys," Larson declared as he broke the label and twisted the cork out of the bottle. He took a swallow and passed it to Bergavin. "One drink for now." Each of the men took a drink. Larson pushed the cork back into the bottle and set it under the truck. "We'll have the rest of that when we finish unloading the truck. Louie, go back up there and start handing those down. We'll stack them on their sides so the corks stay wet. If the cork dries out and shrinks, the whiskey is ruined."

The men formed a work chain and quickly began to stack the boxes in the cool, dark dugout. As they worked, they talked in quiet voices about how much money they had and all the good free whiskey they would be able to drink.

Louie pulled away a box on the third row and stopped. "What the hell?" he asked in a dumbfounded tone, handing the box to Billy and bending down to put his hand into a space between the cases. "There ain't any whiskey in here," he said, "But there's something else. Let's see what it is." He lifted out a canvas bag with a leather band around the top and a leather bottom and handles. "Damn. This thing's heavy."

"Let me see that," Larson said, holding out his hand. "It looks like a small mail pouch."

"You best use two hands," Louie said, swinging the bag to Larson. "This bag's damned heavy."

Larson grunted as he grabbed the bag and it clumped down onto the floor of the truck box. "Son-of-a-bitch." He slowly turned the bag to examine it. "It must be important. Look at this lock," he said as he rattled it. "Only one way to see what's inside." He pulled the knife from his pocket, opened it, and cut a small slit in the canvas below the lock.

The others crowded around as he put his fingers in the cut and pulled it open. Larson looked inside and whistled. "This thing is *full* of gold coins!"

CHAPTER EIGHT

Andy Larson started to laugh. "Damn, will you take a gander at this?" He tore the hole in the canvas wider. "Look at that pretty color!"

"Can I . . . can I feel the gold?" Billy Nestoss asked, putting a hand toward the bag.

Louie Bergavin's brow wrinkled as he dropped to the ground and leaned over for a better look. "Is that real?"

Mike Garske stood with his head cocked to one side watching the others. "Are we rich?" he asked, his gaze moving from face to face.

"Here, Billy," Larson said, tipping the bag toward Nestoss' hand. "Stick your hand in there and feel the gold. There's nothing else feels like that."

Nestoss slowly slid his hand into the bag and brought it out piled high with bright gold coins.

Larson took the top coin off the pile and looked at. "These are Saint-Gaudens twenty dollar gold pieces."

"How many do you think are in that bag?" Nestoss asked.

Louie Bergavin took a coin from Nestoss' hand, looked at it and bit it.

"Why'd you do that?" Nestoss asked.

"Damned if I know," Bergavin answered, "but I've seen my dad do it with gold coins."

Larson laughed. "He was testing to see if it was soft. Real gold coins are supposed to be soft."

"Can we take some, Andy?" Nestoss asked, holding his gold-filled hand toward Larson.

Larson shook his head. "No, these coins are likely more trouble than the whiskey. We can't show any of this stuff for a long time. It's bad enough we stole a truckload of mob whiskey. Now we got their gold, they're gonna pull out all the stops hunting for us. And it ain't gonna be pleasant if they find us. Put those back with the rest."

Nestoss nodded, looked at the coins, and tipped his hand over the hole in the bag. The coins made a soft clinking sound as they dropped from sight.

Louie Bergavin climbed back up onto the bed of the truck. "Let's get the rest of this shit unloaded." He bent down and looked into the dark space between the wooden cases where he'd found the bag of gold. "Damn, look at this," he shouted, dropping to his knees. "I don't believe it, there's *more* bags in here!" He reached in and pulled out another canvas and leather bag and dropped it to the bed of the truck with a thud. "One." His arm disappeared and drew out another bag. "Two." He repeated the movement again and again. "Three, four, five." He leaned down and peered into the space. "That's it, boys, five bags is all we got."

"All we got?" Mike Garske repeated. "Doesn't that mean we're *damned* rich?"

The others laughed.

"Yeah, Mike," Larson answered. "It looks like we're rich, or at least damned well off."

Everyone gave a strained laugh.

"Let's get this heavy work over," Louie Bergavin said, handing down another case of whiskey. "The sooner we get this finished, the sooner we can have ourselves a drink."

Larson shoved the canvas bags to the side of the truck bed

and grabbed the next case of whiskey. "C'mon, boys, let's get this done."

The four men stood around the inside of the dugout looking at the stacks of wooden cases lined up against the far wall.

Billy Nestoss rapped his knuckles on a whiskey case. "Did anybody count these?"

"Not me," Louie Bergavin answered, stepping up and scuffing his feet on the fresh dirt in front of the last row of cases. "We don't want anybody to see where we buried the gold." He stepped back, looked at his handy work, and dragged his feet some more.

"Well, we know the first guess will be off because of the space where those five bags of gold were hidden," Larson said and chuckled. "But who really gives a shit? What was in that space more than makes up for the missing cases of booze."

"What about the gold?" Mike Garske asked. "What're we gonna do with all that money when we dig it up?"

"I've been thinking on that," Larson answered. "We don't dare to spend any of it around here. Gold is too noticeable. I'd say we'll have to go to Minneapolis or some other big city to get rid of it. Someplace where gold coins wouldn't be so unusual."

Louie Bergavin pulled the cork from the bottle in his hand. "How about we drink some of this good *free* whiskey?"

"How much money do you think we got, Andy?" Mike Garske asked as he grabbed up a bottle. "Between the whiskey and the gold, I mean."

"Mike, I don't have any idea. My experience with gold coins is . . . Shit, I don't know anything about gold coins except that it'll be fun to spend them when the time comes. But first things first. We gotta go up to the bluffs to the north of here and get rid of the truck. Don't forget to switch the license plates back. Remember, nobody goes near this place until we decide what to do about the gold. Understood?"

The others all nodded.

"What about Bert?" Mike Garske asked.

The others all looked at each other but said nothing.

"Well, damnit!" Mike shouted, his voice nearly cracking. "We can't just leave him in the back of that damned truck of yours."

"Why don't we take him up and bury him on the hill with your mother and father?" Larson asked. "We can get a stone made in Fargo or someplace."

Mike looked down at his feet and wiped at wet eyes with the back of his hand. "What if somebody asks me where he is?"

"Tell them he's gone to Montana, took a job over there," Larson answered.

"Well, he sure as hell can't stay gone to Montana forever," Mike countered.

Larson squinted and rubbed his fist against his forehead. "We'll have to work on that, Mike. For now the important thing is to get him out of that hot truck."

"We can put him in the root cellar up beside the barn for a couple of days," Mike Garske volunteered. "It's nice and cool in there."

"That's a good idea, Mike," Billy Nestoss said. "That'll give me time to make him a nice box. Old man Herman won't miss a few boards."

Andy Larson clapped his hands. "Okay, boys, we've got things to do. Everybody take a couple bottles of this stuff before I lock it up. Put a couple of extra cases in my truck so we'll have something for later without having to come back out here."

Louie Bergavin grabbed two bottles and stepped back out the door. "I'd like to take a few gold coins too," he joked.

"Tough shit," Larson countered as he pushed the door closed and snapped the lock shut. "All in due time, my friend. For now all you get is some damned expensive rye whiskey."

CHAPTER NINE

William Werner was hanging up his coat and hat when the intercom on his desk buzzed. "Damn, what's going on this early in the day?" he muttered as he straightened his suit coat, adjusted his pince-nez, and turned toward his desk. The door to his office suddenly burst open and Guido Salvatore stepped into the room.

The man in back of him filled most of the door, and he ducked as he stepped into the room behind Salvatore. The huge man's face was totally expressionless. His dark eyes were wide spaced above a nose that had obviously been broken several times. The man with the tight burr-cut head had no neck, and his square jaw had a dark stubble shadow with bare scar lines in it.

"Shut the door, Bruno," Salvatore ordered.

The large man raised a huge ham-like hand and quietly closed the door. His hand disappeared under his coat as he stepped off to one side of Salvatore.

Salvatore removed his hat, tilted his head, and looked Werner up and down. "Did you happen to notice that my trucks didn't come in here yesterday?" he asked, rubbing a knuckle on his skinny mustache.

"No, Guido, I left early and just now came into my office," Werner answered, nervously. "I haven't had a chance to look at any of the reports from yesterday."

"Well you won't find them on any of your damned reports

because they were hijacked and burned yesterday afternoon!" Salvatore exploded.

"What . . . what?" Werner asked. "I didn't know."

"The sheriff from Wilton called me late yesterday afternoon. He'd gone out to investigate some smoke and found two of my trucks, *your* trucks, burning in the road. All four of the men were dead and the trucks were pretty well shot up. They'd been torn up by machine gun fire. The truck with the whiskey was gone."

"Damn," Werner said, softly. "Those were my drivers. I wonder why I haven't been notified?"

"When we drove by there on the way down here last night, the highway patrol, the sheriff, and some other cops were doing an investigation. I managed to talk to the sheriff for a few minutes, and we came into town and got a hotel room. I was on the phone most of the night to people in Minneapolis, Chicago, and Canada. Here's an interesting point. The idiot sheriff up in Wilton actually stopped the stolen whiskey truck and talked to the driver before he let him go."

"He let him go?"

"He didn't know it was my truck."

"Which way was the bastard headed?"

"He was headed south. Toward Bismarck."

"Why here?" Werner asked.

"That's what I want *you* to tell *me*, William," Salvatore answered softly. Suddenly his hands shot out and grabbed Werner's lapels. "Have you got my fucking truck?" he screamed.

Bruno reached out and patted Salvatore on the shoulder. "Easy, Mister Salvatore," he cautioned. "Let me take care of this for you."

Salvatore took his hands away from Werner's lapels. "You're right, Bruno, you're right." He reached out and gently smoothed the wrinkled cloth on Werner's coat.

"Sometimes my temper takes over, and I forget that Bruno is supposed to handle these matters for me."

"I swear to God, Guido, I know nothing about this. This is the first I've heard of any of it."

Guido Salvatore's eyes squinted as he reached up and rubbed a knuckle on his mustache. "I believe you, William. I don't think you're stupid enough to try to pull something like this on me. You also don't have the balls."

"Thank you, Guido," Werner said softly, relief showing in his voice. "You know I would never cross you like that."

"You've heard me mention my Uncle Alphonse, haven't you?" Salvatore asked.

Werner nodded. "I have."

"Alphonse isn't really my blood uncle," Salvatore began slowly. "He is more of a senior partner of mine. You may know him by his full name, *Alphonse Capone.*"

Werner nodded weakly and took a deep breath. "I know of him."

"There was a small addition to the whiskey on that truck yesterday. Uncle Alphonse had sixty thousand dollars in gold coins being transported down from Canada." Salvatore waited for the news to have a full effect on Werner before continuing. "They were hidden, six hundred to a bag, in five canvas and leather pouches amongst the whiskey cases."

Werner dug a neatly folded handkerchief from an inside coat pocket and wiped at his face. "I . . . I . . . I . . ."

Salvatore raised his hand. "Someone here in Bismarck now has three hundred and eighty-two cases of my fine Canadian whiskey and three thousand bright shiny new 1923 Saint-Gaudens twenty-dollar gold pieces that belong to Alphonse Capone. We want them all back. Do you understand? We want them back and some son-of-a-bitch will die for this!"

Chapter Ten

A policeman stuck his head in the locker room door. "Hey, Torkelson, get your partner and report to the Chief's office. Make it quick."

"Yeah, yeah," Fred Torkelson answered and waved his hand at the door.

"Well, Fred, how's it feel to be back working days?" Charlie Norman called across the room.

"It's too early to tell," Torkelson answered and slammed his locker shut.

"Fred, there's a hot rumor around here that your partner made sergeant," David Langemo said from the bench behind him.

"Yeah, I'll tell ya what," Torkelson answered. "You put that rumor in one hand and shit in the other and see which one feels like you got something in it."

"That was funny the first time you said it ten years ago," Langemo retorted. "I'm still trying to figure out if those ninety days of night duty was a punishment detail or a test of your abilities. Most of us only get thirty days on a shift like that."

Torkelson shrugged. "I requested two extensions."

"You two gotta have something in mind. I think you were just sucking up to make sure Andy got that extra stripe," Norman said.

The door opened again and the same policeman shouted, "The Chief ain't in a good mood today, Torkelson. You two'd best get your asses in there."

Charlie Norman made exaggerated kissing sounds. "Go git 'im, boys."

Torkelson finished buttoning his uniform shirt, swung his pistol belt up, and buckled it in place. He checked himself in the full-length mirror by the door and did some minor adjustments on his shirt. He opened the door and turned. "Hey, Charlie."

Norman looked up from his locker in time to see Torkelson raise his middle finger before walking out the door.

"Where in the hell's that damned Andy?" Torkelson muttered as he walked down the hall. "He shoulda been here by now."

Andy Larson sat in a chair outside the door with the window marked in bold letters, CHIEF of POLICE, BISMARCK, NORTH DAKOTA.

"Where in the hell you been?" Torkelson asked with a grimace.

Larson stood up and smoothed his uniform shirt. "When I came in somebody told me the Chief wanted to see us. I just saved myself a walk."

Larson knocked on the door. "Come in."

Larson opened the door and he and Torkelson stepped into Chief Raymond Pearce's office.

"Shut the door," Pearce instructed.

Larson closed the door. He and Torkelson took four steps to the front of the Chief's desk, came to attention, and saluted.

Pearce casually returned the salute. "Stand easy," he said, leaning forward and putting his elbows on the desk. He steepled his fingers under his nose and stared intently at each of them individually. He took a deep breath and let out a long audible sigh. "There are just so many times with you two when I don't know if I should shake your hands or kick your asses."

"Yes, sir," they answered in unison.

"Your work on busting up that car theft ring last week is very commendable. There was a hell of a lot of smart work done for a long time to wrap that one up." He looked at a paper on his desk. "Almost three months. I see from your report that the majority of the stolen vehicles were stripped down and used to transport liquor."

"Yes, sir," Torkelson agreed. "A fully stripped-down Studebaker could carry thirty to forty cases of whiskey. You put four or five cars like that in a convoy and they can carry five to six thousand dollars' worth of whiskey at fifty dollars a case."

"They usually kept to the back roads and trails," Larson added. "Some of those drivers had loops of heavy chain bolted to their back axles so they could drop it down onto the roads and make a cloud of dust so anybody chasing them had to slow down, sometimes almost to a complete stop while the stuff settled."

"You can see in the report they've found some of those stolen vehicles as far south as Denver and a lot of places between here and there," Torkelson added. "The amount of money a man can make running booze gives a lot of incentive to stealing the mode of transportation. There'll be a lot more of that before this whole thing is over."

Chief Pearce nodded. "You two are good at catching the petty thieves and people who work under the cover of darkness. I have a gut feeling you two don't always play by the rules, but as long as I don't know about it and the crime rate is being held down, I don't give a shit."

"Yes, sir," they answered again.

"By the way, you two don't know anything about a still being blown up down in Dog Town a couple of nights ago, do you?"

Torkelson and Larson exchanged puzzled looks and shook their heads.

"I hadn't even heard about it," Larson answered.

"I heard about it for the first time a little while ago," Torkelson added.

Chief Pearce's eyes narrowed. "Uh huh." The Chief stood up and held out his hand. "Congratulations, Larson, you've been promoted to sergeant."

Larson shook the Chief's hand and smiled. "Thank you, Chief. I didn't know . . ."

"Cut the bullshit, Larson," Chief Pearce interrupted. "There are no secrets around here on things like this. We'll do a formal ceremony sometime in the next couple of weeks. The pay increase goes into effect today."

Larson smiled. "Thank you, Chief."

"I've pulled you off nights because I want you to do some special work for me."

"Sir?" Torkelson asked.

"It's a known fact Minot is a hotbed of big-time crime. I don't want it down here," Chief Pearce said, sitting back down in his chair. "I want the two of you to keep an eye on something for me. You'll be wearing civilian clothes for this."

"What is it?" Torkelson asked.

"There was an incident up north of Wilton yesterday where four men were killed. Three of the men worked for Werner Transportation. Or at least they had papers on them that indicated that."

"What do you mean by incident?" Larson asked. *Let's see what anybody knows.* "Were they Werner trucks?"

"I'm not too clear on much of it," the Chief answered. "I saw a preliminary highway patrol report this morning that said there were four dead men. All killed by gunshots. There were two burned and shot-up trucks. We don't have any jurisdiction up there, but I want to know about the Werner drivers. It may not be a big deal, but why were they driving somebody else's trucks?"

"What about the fourth man?" Torkelson asked.

"He had a Minot driver's license," Pearce answered. "But nothing that indicated he worked for Werner."

"What was in the burned trucks?" Torkelson asked.

"Hay."

"Someone killed four men and set fire to a couple of hay trucks? That's an odd crime," Larson said. "There's gotta be more to it than that."

Chief Pearce nodded in agreement. "The sheriff up there's named Ed Walker. I've met him a few times. I don't think he's the brightest bulb in the chandelier, but then again he might be putting on that act for show," Chief Pearce said. "Kind of the good-old-boy-small-town-sheriff thing. He told the highway patrol that he thinks there was another truck involved."

"How'd that be?" Larson asked.

"From what I read, it's kind of vague. The sheriff said it might be part of a whiskey-running operation and that's why the trucks were shot up. The bullet hole patterns in the vehicles indicate there were some automatic weapons involved."

"You mean machine guns?" Torkelson asked.

"Uh-huh. That's usually something that comes in from the big cities," the Chief answered. "One of the men had his arm blown off by a shotgun, and everybody in North Dakota's got one of those. They didn't find any guns, but three of the men had holsters on their belts, and the man with the Minot driver's license had a shoulder holster."

"You want us to go up and talk to Sheriff Walker?" Larson asked.

"No, we'll let the highway patrol and the State Marshal handle it up there. I want you two to go down and talk to Werner. See what you can find out about the dead drivers and what they were hauling. See if he knows anything about the other dead man. Throw out some whiskey-running hints and see if he gets nervous. He might be running booze. There's enough money in that stuff to tempt even an honest man."

Damn, that was close, Larson thought as they left the Chief's office.

"Well, let's get changed," Torkelson said, as they walked down the hall. "I guess this promotion means you'll be buying the drinks tonight."

Larson glanced out of the corner of his eye at Torkelson. "Don't you know that drinking's illegal?"

Both men laughed.

"It'll be easier to get a drink in civilian clothes anyway," Larson joked. *This is gonna get interesting now. I wonder what'll happen if I ever have to go talk to Sheriff Walker?*

CHAPTER ELEVEN

Sergeants Fred Torkelson and Andy Larson walked through the front door of the Werner Transportation offices just as Bruno Campagna threw open the door of William Werner's office and stepped aside to allow Guido Salvatore to walk out.

"You'd better have some answers for me, damned quick!" Salvatore shouted over his shoulder as he squared his hat, glared at the two men by the door, and stomped across the room. "I'll expect a phone call from you when I get back to Minot."

"Yes, Guido," William Werner answered fawningly, wringing his hands as he followed Salvatore to the front door. "I'll be on it immediately."

"Damn, that one ol' boy's big enough to hunt ducks with a rake," Larson intoned and smiled as he watched Bruno duck out the door. "I don't think I've ever seen anybody that big before."

"May I help you?" the secretary asked the two men who had just entered.

"We're here to talk to Mister Werner," Torkelson answered, pointing to the man standing by the door watching Salvatore and Bruno move across the parking lot.

"What do you want?" Werner asked, without turning around. "Are you men drivers?"

"Are you looking for drivers?" Torkelson answered.

Werner turned, took a deep breath and let it out slowly. "Well, damnit, are you drivers?"

"Not exactly," Torkelson answered, pulling open his coat to reveal his badge. "We're here to talk to you about three drivers you lost yesterday."

"Ah, yes, I was just told about them," Werner said softly. "Such a shame."

"What was the man's name who just left?" Torkelson asked. "The normal sized one."

"Ah, Guido Salvatore," Werner answered.

"You ship something for him?" Larson asked.

"We do business from time to time."

"That's not what I asked you," Torkelson retorted. "I asked you what you ship for him."

"He's got some doors going to Minneapolis."

"Hmmm," Larson began. "You know, Mister Werner, Guido there doesn't look much like a door salesman to me."

"I'll agree," Torkelson continued. "He's a bit too polished for a lumber man. He doesn't strike me as someone who'd like to get slivers. That big fella with him for loading trucks?"

"You told me you were here to talk to me about my murdered drivers," Werner said. "Why don't we step into my office and talk?"

"Good idea," Torkelson agreed. "Lead on."

Werner closed the door and pointed to a table. "Can I get you some coffee?"

"No, thanks, and we'll stand," Torkelson answered. "What can you tell us about the men who were shot yesterday?"

"In what way?" Werner asked.

"Those men worked for you, didn't they?" Larson asked. "According to the report they had pay stubs from your company in their wallets."

"Yes, they sometimes work for me, but those weren't my trucks they were driving when they were killed."

"Whose trucks were they?" Larson asked.

"I have no idea. From time to time my men will drive for other companies when I have no work for them here."

"The highway patrol's going over records right now to see who those trucks belong to," Larson said.

"I would hope that's part of their job," Werner agreed with a weak smile.

"The trucks they were driving look like they were loaded with hay. Why were they carrying guns to guard hay?" Larson asked.

Werner walked behind his desk and sat down. "How would I know that? I don't even know who they were working for."

"Did we mention that the fourth dead man was from Minot?" Torkelson asked. "Mister, ah . . . , what's his name that just left, said he was going back to Minot, didn't he?"

"You remember, the door salesman," Larson added with a menacing smile.

"Yes, Mister Salvatore is from Minot," Werner agreed.

"He didn't seem to be in too good a mood," Larson noted.

Torkelson asked, "Those wouldn't happen to be his trucks that're all shot up and burned, would they?"

Werner shrugged and answered weakly. "I really couldn't say."

"Couldn't or wouldn't?" Larson countered.

"What does Salvatore do for a living?" Torkelson asked. "Besides sell doors."

"I believe he's in the import business. I think his main offices are in Minneapolis. At least that's where the doors are going to be shipped."

"You don't seem to know very much about Mister Salvatore," Torkelson said.

Werner shook his head.

"The highway patrol will be able to tell us if he owns those trucks," Larson said.

"Let's go back to the dead drivers for a minute," Torkelson said. "Your three drivers were wearing belt holsters and the man from Minot had a shoulder holster. But they didn't find any guns. That seems a bit odd, doesn't it?"

"I told you they weren't driving for me yesterday," Werner countered.

"The sheriff up in Wilton thinks there was another truck," Larson said. "Maybe that truck was stolen from the scene, but who'd steal a truckload of hay? I mean if it *was* a truck of hay. Who knows what could have been hidden in the hay? Wait, a thought just hit me. What if it was whiskey?"

Torkelson glanced at Larson and nodded. "The report says the trucks were shot up by machine guns and burned. Don't you think that's overdoing it a bit for stealing hay?"

Werner stared at him blankly. "I told you, I first became aware of the terrible deaths of my drivers about an hour ago. I have no answers, only questions myself."

Torkelson nodded, walked over to Werner's desk and slid a business card toward him. "If you think of anything or hear something you think might be important to us, give us a call."

Werner looked at the card and started to stand.

"Don't get up. We know the way out," Larson said, and opened the door.

CHAPTER TWELVE

A bank of dark thunderhead clouds was beginning to bring shadows across the evening sun on the North Dakota prairie when Billy Nestoss dropped the tailgate of the truck with a thud.

Louie Bergavin leaned in, grabbed one of the rope handles on the rough-sawn wooden box, and pulled it toward them. "You did a nice job on this," he commented as they lifted the coffin out.

"Yeah, old man Herman won't miss these boards. I built it while he was gone to lunch, and Andy picked it up before he got back."

"I hope the rain holds off," Mike Garske said wistfully, pointing at the approaching clouds. "I'd like to get Bert buried before that damned storm hits."

"It looks like a bad one," Andy Larson agreed. "Let's get moving."

Mike Garske lifted the board from across the weathered wooden door of the root cellar and it creaked as he pulled it open. He propped the board against the door to keep it in place as they entered the dark, dank, rock-faced hole dug in the side of the hill. "We're here to git ya, Bert," he said softly as they all waited for their eyes to adjust to the darkness.

A break in the clouds allowed a beam of light to shoot in and stand their shadows against a blanket-wrapped bundle laid on boards spanning two sawhorses. The bright sun reflected off rows of jars of canned fruits and vegetables on the shelves behind the bundle.

"Should we bring the box in here or will it be just as easy to carry him out there?" Billy Nestoss asked.

"You and I can carry him out on those boards," Louie Bergavin answered, stepping to the head of the shrouded body. "Lift him on three."

They laid Bert Garske's body gently in the wooden box and stepped back. "I'm gonna nail it shut, Mike," Billy Nestoss said softly. "Anything you wanna do or say first?"

Mike Garske knelt beside the coffin and pulled the corner of the blanket back from his dead twin brother's face. "I'm sorry, Bert," he whispered. "You tell Ma an' Pa, I'll be over there on the other side to see all of ya someday. Tell 'em I'll take damned good care of the farm." He turned and wiped his eyes before looking up at Larson. "You got any of that whiskey with ya, Andy? The stuff he got killed for."

"Ah . . . sure, Mike," Larson answered, a slight catch in his voice. "I'll get you a bottle out of the truck." He returned shortly and handed the liquor down to the kneeling man. "Here you go, Mike."

Mike Garske took the bottle and looked at each of the somber standing men. "You all know my brother's life wasn't worth a whole damned trainload of this Canadian piss, don't ya?" With tears coursing down his cheeks, he pushed the bottle in beside his dead brother's arm and lifted the corner of the blanket up over his face. He stood and wiped his sleeve across his face. "Let's git this done," he sobbed. "Let's put him in the ground 'fore that damned storm hits us."

A low rumble of thunder seemed to emphasize his words, and they looked up to see sections of the clouds light up with static lightning.

"One last thing," Larson said. "I've got three bags of rock

salt in my truck. Help me bring it over here."

"What the hell's that for?" Bergavin asked.

"It'll dry the body out, and it won't stink so bad," Larson answered.

"Hell, nobody's gonna dig him up and smell him," Nestoss said, glancing at Mike to see if he'd reacted to his poor attempt at humor.

"Let's not argue this," Larson said. "Just help me bring the salt over and put it around him. I don't want to take any chances."

"I think you're worrying too damned much about unimportant shit," Bergavin mumbled.

Minutes later the body was covered with salt. Billy Nestoss knelt and hammered in a series of nails around the edge of the lid.

Without a word the four men leaned down, and each grasped one of the rope handles. They lifted the wooden box and began the trudge up the hill to the metal fenced area that contained two carved headstones and the freshly dug hole for the final resting place of Bert Garske.

"Damned salt's heavy," Bergavin muttered.

As they walked, Mike Garske began to sing, "Onward Christian Soldiers" softly, and the others soon joined him.

At the small family cemetery they gently set the coffin down beside the hole and the pile of dark earth. They stepped back, took off their hats, and folded their hands.

"Who's gonna say something?" Billy Nestoss asked, and they all looked at each other, waiting for a volunteer.

"Let's lower him into the ground," Andy Larson said. "Then I'll say a few words." *I saw this too many times in the war.*

They looped ropes under the coffin, lowered it slowly into the hole, and tossed the ends of the ropes down to clump on the wooden lid.

Andy Larson picked up a handful of dirt and slowly dribbled it through his fingers to make a rattling noise on the coffin. "Ashes to ashes," he started.

The others lifted handfuls of dirt and mimicked Larson's action as they joined in. "Dust to dust."

Mike Garske pulled the shovel he had used earlier in the day from the pile and dropped a shovelful of dirt into the hole.

Larson nodded and began, "Yea, though I walk through the valley of the shadow of death, I will fear no evil. . . ."

When Larson finished, he looked up at the others as they raised their heads. "May Bert rest in peace."

"Amen," the three men echoed in unison when he finished.

The four men took turns with the shovel, quickly filling the hole and mounding the dirt above it.

The thunder grew louder and more frequent as jagged lightning bolts crashed from the clouds to the dry ground. The air grew chilly and smelled of rain and cordite. The men could see a dark wall of rain moving toward them as they started down the hill toward the farm.

"Let's go!" Billy Nestoss shouted and began to run.

When the first three of them reached the barn, rain was already beginning to beat loudly on the roof. They turned and looked back to see Mike Garske walking slowly toward them, the rain blending with his tears.

"He ain't doin' well, is he?" Louie Bergavin asked.

"It's got to be pretty damned rough to be burying your twin brother," Andy Larson said flatly. "We have to do something to take his mind off this."

Mike walked in out of the storm and smiled weakly. "Think it'll rain?" he asked, wiping his hands down his face. He walked over to a pile of cloth feed sacks, pulled one off the top, and began to rub it vigorously on his face and head. "Ya got more of that whiskey, Andy?" he asked. "I think it's only fittin' we throw ol' Bert a wake. He'd a liked that."

Relief showed on the faces of the other three men and they gathered around Mike.

Louie pulled his hat down and dashed out to the truck. He quickly returned with an armload of bottles and handed one to each of them. He wiped at his face with a shirt sleeve before twisting the cork from the bottle in his hand and raising it above his head.

"Here's to Bert," he shouted.

CHAPTER THIRTEEN

William Werner leaned over and placed his mouth next to the mouthpiece of the candlestick phone sitting on his desk. The hand holding the receiver next to his ear trembled slightly. He didn't have any good news for Guido Salvatore, which was bad news for him. "Please tell Mister Salvatore that Mister Werner is calling," he instructed the secretary when she answered the phone.

"This is Salvatore," the gangster growled.

"Guido, this is William Werner."

"I know, my secretary told me," Salvatore snapped. "What've you got for me?"

"I haven't been able to find out anything," Werner answered weakly.

"I'll tell you something, Werner," Salvatore shouted. "The longer I think about this shit, the madder I get!"

"Those two men who were coming in when you were leaving my office were cops."

"What'n the hell did they want?"

"What do think they wanted?" Werner replied, sharply. "They wanted to know why my drivers were wearing holsters. . . . No, wait a minute, first they wanted to know why my drivers were driving your trucks."

"How'd they know they were my trucks?"

"Well, they didn't. I mean they said the highway patrol would look at the records and find out whose trucks they were."

"Ha," Salvatore laughed. "Those trucks are registered to a grain company over in Fargo. It's a legitimate company that hauls wheat, oats, and flax to Minneapolis."

"Then why don't you use them to haul your damned whiskey to Minneapolis?" Werner demanded.

"Who says I don't use them?" Salvatore asked. "Do you really think the whiskey you haul for me is all the booze I move these days? Your action is less than a quarter of what I run into Minneapolis. You know what they say about all your eggs in one basket? Well, the same goes for all your booze in one truck."

Werner took a deep breath and let it out slowly. "Why do I get the feeling that you're pissing on my leg and telling me it's warm rain?" he asked dejectedly.

"Those two burned up trucks aren't going to tell them anything," Salvatore said. "Burned hay is burned hay.

"Can't we pay those two cops off?" Salvatore asked. "Get them to run in circles for a while? Have them keep us posted on the police activities, things like that."

"Shit, I don't know," Werner answered. "I've got a couple of cops that'll do anything for a little cash under the table, but I don't know about these two."

"Every man has his price. Find out what theirs is."

"I don't know, Guido . . ."

"Listen to me, Werner, you little pissant!" Salvatore shouted. "I'm tired of *fucking* around with you. You get me some answers or you might start having some serious real estate problems. Like those big barns of yours burning. Understand?"

Werner's hand began to tremble again. "I understand," he answered hopelessly.

"I pay for my whiskey in advance. The Bronfman brothers won't even send it to the border for me to pick up unless they have cash in hand before it's loaded. There were three hundred and eighty cases of top quality *Superior* whiskey on that truck. I pay two bucks a bottle up front for it and wholesale it to Minneapolis dealers for three and a half. That means I had over nine thousand of my own money invested in that truck as soon as it was loaded. Sold to my dealer, I make a seven thousand dollar profit. Sold on the street it's worth almost *twenty-three thousand dollars!*" Salvatore exploded. "I paid up front, the dealers in Minneapolis paid up front. Now I've got to pay them back, either in cash or booze. Who's going to pay me back? Huh, who's going to fatten my wallet?"

"Guido . . ."

"Don't interrupt me!" Salvatore screamed into his phone. "Some bastard is making a fat profit off something he stole from me and I don't like that. Now here's the big rub. Uncle Alphonse is livid about his stash of gold being stolen and you don't want to be the object of Uncle Al's ire. His boys and their Chicago typewriters aren't folks you want to come calling. Do you get my drift?"

William Werner shuddered. "It's very clear, Guido."

"Good. Now you talk to those cops and find out if they know anything. I'm sending Bruno and a couple of my other boys over there to do a little investigating for me. Somebody's about to find out they fucked with the wrong man!"

Werner heard the phone line click dead, and his shaking hand hung the receiver from his phone back on the hook. He shuffled papers on his desk until he found the card Sergeant Torkelson had given him that morning.

CHAPTER FOURTEEN

The rain beating on the tin roof of the lean-to beside the barn was a steady din to the four men resting back in a pile of hay. Each of them held a whiskey bottle loosely in his hands. Through streams of water running off the roof, they watched a bright lightshow flashing in the night clouds around them. From time to time, rolling crescendos of thunder would add music to the show.

"Hey," Louie Bergavin shouted, over the rattle of the rain. "Have you boys noticed that this is a pretty damned good-tasting whiskey?"

"Sure is," Billy Nestoss agreed, waving his bottle in front of him.

Mike Garske just nodded.

"I told you *Superior* is a hell of a lot better than the usual goat piss we've been drinking," Andy Larson said.

The men all tilted their bottles up so they could see the label in the occasional flash of light from the sky.

"I always said, if yer gonna steal, steal the best," Nestoss said, and they all laughed.

"This stuff runs around five bucks a bottle," Larson said. "We've seized a few bottles of it in raids around town, but you don't find too many places serve anything this good."

"Yeah, the places that serve stuff this good have paid the cops off to stay away from their doors," Bergavin said and laughed.

"How much do you cops keep after a raid?" Mike Garske asked.

"What makes you think we keep *any?*" Larson returned. "Haven't you seen all the pictures in the papers where the Chief or somebody else of high moral standing is busting a keg or smashing a bottle?"

"That answers my question," Garske said with a thin laugh.

"Did you think I was buying *all* the stuff we've been drinking around the fires at night?" Larson asked.

"Hey, Andy," Nestoss called above the din of the rain on the tin roof. "You said you was gonna tell us about your meeting with old man Werner this mornin'."

Andy Larson stood up so he could face the others. "That man was a back-pedaling fool," he began. "We could see right away that he wasn't going to tell us anything. He admitted three of the dead men were his drivers but said he didn't have any idea who the fourth man was. He claimed he didn't know whose trucks they were and said his men drive for other people on their days off. Tork hit him with the fact that all of the men were wearing holsters, but there weren't any guns to be found. You boys did a good job on that one."

"Wasn't it kinda hard to listen to him, when you know the true story?" Nestoss asked and took a drink from his bottle.

"Yeah, keeping a straight face was a little rough at times," Larson admitted. "Then again, there were times I wanted to slap the piss out of him because I knew he was lying to us. From the reports I know the sheriff up in Wilton thinks he saw the third truck. He saw the third truck all right, and me driving it. I'm going to have to shave off my mustache and do everything I can to keep from meeting with him. He puts on a great act about being a good-old-boy small-town sheriff, but I think he's smarter than that."

"What're you gonna do?" Mike Garske asked.

"I guess we'll just have to wait and see what happens. I know the truth, but I sure as hell can't tell Tork about it."

"It's gonna be rough, Andy," Bergavin said.

Larson nodded and took a drink from the bottle in his hand. "When we were going into Werner's office, there were a couple of guys leaving. One was a short, dark, snappy-dressed man with one of those little pimp mustaches. The other guy was one of the biggest men I've ever seen outside of a circus. We asked Werner who they were, and he told us the little man was a lumber salesman or something like that, from Minot."

"Who was the big guy?" Nestoss asked.

"He didn't say, but my guess is, from his size, that he's some sort of a bodyguard or an enforcer," Larson answered. "The little guy was pissed about something and told Werner he'd better have some news for him by the time he got back to Minot."

"You think those were his trucks?" Bergavin asked.

"I'd put money on it. His trucks, his whiskey, and his gold."

"Then he's the one we'd best be watching out for," Nestoss said.

"We're waiting to hear from Minot about our little friend," Larson said. "Tork put in a call to the only person he trusts on the force up there, but he was out. He'll get back to him in the morning and then we'll know more about the lumber salesman. Damn, look at it rain."

CHAPTER FIFTEEN

Sergeant Fred Torkelson hung up the phone and looked at his notes as he lit another cigarette from the smoking butt of his last one. "C'mon over here, Andy," he called and waved to Larson.

Larson picked up his steaming cup of coffee, walked over, and flopped down in the chair beside Torkelson's desk. "What'd your pal in Minot have to say?" he asked as he looked at the scrawled notes on the pad in front of the sergeant.

"Werner was telling us the truth about Salvatore's lumberyard yesterday. The guy's also got a jewelry store, clothing store, pool hall, used car lot, a grain trucking firm, and a junkyard or two. Those are the legitimate businesses they know about. There's also little doubt that he's running booze on the side. His friend says he has to be very careful who he talks to on the force up there because so many of them are on the take from the booze runners."

Larson whistled softly. "Seems like the man keeps himself busy."

Torkelson nodded. "The big man is Bruno Campagna. He's the muscle for Salvatore. He's known by the nickname Bear."

Larson nodded. "Gee, I wonder who came up with that snappy clever name?"

Both of the men laughed.

"I've got a note here that Werner wants to talk to me. I called him, and he says he'd rather talk to me alone," Torkelson said.

"Maybe it's bribe time."

"Wonder what I did to piss him off yesterday?" Larson joked. "I'll go wander around town and look for crime while you go talk to Werner. If he makes you an offer, be sure to get some for me too."

"Good plan," Torkelson agreed. "Let's meet at Rosie's for lunch."

Fred Torkelson opened the door to William Werner's office to find him sitting casually on the edge of his desk, sipping a cup of coffee.

Werner set the cup of coffee down, stood and held out his hand. "Good to see you, Sergeant Torkelson. Can I call you Fred?"

"That's fine," Torkelson answered, shaking Werner's hand.

"Coffee?" Werner asked.

"No, thanks," Torkelson answered, taking a seat on the edge of a large table.

"Good enough. How are things coming on the burned trucks?"

"Nothing new, we're still waiting to hear from the highway patrol. What have you found out about your drivers? Why were they wearing guns?"

"I thought you said there weren't any guns to be found," Werner countered.

"Oh, yeah, that's right," Torkelson agreed. "Holsters, but no guns. What can you tell me about your friend . . . ?" Torkelson flipped open a notebook and thumbed it. "Ah yes, Salvatore."

"Like I told you, he's having me ship some doors to Minneapolis for him."

"It's odd he doesn't use one of his own trucks. He has a truck line, you know."

Werner coughed, rubbed his chin, and looked down at his

coffee cup to stall and gather his thoughts. "It was probably easier and cheaper to have me take them to Minneapolis for him. The doors were coming in from a factory in Montana. Saved him having to haul them up to Minot and then over . . ."

He's going to sweat bullets in a minute, Torkelson told himself and tried to keep from smiling. *If this guy backpedals and spins around anymore, he's gonna get dizzy.* "I understand. These days you have to save money anywhere you can."

"Exactly," Werner agreed and smiled weakly.

"It can be tough to get by these days," Torkelson said. *There's the bait.*

"Yes, I suppose it is a bit rough making it on a policeman's wages these days," Werner said.

Torkelson sighed dramatically. "Yeah, you can say that again," he agreed.

Werner's eyes drifted up toward the ceiling and then back to Torkelson. "I suppose you could always use a little extra money," he volunteered slowly.

Torkelson looked down at his hands. "Yeah," he answered, without looking up. "Even a sergeant's pay leaves a few tight spots around the end of the month."

"What . . . what if I were to offer you a small stipend for . . . ah . . . Oh, let's say . . . ah . . ." Werner stuttered as he looked for the words to make the offer.

C'mon, Torkelson thought, still looking down at his hands.

"Oh, hell," Werner blurted. "Would an extra . . . oh, let's say twenty bucks a week help you?"

Torkelson slowly raised his eyes. "Cash, in old five-dollar bills?"

Werner smiled. "Sure, fives would be easy."

"I'll call you tonight. Seven o'clock," Torkelson said, keeping a straight face as he stood and proffered his hand. "You want to

know what's been found about the burned trucks, right?"
"Exactly," Werner agreed and smiled.

Chapter Sixteen

Fred Torkelson slid into the booth across from Andy Larson and smiled.

"Good meeting?" Larson asked.

"He's gonna pay me twenty bucks a week for inside information," Torkelson said and chuckled. "Old fives."

"Old fives?"

"Harder to identify and trace."

"Shit, who in the hell is gonna screw around with twenty bucks?"

Torkelson shrugged and chuckled. "When I get back to the office I'll write this up. I'll put the money in the envelope every week, along with the initial write-up of this plan. I'll have to figure out a safe place to keep it. I think it's best we keep this between the two of us and by doing it this way, our asses will be covered if it ever comes up."

"I agree."

"I'll have to decide what kind of information I'm going to feed him tonight."

"Was it tough to get him to make an offer?"

"Nah, the guy's a natural crook. He stammered and stuttered around for a bit, but finally came through and tossed a number at me. Hey, you shaved off your mustache."

"It was beginning to itch so I decided to get rid of it for a while. Let's eat."

★　★　★　★　★

William Werner blew a smoke ring, tapped the ash from the end of his cigar, and glanced up at his clock just as the phone rang. He smiled, slid the phone close, and lifted the receiver to his ear. "Werner here."

"This is Torkelson."

"I like a man that's punctual. What have you got for me?"

"According to the highway patrol report, those two burned trucks belong to your friend from Minot, Salvatore," Torkelson answered.

"Really?" Werner asked. "That brings up a lot of questions, doesn't it?"

"Yeah, but there's not much more right now. I'm still looking into the possibility there was a third truck."

"I wonder why anyone would steal a truck of hay?" Werner said. "You did you say it was a truck of hay, didn't you?"

"No, I didn't. We don't know what was in that truck or even if there *was* a third truck. A lot of this rests on the fact the sheriff up in Wilton says he stopped a hay truck about that time and asked the driver if he'd seen the fires back up the road. The driver told him no, all he'd seen were two hay trucks and some men arguing beside the road. The sheriff let him go, but he thinks he can identify the man if he sees him again."

"Well, I appreciate what you've told me. It's interesting to learn those trucks belong to Salvatore. I didn't know he was in the feed business. Lumber is about the only thing he's dealt with me on."

Yeah, I'll bet. "If I hear anything of interest, I'll be sure and give you a call. Things are usually slow in the beginning of an investigation like this," Torkelson said. "There are a number of people and agencies working on it. It takes time to get everything compiled and put together. When can I pick up my money?"

"Stop by tomorrow morning," Werner answered. "My secretary will have an envelope for you out front. It's best we not be seen together."

"I agree. Good night."

Werner took another puff from his cigar, ran his finger down a list of numbers, dialed his phone and gave the operator the Minot number he wanted.

"This is Salvatore."

"Guido, this is Werner."

"What've you got for me?"

"First off, I've got a policeman that'll sell me information."

"For how much?"

"Twenty dollars a week."

There was a pause and a soft chuckle. "You've got to be shitting me," Salvatore exclaimed. "Is this guy a janitor at the police station? Twenty bucks a week. I pay one cop in Minneapolis that much a day."

"I started with a low offer and he took it right off the bat. To some guys twenty bucks is a lot of money. A cop here in Bismarck doesn't make much."

"Yeah, yeah," Salvatore agreed. "So what's he given you?"

"He says that a lot rests on the word of the sheriff up in Wilton. He says he can identify the driver of the third truck."

"I talked to the old bastard on the way through Wilton the other day. He didn't tell me he could identify the driver. Hell, I've been giving him fifty bucks a month to leave my trucks alone when they go through his little shit-kicking town. Uncle Alphonse has sent four men over from Chicago to help find his gold. Bruno will take them through Wilton on the way down to see you tomorrow. I'll have them stop and have a little chat with the sheriff."

"Ah, why . . . why . . . why are they coming down to see me?" Werner asked, fear showing in his voice.

"Uncle Al wants you to see that he means business."

The phone clicked and the only thing Werner heard was a soft hum. "Oh, my God," he whispered.

Chapter Seventeen

The truckload of whiskey theft debacle had never been far from Andy Larson's mind since the day it had happened. The unnecessary death of Bert Garske tore at his heart, and he had gotten little sleep. *I've ruined these men's lives,* he told himself as he threw another small log on the bonfire. He held his hands out toward the flames and felt the warmth. *How was I to know they'd be that well armed? We'd watched them for over a month and never saw any signs of that kind of firepower. We just happened to pick the day they were hauling that damned gold.* He turned his back to the fire, rubbed his bare upper lip, and looked out into the darkening woods for the others. The fire wasn't necessary for a warm summer night like this, but it had become a ritual of their weekly meetings. *If they bring this whiskey heist case down here to Bismarck, there's no way in hell I'm going to be able to avoid Sheriff Walker. They don't even know yet that it's a truck of stolen whiskey and gold. They're looking at it as a case of four murdered men.*

"Hey, Andy," Billy Nestoss called from the trees. "I'm comin' in."

"Well, c'mon," Larson shouted. "I'm not gonna shoot you."

Billy Nestoss strode out of the darkened trees into the circle of light and stuck out his hand. "How are ya, Andy?"

Larson shook his hand. "I'm doing very well, Billy. I got promoted to sergeant yesterday."

"No shit? Well, congratulations *Sergeant* Larson," Nestoss

said, pumping his hand harder. "Did they make you shave off your mustache to get the rank?"

Larson laughed. "No, I did this in case I've got to meet with Sheriff Walker up in Wilton. Hopefully he won't recognize me without it."

"I suppose we'll have to drink to your promotion, won't we?" Nestoss asked with a grin.

"Yeah, I reckon we will," Larson agreed. "There's a seized bottle of some good stuff down there by the log."

"We all think it's great, you seeming to have an unending supply of *seized* whiskey for us to drink at our little get-togethers. We can stay away from our own private stash in the dugout," Nestoss said as he twisted the cork out of the bottle. "Here's to you, Sarge." He took a drink and handed the bottle to Larson.

Larson took a small drink and handed the bottle back to Nestoss. "Where's Garske and Bergavin?"

"They'll be here in a few minutes," he answered and took another drink.

Larson motioned for the bottle. "Who's got all the pistols from the other day?"

Nestoss took another sip and handed him the bottle. "I've got all four of 'em hidden down at the lumberyard. You've got the Tommy gun, don't ya?"

"Yeah, I keep it wrapped in canvas and hidden under the floor of my house. I sure as hell hope I don't have to use that thing. How's Mike doing?"

"He's awfully quiet, but he's staying busy getting ready to start the harvest. We might have to go out and help him a bit."

"That's only fair." Larson handed Nestoss the bottle without taking a drink. "We'd best save a little for Louie and Mike."

"Hello the fire," Louie Bergavin shouted. "You got any whiskey left?"

"Yeah, but much later and you wouldn't have gotten any,"

Nestoss called and waved the bottle above the fire.

Bergavin and Mike Garske walked out of the trees smiling.

"We stopped an' got us some ham an' bread," Garske said, holding up a brown paper bag. "I'm hungry an' nothin' beats a good ham sandwich."

"Andy here, made sergeant yesterday," Nestoss announced proudly. "And shaved his mustache off."

"Damn, that's great," Bergavin said, pumping Larson's hand. "Did you have to shave for . . . ?"

Larson raised his hand. "That's already been asked, and no, I did it in the hopes that the sheriff from Wilton won't recognize me with a smooth lip."

"Way to go, Andy," Garske said offering his hand. "You've worked hard for it."

"Drink up, boys," Nestoss said, handing Bergavin the bottle. "We'll have a sandwich in a few minutes."

On the second pass of the bottle, Mike Garske took a swallow and held the bottle against his chest. "Do you think we're going to have a lot of trouble because of the whiskey and gold, Andy?" he asked.

"Mike, that's a damned stupid question. It's bad enough we stole Salvatore's whiskey. If it's his gold, there won't be any resting on his part 'til he gets it back. We're gonna have to keep this quiet as hell. He's a bad man and nobody to be messed with."

"What if we gave it back to him?" Garske asked.

"How'd we do that?" Bergavin asked. "Tell him where the stuff's hidden and let him go get it?"

"That wouldn't make any difference to him. Guido Salvatore's not the forgiving kind," Larson answered. "Even if he got all the whiskey and gold back, he'd kill to make an example of someone. Remember what happened to those guys up in Minot? The man rules by brute force just like Al Capone and all those like him."

"Andy's right," Bergavin agreed. "We've got to be very careful about this. Gimme the damned bottle, Mike, I need a drink."

"Everybody sit down," Larson instructed, pointing at the logs around the fire. "We've gotta have a talk."

The four men sat down and continued to slowly pass the bottle.

"Louie, how are you doing? Is killing that man bothering you?" Larson asked.

Bergavin looked around at the others and shook his head. "I dreamed about it the first night or two, but I don't think it's bothering me now. He'd killed Bert and he'd have killed more of us, so I had to do what I did to stop him. I'm okay with it."

"Mike, what about you?"

Garske looked deeply into the fire, then up at Larson. "I dream every night about that bastard shooting at me," he said slowly. "I . . . I see the flash from the end of the gun barrel, and then I hear the Tommy gun firing and see him fly though the air to flop into the tall grass in the ditch. Then I dream about Bert being dead and us burying him up on the hill beside Ma and Pa." Garske blinked several times and rubbed the back of his hand under his nose. "I know it'll go away some day."

"I'm sure it will, Mike," Larson answered. "What about you, Billy."

Nestoss took a long drink and set the bottle on his knee. "Hell, Andy, I think about all that happened in those few minutes and wonder if it's true. We're in a pile of deep shit, aren't we?"

Larson held out his hand for the bottle. "Yeah, Billy, we are," he agreed and took a drink. "I'm sorry I got you boys into this mess. I truly am. I thought they'd just let us take the whiskey when they saw the guns. I didn't plan on the shooting. And I sure as hell didn't think any of us'd get killed. How were we to know there'd be all that gold on the truck and they'd be armed to the teeth to protect it? I made the mistake of underestimating the enemy. I don't know what to tell you, boys. I'm sorry, but I just really fucked up."

"Nobody forced us into this, Andy," Bergavin countered. "We all came on board of our own free will."

"Yeah," Garske agreed. "We were all gonna be whiskey rich. . . ."

"Now we're whiskey *and* gold rich," Nestoss interrupted. "We just gotta figure out a way we can live to spend it."

"I want you all to stop by the lumberyard tomorrow and pick up a pistol," Larson said. "I've just got a feeling that we'd best be packing heat from now on. Find some time to practice with the gun until you get good with it. Like Billy said, we're in a pile of deep shit. So we have to be prepared. Once again, boys, I'm sorry for what I've gotten you into."

CHAPTER EIGHTEEN

Chief Pearce stepped into the door of the Bismarck Police Department squad room. "Could I have your attention, please," he called out over the early morning din. "I just got a phone call that Sheriff Walker up in Wilton died last night. It was a heart attack. There'll be a funeral on Friday. We'll send a delegation up. Torkelson and Larson report to my office."

Larson looked over at Torkelson who shrugged and pointed his thumb down the hall. "Let's go see what he wants."

"Sit down," the Chief instructed, pointing at chairs beside his conference table. "Like I told you, Sheriff Walker died of a heart attack last night. What I didn't tell you is that it looks like he was worked over a bit before he died."

"Worked over?" Larson asked. "You mean beat up?"

"The highway patrol report says his face has the shit smashed out of it, and his clothes have been torn. One hand has two broken fingers. That could be pretty damned painful."

"Do you suppose it had to do with the shootings?" Torkelson asked.

"It all seems to fit," the Chief agreed. "A sleepy little town like that suddenly has a crime like Minot and Grand Forks. There's no doubt it has to do with booze running."

"We'll go down and talk to Werner," Larson volunteered.

The Chief nodded. "That's what I want. Turn up the pressure on him. I read your report about Salvatore, from Minot, being down there talking to him. I'd say the story about the third hay truck and whiskey are probably right on the money. Salvatore seems to keep a low profile with the law up there."

"Money works wonders," Larson interjected. "In some cases it's better than soap for keeping a person clean."

The Chief leaned forward and looked at Larson over the tops of his glasses. "That's good. I may have to use it. Now," he said, pointing at the door. "Go see Werner."

Larson drove the unmarked police car to the south side of Bismarck and parked it in the lot outside Werner Transportation.

"Damn, look at that fancy car parked in front," Larson remarked as they sat preparing to get out of their car.

"Yeah, that's a Packard Touring Salon. It's not from around here. It's got Illinois plates. Let's wait a few minutes and see who drives that thing."

Fifteen minutes later the front door of the building opened, and Bruno Campagna pushed out. Four smaller men, all dressed in dark suits and hats, walked silently with him to the Packard. One of them opened the door and slid behind the steering wheel. Bruno entered the other side and the other three men crawled into the back seat of the long automobile.

"I'll be damned," Larson said softly as he slouched down in the seat. "It looks like the Bear's been visiting Werner. I guess his boss isn't along on this trip. I don't recognize any of his friends. Those guys being here in the area might explain the sheriff getting worked over."

"Yeah, they'd be the ones to do it. Definitely a hard-looking bunch. Well, let's go visit Werner," Torkelson said as he opened his car door. "Maybe he can tell us where Salvatore is. Since I'm on the take from him, I'm going to have to let you be the hard-ass on this call."

Larson grinned. "I think I can handle that."

William Werner wiped a large handkerchief across his sweating face with trembling hands. "God, what have I gotten myself into?" he mumbled, as he thought about his conversation with Bruno and his four companions. "Those men wouldn't even think twice about killing me if Salvatore gave them the word. I've got to come up with some answers pretty damned soon."

The sharp rapping on his office door startled him. *My God, they're back.* He took another fast wipe at his face and stuffed the handkerchief in an open drawer. "Ah, come . . . come in," he called meekly. He was surprised when the door opened and the two policemen walked in. He cleared his throat and put on a weak, almost relieved, smile. "Well, do you have any word on my drivers?" he asked, starting to stand.

"No need to stand up, Mister Werner," Torkelson began, motioning with his hand.

"We ain't staying long," Larson finished. "We just saw Bruno and four of his friends leaving as we were coming in. What'd they want?"

Werner seemed to gather strength. "Ah, they were here to check on Mister Salvatore's door shipment."

"C'mon, Werner," Larson growled. "You can't bullshit an old bullshitter and I pride myself in being one of the best. What'd they really want?"

"Ease up, Andy," Torkelson said, putting a hand on his shoulder.

Larson shrugged his hand off and stepped closer to Werner's desk. "I want some straight answers. Now, what'd they want?"

Werner seemed to be trying to find an answer as he slowly shook his head. "I told you, they were here. . . ."

Larson slammed his hand down on Werner's desk. "Bullshit!" he shouted. "That fancy car they got into was from Illinois. They don't send a car from way over there to check on a damned door shipment!"

Torkelson again put his hand on Larson's shoulder. "Andy, he's not going to cooperate if you keep bullying him."

Larson reached up and pushed Torkelson's hand from his shoulder. "If I stay in here any longer I'm gonna rough him up," he muttered, pointing at the man behind the desk. "I'll be in the car."

When the door closed, Torkelson sat on the corner of the desk and smiled. "You'll have to excuse him, Mister Werner. He's a veteran of *The War* and he's a bit testy this morning. We just found out Sheriff Walker up in Wilton died of a heart attack last night. They're old friends, and it seems somebody had beaten the sheriff before he died."

Werner pulled the handkerchief from the drawer and gave his face two quick wipes. "That was no reason for him to treat me like that," he said slowly. "Do you suppose he could use a little extra money?"

Torkelson shook his head. "I doubt it, but I'll talk to him. He just made sergeant and he's trying to prove himself."

"Do they know who beat the sheriff?" Werner asked and took another blot at his sweating face.

"No, but I'd say those men who just left are likely candidates. They looked like real hard cases to me. Not the kind of people to be crossing or fooling with. I'll keep you posted on what the police find out, and you let me know if you hear anything that might be helpful in our investigation. And I'll have a little talk with Larson."

Werner stood up and proffered a shaking hand. "Thank you, Sergeant. There'll be an envelope out front for you Monday."

CHAPTER NINETEEN

Sergeant Torkelson chuckled as he slammed the car door. "Mister Werner is definitely convinced that *you* are one bad-ass and nobody to mess with."

"I really did want to slap him around a little," Larson said.

"He wants to know if you want to make a little extra money too."

"Sure, who wouldn't?"

"You want me to tell him that?" Torkelson asked.

"No, one of us being on the take is enough."

"I think Bruno and his friends had put a scare into Werner before we showed up. When I told him about somebody beating up the sheriff, he really paled and started to sweat."

"Yeah, I didn't think we made him that nervous just by walking in the door," Larson agreed. "But he wasn't looking too good when we arrived. I've got a little personal business to take care of. Can you cover for me for a couple of hours?"

"Sure, I've got a lot of paperwork to catch up on."

Andy Larson drove out on the road that bordered the Blackstead Ranch and admired the lush green countryside. *You can sure tell when North Dakota is having a good, rainy summer.* From time to time he could see the tan sandstone outcroppings where the stones had been broken out by his grandfather for his dugout. *Most people don't even realize that those stone formations have been cut,* he told himself. His grandfather had told him how he used hammers and chisels to break the stones loose, loaded them on a horse-drawn stone boat, and hauled them to his building site where he broke them into the proper sizes for his walls.

Larson drove past the gate and the trail that led down to the sandstone dugout where the whiskey and gold were hidden. He slowed and studied the area. The grass around the ditches stood tall and firm. There were no signs of tire tracks or any activity at the gate or the downhill trail beyond it. He parked a half mile down the road, jacked up the rear of the truck, removed a tire, carried it across the road, and hid it in the tall grass. *Now anyone passing here will think someone's gotten a flat and walked or caught a ride into town to get it fixed.* He looked both ways, lifted a shovel from the back of the truck, put it up over his shoulder. "Lots to do, lots to do," he chanted softly as he walked back up the road toward the gate.

A short time later, Andy Larson stood in the trees across from the sandstone dugout and studied his grandfather's work. The front was a stone wall with two windows and a door. The slope of the hill covered most of the side walls. The visible sandstone squares of various sizes and shapes were neatly placed and mortared. The short, soot-darkened sandstone chimney that protruded up through the old sod roof was hardly noticeable with all the grass that had grown up around it. Large rusty handmade hinges held the heavy, gray hand-hewn cottonwood door and shutters in place. Tee-shaped gun ports were cut into the door and shutters for use in case of an attack.

The old man could probably have forted up in there for a long while if necessary.

Larson walked to the front of the dugout, leaned the shovel against it, and groped around the eaves until he finally found the key for the large padlock on the door. *This damned thing isn't really for anything but show,* he thought as he worked the key in it. He swung the door open and looked at the rows of boxes against the far wall. *Damn, there's a fortune in booze and gold in here,* he told himself. *And right now all it can buy us is trouble.* He swept a cobweb out of the way with his hand and walked into the cold, dank interior of the dugout. He raised the wooden drop bars on the inside of the shutters and pushed them open to allow more light to stream in. *I really didn't look around in here too much the other day and it's too bad I haven't taken the time, since I was a kid, to come out here to appreciate all the effort and work Gramps put in this place when he built it,* he thought as he looked up at the massive hand-hewn cottonwood beams supporting the roof. A stone fireplace took up the far right corner of the room, and a set of bunk beds filled most of the left wall. *It's a piece of living history.* He tested the strength of a heavy wooden table set in a corner of the room. Satisfied, he dragged it over and positioned it under a window. He grabbed the legs of one of the two chairs hung on pegs from the rafters, wiggled it free, and set it beside the table.

He walked out the door and took a deep breath as he stood blinking in the bright sunlight. *It's actually kinda cool in there,* he told himself as he retrieved his shovel. He walked back in, leaned the shovel against the table, and lifted the top case from a stack of wooden whiskey boxes. *The two stacks from this corner'll be all I need to move.* When the last case was shifted, he pried it open with the blade of the shovel, pulled out a bottle, and set it on the table.

Larson put his foot to the top of the shovel blade and pushed it down into the soft earth where the wooden cases had been sitting. He lifted a shovelful of dirt and dropped it to the side. The fourth time he pushed the shovel into the deepening hole, he felt it hit the top of a canvas and leather bag. He set the shovel aside, dropped to his knees, and began to scoop dirt from the hole with his hands. His fingers closed on the leather handle of the bag. *Good.* He gripped the handle with both hands and began to wiggle and pull on it until he felt the bag begin to loosen and it suddenly pulled free. He hefted it from the hole, swung it over beside the table, and looked at it before beginning to brush the dirt from it with his hands. He wiggled the padlock on the leather band, let it drop, pulled a knife from his pocket, opened a blade, and slit a long hole in the canvas under the lock.

Larson pushed his hand down into the bag, brought up a handful of gold coins, and set them onto the table beside the whiskey bottle. He repeated this process until the bag was empty and large piles of shiny gold coins surrounded the bottle. He stood, brushed the dirt from his knees, pulled the chair out, and sat down. He twisted the cork top from the bottle, took a drink, and started to hum a French drinking song as he began to pile coins and stand them in even rows. When all of the gold coins were stacked, he sat back in his chair, smiled, and took another drink. *"Mademoiselle from Armentieres, parlez-vous? Mademoiselle from . . ."* he sang softly and started to laugh uproariously as he began to count the golden columns.

CHAPTER TWENTY

Andy Larson walked into the police squad room and flopped down in the chair behind his desk.

Sergeant Fred Torkelson looked up and tapped his pencil on the pile of paperwork in front of him. "Where'n the hell you been?"

"I went out to my grandfather's old place across the river."

"You've been gone over four hours."

"Geez, Tork, I told you I had some things to do."

"Yeah, well the latest report on Sheriff Walker's death is somewhere in that pile of papers on your desk. The rest is sergeant shit. Along with that massive pay raise comes a lot more paperwork."

Larson nodded and began to shuffle papers. "Here it is," he muttered, bringing up several clipped sheets of paper and reading briefly. "It doesn't tell us a hell of a lot more than we already knew."

"Yeah," Torkelson agreed. "And there's not much we can do from here. Go over my final report on the car theft ring. You'll see I put in there we're pretty sure most of the cars ended up being stripped down, sent north, and used to run booze on those back roads out of Canada."

"Okay. Did we get a final count on captured and confiscated cars from the Border Patrol? Anything new in the fire?"

Torkelson laughed. "There's an item in there I got this morning. One of the Studebakers stolen from here in Bismarck was found stuck in the mud on a back road just this side of the border two days ago. It'd been stripped down and had forty cases of that piss-poor imitation rum inside it. Tracks showed the driver had headed off across country on foot."

"I wonder if the driver has to pay when they lose something like that?" Larson joked.

"Those people moving the booze aren't very forgiving about much of anything," Torkelson answered. "My guess is that if the driver knows what's good for him, he's still going."

"From what we've seen in the past, I'll have to agree with you."

"Do you have any new ideas about the dead men and burned trucks?" Torkelson asked.

"No, but I'll have to go along with the idea it was probably a whiskey heist. We've seen that kind of violence up around Minot and Grand Forks, and it was just a matter of time before it moved down here."

"When we see people like Salvatore and his goons visiting in Bismarck. . . ."

"It's time to break out the bullet-proof underwear," Larson interrupted. "Let me finish reading your report and sign off on it."

"Okay, I've got a search warrant for Werner's garages and old barns. As soon as you're done, we'll get a few other men and go down there and poke around."

Larson fanned through the report, signed it, and stood up. "It's fine. Let's go."

"That didn't take long," Torkelson admonished. Standing, he shrugged into a jacket and pushed a sheaf of folded papers into a pocket. "I'll have the dispatcher get some men to meet us down there."

The intercom on William Werner's desk buzzed. "There are two policemen here to see you, Mister Werner."

Before he could stand, the door opened and Torkelson and Larson entered.

Torkelson dropped the folded papers on Werner's desk and smiled. "We're here to take a look around in some of your outbuildings," he announced. "Those are the search warrants." He leaned closer to Werner. "I guess I'm off your payroll," he whispered.

Werner adjusted his glasses, glanced through the papers, and glared up at Torkelson. "I'll be calling my attorney."

"Suit yourself. He's got ten minutes to get here," Torkelson said. "We'll wait down by the first garage. Ten minutes and we're starting."

"He can't get down here that fast," Werner argued.

"Tough shit," Larson growled over his shoulder as he followed Torkelson out the door. "Ten minutes."

William Werner ran across the asphalt lot in front of his main garage, waving his hat above his head. "Wait, wait!" he shouted. "My attorney'll be here in about five more minutes."

Torkelson pulled a watch from his pocket, glanced at it, dropped it back out of sight, and shrugged. "Like the Sergeant said, tough shit. Let's go."

"What're we lookin' for, Sarge?" one of the uniformed policemen asked.

Torkelson motioned with a hand above his head. "You four go around the outside of these buildings and look for something that might be a stolen truck of booze. It's probably hidden in a load of hay." The men spread out and disappeared around the corner of the building.

"Let's take a look inside, Andy," Torkelson said, leading the way into the cavernous garage that smelled of gas, oil, rubber, and unidentifiable strong odors. Several trucks with the easily recognizable Werner Transportation blue and yellow paint jobs were parked in the main room. Four men peered out of the darkness under two of the trucks that were straddling grease pits, and several other men turned from workbenches and looked at the two policemen outlined by the light streaming in through the door behind them.

A large man came out the door of the office and stood with his hands on his hips. "Can I help ya?" he boomed.

Torkelson pulled back his jacket to reveal his badge.

The man's voice softened considerably when he asked, "What can I do for you?" He glanced past the policemen and saw Werner and another man come into the garage.

"Good afternoon, Mister Werner," he called, touching his fingers to his hat brim. "Are these gentlemen with you?"

"Go back into the office, George," Werner instructed. "I'll call you if I need you. As a matter of fact, all you men go into the office and close the door." The men quickly complied with Werner's orders and the door was closed.

"Officers, this is my attorney, Cyril Shark," Werner said, motioning toward the short, pale, nattily dressed man beside him.

"I know who he is," Torkelson answered. "I see his picture in the papers a lot."

"I'm gonna look around," Larson announced and walked off toward the far end of the room.

"What is the reason for this search?" Shark demanded, puffing up his chest and standing as tall as he could.

Torkelson tipped his head back and looked down his nose at the lawyer. "You can read it in the search warrants. I've got work to do." He turned to go and stopped when Shark reached out and grabbed him by the elbow.

"I wasn't finished talking to you," Shark said, in a gravelly voice.

Torkelson looked down at Shark's hand, smiled insincerely,

and clamped a hard grip on the man's wrist. "You being the high profile attorney you are know the penalties for interfering with a police officer while he's attempting to conduct an investigation, *don't* you?"

The lawyer's eyes grew wide from the pain and he sucked in a deep breath. "Yes," he answered.

"Fine," Torkelson said, and released his grip on the man's wrist. "You *are* a smart man."

Shark grimaced as he rubbed his wrist. "I'll . . . I'll be calling the Chief about this," he threatened.

"While you're at it call the Mayor and the Police Commissioner and send a letter to the President, you pompous little asshole," Torkelson hissed. "Now get out of my way."

"You probably shouldn't have done that," Larson said as he rejoined him.

"Yeah, I'm sure that'll come back to bite me in the ass," Torkelson agreed. "But it sure felt good."

Chapter Twenty-One

William Werner stood in the door of the last old horse barn and wiped at his face with a large handkerchief. "Are you satisfied now?" he called to Andy Larson as he crawled down the ladder from the hayloft.

"Yeah," Larson answered, wiping his hands on his pant legs. "Where'd Tork go?"

"I think he's outside smoking a cigarette," Werner answered.

"This wouldn't be a smart place to smoke, would it?" Larson asked, looking back up into the loft. "You pay a lot of insurance for these buildings?"

Werner wiped at his face again and nodded. "Maybe too much."

"It'd be a shame if this place caught fire," Larson said. "I imagine all of these buildings would go up in flame in no time."

Werner nodded and shuddered when he remembered the words of Guido Salvatore: *"You get me some answers or you might start having some serious real estate problems. Like those big barns of yours burning."*

"Would you mind if I went back to my office now?" Werner asked meekly.

"Go ahead," Larson answered and made a shooing motion with his hands. "Shit, you didn't have to come along in the first place. Beat it."

Torkelson ground out his cigarette under his shoe heel and walked over to join Larson and Werner. "Clean as a whistle,

Werner," he said. "Sorry we bothered you. Tell your little attorney, Sharkey or Shark Bait or Shark Butt or whatever his name is, I hope his wrist's okay and that he learned a lesson about places he can and can't put his hand."

Werner walked away shaking his head, wiping at his face and muttering to himself.

Larson began to chuckle. "I don't think he's a very happy fella."

Torkelson nodded and grinned. "So, what've you got going tonight?"

"Believe it or not, I've got a date with Becky," Larson answered. "We haven't had a date in over three months because of my being on that damned night shift work. Now I've got the whole weekend off."

"Are you going to tell me that a young stud like you hasn't been sneaking over to her place at night after you got off?"

"She lives in Daniels' rooming house, and that old lady would've put a load of buckshot in my ass if I'd have tried to sneak in there. Besides Becky's been up at the University most of the summer going to classes."

"Where're you taking her?"

"Damn, you're getting snoopy about my private life all of a sudden, ain't you?" Larson countered.

"Well, where are you going?"

"We're going out to Samples' blind pig south of Mandan. They've got a band there tonight. We'll be able to do a little dancing."

"And drinking," Torkelson added, with a smirk.

"Yeah, why, you gonna raid the place?"

"No. I just didn't wanna go someplace and catch you drinking. Now I know to stay away from Samples'."

"That's a hell of a good plan, Tork. I'll see you Monday morning."

CHAPTER TWENTY-TWO

Andy Larson knocked on the door of Mrs. Daniels' rooming house. A curtain over the window in the door was pulled aside, and a round-faced white-haired woman peered out. She broke into a wide smile and the door swung open. "Why, Mister Larson, it's been ages," she chortled as she grabbed his hand. "Please, do come in. Becky should be ready in a minute."

"It's good to see you again Missus Daniels," Larson said as he followed her into the living room. "It has been a long time, hasn't it? Your house always smells so good. Is that fresh bread I smell?"

"Fresh made dinner rolls," she answered. "Would you care for one?"

"No thanks, Missus Daniels. Becky and I are going down to Rosie's for tonight's special. Pot roast, if I'm not mistaken. Then I'm taking her out dancing."

The little white-haired lady patted his arm. "That sounds like a fun night. Let me go call her."

But before Mrs. Daniels could turn, Andy saw a pair of black shoes and well-turned ankles appear on the top step. As the young woman walked quickly down the stairs and into his full view, he felt a warm glow spread over him.

Becky Dansworth wore a short, red "flapper" dress that clung to the curves of her body and exposed her silk-stocking–encased ankles and knees.

Damn, she's even prettier than I'd remembered, he thought when he saw her full red lips, soft blue eyes, and bobbed blond hair. *It looks like she's picked up a few new makeup tricks while she was away at college this summer.*

Becky arched an eyebrow and smiled as she strode across the room. "Hi, Andy." Her voice was strong and smooth.

"Damn . . . ah, I mean, dang, you look good, Becky," Andy finally managed to say.

"Well, Andy Larson, you don't look so bad yourself," she said, with a soft laugh. "All dressed up in that jacket, fancy tie, and shined shoes. And no *mustache.*"

Andy rubbed his upper lip and felt himself blush as he completely forgot all the catchy lines he was going to woo her with. "Um . . . Well, thank you, Becky." *Damn, where'd my mind go?*

"You two sure make a fine-looking couple," Mrs. Daniels complimented. "I'm sure everyone on the dance floor will be giving you two the eye."

"Why, that's most kind of you to say, Ruby," Becky answered and took hold of Andy's arm. "I won't be too late."

"You two just go out and have fun," Mrs. Daniels instructed. "The front door'll be open whenever you get home, Becky."

Larson opened the door of his truck and helped his beautiful date step up into the front seat. "I'm going to have to buy a car one of these days," he said lamely as he closed the door. *Why'n the hell'd I say that?* he asked himself as he ran around and climbed in behind the steering wheel. *The girl's turning me into some kind of blubbering idiot.*

Andy and Becky had a pleasant meal, interspersed with questions and answers about how each of them had spent their summer and about their future plans.

Becky locked her arm through Andy's as they walked slowly back to his truck. "There's something that was never brought up while we were eating. How do you like being a policeman?" she asked.

He reached out and opened her door. "It's probably not the best job in the world, but I like it. I've moved up through the ranks pretty fast and have an understanding partner. It's a good job. Now let's head out to Samples' for the dance. I'm told they have a great band tonight."

Again they made small talk as they drove across the bridge over the Missouri River and turned south down the winding road through the river bottoms.

"I wonder where Whitney is? He should be stepping out of the trees to check us," Andy said, leaning forward above the dash to get a better view of the road.

As if in answer to his question, a flashlight beam suddenly appeared in the middle of the road ahead and wig-wagged them to a stop. The beam washed back and forth across the truck as the man carrying it approached.

"Hey, Whitney," Andy shouted.

The beam was lowered, and a young man stepped forward to put his foot on the running board. He raised the beam briefly across Andy's face and then across to Becky.

"Is this a raid, *Sergeant* Larson?" the man asked, putting the beam onto his own face before snapping off the light. "Good evening, Miss Becky," he continued, and they could see his grin from the dash lights. "I heard you got promoted, Andy. Con-gratulations."

"Now why would I go and raid my favorite gin mill?" Andy asked.

"I don't know, boredom?" Whitney answered. "We've got a damned good band down there tonight. Called The Red River Ramblers. Brought 'em in all the way from Fargo. Six of the hottest musicians around. I'm waiting for somebody to come up and relieve me for a while so I can go down and listen. You'll be able to dance the soles right off yer shoes, Miss Becky."

"How big of a crowd you got tonight, Whitney?" Andy asked.

"Somewhere around eighty, eighty-five."

"Good crowd! You Samples Brothers must be getting rich," Andy declared. "I'll buy you a drink when you come down."

"That's a deal. I get a break around eleven, and I'll be in need of a drink by then," Whitney answered. "I'll take a turn or two around the dance floor with Miss Becky, too."

"Only if she's got soles left on her shoes," Andy said as he put the truck in gear. "See you down there."

"The brothers have quite a system of road blocks along here," Andy said as they drove away. "Did you hear that rattle and little bump just now? That's part of the system. The man on guard back there has an ax he uses to cut a rope in case of a raid by the Feds. The rope releases three big, well-spaced cotton-wood logs that fall across the road. When the logs drop, they pull a rope hooked into a pulley, and the rope from the pulley drags a steel plate off the road. That leaves a three-foot wide trench for a tire to drop into. An alarm goes off in the barn, the booze disappears, and all that's left is the keg of beer. Beer is a minor expense and only a small fine."

Becky laughed. "That's pretty neat. How do you know all about it?"

"I helped dig the trenches."

"Andy, you're a cop."

"I've known the Samples brothers since we were crawlers. A lot of times friendship is stronger than the law."

Becky studied Andy's profile in the lights from the dash. *He's a good man, I can tell.*

CHAPTER TWENTY-THREE

The Samples brothers had converted a sprawling milk barn into a dance hall and the big double doors opened out onto another open-air concrete dance floor. The inside of the barn was well lit, with a wooden stage in addition to the dance floor. Three bars were placed along the walls, and a large keg of free beer took up a portion of one corner. Tables and chairs ringed the dance floor. The outdoor area was surrounded by benches and dimly lit by a surrounding string of small light bulbs that twinkled in the moonlight. This area was more for slow dancing and necking.

Admission to the Samples brothers' barn was a dollar a person, and that included the free beer. Couples were a dollar and a half.

Andy parked his truck off in the trees by itself. "I don't like to get hemmed in," he explained as he opened the door for Becky. "Being a cop, I might have to leave in a hurry, so I always park over here." They could hear the music from the barn as they walked arm in arm to a man sitting at a table by the door.

"That'll be a buck and a half, Andy," Julian Samples said, admiring Becky.

"Looks like quite a crowd," Andy observed as he handed him the money.

"Not as big as last Saturday, but dang close. Enjoy yourselves."

Andy and Becky stood inside the doors to let their eyes adjust to the brightness.

"Hey, Andy," Louie Bergavin called, as he stood and waved. "C'mon over, we got room at our table."

Andy led as they weaved their way between the tables to join Louie and his date. Andy and Louie stuck out their hands and put on a mock show of wrestling.

"Andy, this is Jean Bancroft," Louie said, pointing to an attractive dark-haired woman sitting at the table.

"Jean and I know each other," Becky interrupted. "She just started teaching at Will Moore, and I teach at Roosevelt, so we've met at the teachers' orientation meetings."

The two women smiled and shook hands.

"Hello, Jean."

"Hi, Becky."

Andy laughed. "Do you suppose we'll get any smarter since we're both dating teachers?"

Louie gave Becky's hand a light shake. "Gee, Becky, it's good to see you. You've summered well. College life in Fargo must agree with you. Of course, Andy talked about you all the time you were gone. Everything good," he added quickly.

"It's good to meet you, Jean," Andy said and touched his fingers to his forehead.

"Now that we all know each other, how about me getting us all a drink?" Louie asked. "What'll you have?"

Andy and Becky were laughing as they returned to their table, followed closely by Louie and Jean.

"They're quite a band," Jean said, pointing to the men jumping around on the stage. "They really get into it."

"They sure do," Louie agreed and nodded at the large clock on the far wall. "It's after eleven. I'd best be gettin' out of here. Dad starts banging on his anvil at sunup, and I've gotta be there to make echoes."

Andy nodded. "Yeah, I think it's about time for all of us to be heading into town. One more and I'll have to sleep out here in the truck, and I don't think Becky's up for that."

Becky laughed. "Oh, I don't know. I wonder where Whitney is? He said he'd be down for a drink about eleven, and we haven't seen him."

"He probably fell asleep," Andy said.

Suddenly the sound of the band was drowned out by the staccato burst of a machine gun being fired in the barn. Women screamed and men swore. The members of the band dropped to the floor.

Andy shoved Becky to the floor and lay across her. Out of the corner of his eye he could see Louie doing the same with Jean.

Another burst of gunfire tore through the roof, and the only sound was the last of the empty cartridge cases from the machine gun clinking on the concrete floor.

"All right, listen up, people!" a voice boomed.

Andy turned his head and tried to see who was shouting.

Four men in dark suits and hats stood inside the doors to the barn. Each of them had a black cloth with eye and mouth holes cut in it tucked up under the front of their hats. One man held a sawed-off pump shotgun at his shoulder pointed at the crowd, while two of the men waved Thompson machine guns at them. A third man with a smoking machine gun on his hip inserted a new clip of ammunition in it and worked the action. The small group of people from the outside dance floor crowded through the door with their hands clasped behind their heads. The men's faces were flushed with fear and anger, and tears ran down the faces of the women. A short man with a shotgun prodded the back of the last man through the door and stood off to one side.

One of the men swung his machine gun up under his arm, stepped up onto the bandstand, walked over to a microphone, and tapped his finger on it. "Now, I know you can all hear me," he said, in a taunting voice. "I don't like to shout. It affects my temper. Everyone back up on your feet. One of us is going to pass among you with a large canvas bag. Ladies, you can keep your wedding rings, but put your purses in the bag. Gents, I want your watches, wallets, and car keys put in there. When you've dropped that stuff in, I want you to pull out your front pants pockets. We just want to make sure you gave everything. You bartenders, bring the cash drawers over to the table by the door. Now everyone get on your feet and put your hands behind your head. I should warn you, these men aren't afraid to shoot, so don't try anything funny. A shotgun or a machine gun will usually take out more than one person. Think about it."

Andy rose to his feet and held out his hand to Becky, who grasped it and stood.

Louie stood and lifted Jean to her feet. Everyone in the room quickly joined them.

"I told you to put your hands behind your heads," the man at the microphone shouted. "When it comes time to put your things in the bag and pull out your pockets, you can bring your hands down and then I want them right back up behind your head."

"What're we gonna do?" Louie whispered.

"We're outgunned. Do as they say," Andy answered. "Just do as they say."

"Have you got a gun?" Louie asked, quietly.

Andy nodded his head slightly.

"No talking," the man at the microphone growled.

CHAPTER TWENTY-FOUR

The man on the stage stepped to the front of it and moved his machine gun slowly back and forth across the crowd. "Go get it, boys!" he shouted.

The shortest of the masked men tucked the shotgun under his arm and flapped a large canvas bag open. Another man joined him, and they stepped to the front of the people from the outside dance floor and said something. The first man slowly put his hands down and dug a wallet out of his back pocket and dropped it in the open bag. He pulled a large gold pocket watch out by the gold chain, unhooked it and let it fall in behind his wallet.

The man holding the bag nodded and motioned for more.

The man reached into his front pocket, brought out a handful of paper money and coins and tossed them into the bag. He pulled out both of his front pockets, shrugged and raised his hands.

The bagman sidestepped to a woman, who quickly dropped her purse in with the man's things.

The process continued on through the crowd.

"We gotta do something," Louie whispered.

Andy slowly shook his head. "You girls be calm," he said softly. "Just let them take the money and things. We don't want to do anything to make them start shooting."

A short burst of machine gun fire broke the silence, and several women screamed.

The man on the stage, with a smoking weapon pointed at the ceiling, lowered the gun and stepped back to the microphone. "Some of you people are beginning to irritate me," he said softly. "Next time I have to do that, I won't be putting holes in the roof. Now, no talking, understand?"

The man with the bag was holding his shotgun up under a man's chin, and all the other armed men were swinging their weapons nervously back and forth at the crowd.

The man on the stage continued. "See, now all my men are nervous. That's not a good thing."

Andy stared at the back of the man at the next table. *They're getting edgy. Please people; don't do anything stupid,* he thought and took a deep breath. *If he pats my jacket will he feel the gun in there? What'll I do then?*

The bagman, standing in front of Louie, looked up at him. "Gimme vat ya got, beeg man," he said, in a guttural voice.

Do like he says, Andy fervently hoped.

Louie's eyes were thin slits of anger as he looked down at the little man and slowly obeyed.

The bagman sidestepped to Jean, who quickly dropped her purse into the bag. He reached out with his free hand and stroked Jean's breasts. "Ya got anyting in der I could use, cutie?" he growled.

Out of the corner of his eye, Andy could see Louie grow tense. *Don't do it. He's trying to provoke you.*

The bagman turned his masked face and looked at Louie as he again stroked Jean's breasts. "Vat ya tink, beeg man? I tink I could use some a dis."

"C'mon, Rudy," the other masked man said. "We're almost done an' the boss ain't gonna like it if you start any shit with this guy."

The bagman nodded and sidestepped to Becky. "Vell, vat ya

got fer me?" he asked, holding out the bag and eyeing her breasts.

Becky dropped her purse, stood taller, pursed her lips, and spit on the man's mask.

Oh, God, here it comes, Andy thought, as he tensed and prepared to fight.

The bagman wiped at his mask with the back of his hand and laughed. "Vell, now ve know who's got da balls in dis place," he growled as he sidestepped to Andy. "Dat's vun helluva voman ya got der, buddy."

Andy quickly dropped his wallet and watch, pulled out his pockets, and let a handful of money fall into the bag.

"Dat vun's wert keepin'," the bag man said, nodding toward Becky as he sidestepped away without patting Andy's coat.

Andy let out a deep breath and felt the adrenaline rush flow out of him.

When the bagman had finished, he emptied the cash drawers into his bag, slung it over his shoulder, tipped his fingers to his hat brim, and walked out the door.

The other masked men backed to the doors and waited, casually waving their weapons back inside at the crowd.

The man on the stage stepped back to the microphone. "I want to thank all of you ladies and gentlemen for your co-operation and generous contribution to our retirement fund. I would advise all of you to stay in here for at least a half hour. You don't have any idea how long one of my boys might be out there waiting for an excuse to shoot someone." He walked to the door, waved his hand, and disappeared into the darkness.

Suddenly the outside air was shattered by staccato bursts of machine-gun fire, followed by a large whooshing noise and a burst of bright flame.

"Son-of-a-bitch!" Andy shouted. "They've shot up and set fire to the cars out front."

CHAPTER TWENTY-FIVE

The building was a cacophony of screams, yells, tipping furniture, and breaking glass.

One of the bartenders ran to a wall phone, lifted the receiver to his ear, and twisted the crank. "Shit, they've cut the phone lines!" he yelled, dropping the receiver to swing below the phone.

Suddenly the building was dark except for flickering firelight from outside. "There go the electrical lines," Andy shouted. "Louie, you help where you can." He put his hand on Becky's back and gave her a gentle shove. "C'mon, you and Jean take my truck and go for help. Find the closest phone."

"What if they're waiting out there like they said they'd be?" Jean asked.

"They said that to make people stay here," Andy answered. "Trust me, they'll get out of the area as fast as they can."

"Do you still have your keys?" Becky asked as she and Jean ran alongside him out the back door of the barn to avoid the burning vehicles.

"I never take them out in the hopes somebody'll steal it," Andy answered as he yanked the passenger side door open and ran around the front of the truck to open the other door. "Get in!"

Jean jumped in and pulled her door shut.

Becky stepped up onto the running board, leaned back, and gave Andy a quick kiss on the cheek. "That's for luck," she said as she slid in under the steering wheel and reached for the keys.

Andy grinned as he slammed her door shut and touched his cheek where she had kissed him. "Get going! Call the sheriff and the fire departments. Go!"

Becky started the truck, slipped it into gear, and spun the wheels in a tight circle to get it to the road. "Hang on," she called to Jean who had her hands braced against the ceiling to keep her place on the seat.

Andy gave a quick wave and ran back toward the fires.

Someone had started a bucket brigade and sloshing pails of water were passed from man to man to be thrown on the line of burning vehicles. Two men had found fire extinguishers in the building and had meager streams of water shooting at the flames.

"This is a waste of time," Julian Samples shouted. "You can't put out that damned gasoline. We've got to try to save the building."

As if to emphasize his point, gas tanks in two of the vehicles exploded, throwing huge, brilliant balls of flame and burning residue higher and farther out from the line. Men drew back, putting their arms up to their faces to protect them from the heat and flames.

Andy saw Louie wave at him and returned the gesture. "C'mon with me. I've got to go find out what happened to Whitney."

As Andy dog-trotted up the road, Louie caught up with him and matched his stride. "The girls get out of here okay?" he asked.

"Yeah," Andy answered. "They'll get help. Those guys were smart. This isn't the first time they've made a hit like this. Phone wires cut so we can't call out. Shooting up the vehicles, knowing there'll probably be a fire. Taking out the electricity when they're through."

"That Becky's quite a gal," Louie commented. "I find it hard to believe that she'd spit in that guy's face."

"That was one of the most stupid things I've seen in my life," Andy said. "I was sure I was gonna be in a fight. A fight I probably couldn't win."

"You've got a gun."

"In case you hadn't noticed, so did they. They had me outgunned with two shotguns right there and the men with the choppers watching over the whole thing."

"Yeah, you're right. Sorry, I wasn't thinking. Whitney should be up here pretty soon."

"At least they didn't cut the rope for the road blocks. They didn't know about them or they'd have done it for sure."

"What road blocks?"

"I'll tell you later. Whitney was right up here when I saw him last." Andy slowed to a walk and stepped off the road to the guard post. He found the flashlight hanging from the tree, switched it on, and swung the beam in a short arch. "Son-of-a-bitch," he said softly when the light found Whitney hanging by his neck from a nearby tree branch. "Those dirty, rotten bastards. Help me cut him down."

Louie grabbed Whitney around the legs and lifted him so Andy could cut the rope, and the two of them lowered him gently to the ground. He ran the beam of light over him briefly and snapped it off.

"He's been shot, but it looks like he was still alive when they hanged him."

"What makes you say that?"

Andy snapped the light on again, knelt, and lifted Whitney's hand. "Those are rope burns on his palms and fingers. Like he tried to lift himself but wasn't strong enough. Those are fingernail marks on his neck." He turned the light off, stood, and threw the flashlight as hard as he could into the woods. "Bastards!" he screamed. "Dirty-rotten-son-of-a-bitching-bastards!"

"Take it easy, Andy," Louie said, patting his friend on the shoulder.

"Yeah," Andy agreed, his voice barely a whisper. "Now they've added murder to the robbery charges. That little bastard Rudy and I are gonna meet again. I haven't seen his face, but I'll never forget his voice or his accent. Trust me, I'll find and kill that murdering little shithead if it's the last thing I do, so help me God."

"But you don't know he did it," Louie objected.

"No, but I'm going to make an example of him. Kind of like what those people up in Minot do with the guys who steal their booze."

CHAPTER TWENTY-SIX

Chief Pearce sat at his desk staring intently at some papers before he looked up at Sergeant Andy Larson, standing in front of him. "Larson, I've been trying to decide what to do about you and all the shit that happened over at Samples' blind pig Saturday night. Mandan and Morton County's not in my jurisdiction, so there's not much I can do officially to help them."

The Chief lifted the sheets of paper he had been studying and waved them at Larson. "This is a good complete report you filed on the whole incident, and I sent a copy of it over to Sheriff Wenzel. I'm sure he'll call as soon as he reads it. Now this is a question I know will be coming at me from the newspapers and a number of pious sons-of-bitches above me: What in the hell was a sergeant from the Bismarck Police Department doing in a place like that?"

"To be honest, Chief, I was dancing and drinking," Larson answered. "I had a date with a very pretty lady and we were enjoying ourselves, up until those masked assholes with the guns showed up."

Chief Pearce sighed and steepled his fingers in front of his chin. "Larson, you and I know there aren't a lot of saints on this police force, but I don't have any choice. I'm going to have to suspend you for thirty days. If I can get you a faster hearing, it won't be that long and you'll be back at work."

Larson nodded. "I understand, sir."

"Turn your badge and gun in to Sergeant Torkelson. You're a damn fine cop, but I have to do something since it's all over the news that you were there when the robbery and murder happened. Have you got any idea who these hoods were?"

"No, sir, they were masked. I don't have a guess, but I know they weren't locals."

Chief Pearce looked hard at Larson and nodded. "Now, get your ass out of here and go see Torkelson. Make sure he knows where he can reach you if necessary. I'm sure Sheriff Wenzel'll want to have a talk with you."

Larson saluted. "Yes, sir."

The policeman in charge of the property room looked up from a pile of paperwork to see Andy Larson walking up to his wire cage. "Hi, Andy," he said. "What's this rumor I heard that you're being suspended for that crap over at Samples' on Saturday night?"

Larson shook his head. "There're no secrets around here, are there, Chuck?" he asked, opening his coat to show his shoulder-holstered pistol. "So far, I'm still on duty. You wanna see my badge? I've got that too."

"No, Andy, I believe you. Was it as bad over there as the stories make it out to be?"

"Some punk hoods robbed everybody, shot the place up, burned most of the cars, and killed a friend of mine. End of story."

The policeman raised his hands. "Okay, sorry I asked. You need something in here?"

"I'd like to look at some of that shit we brought in from the car theft case. I think it's in boxes on a shelf in back."

The policeman reached over and unlatched the door. "If you know where it is, go help yourself. I don't think I'll ever get caught up with this damned paperwork. Holler if you need anything. You look kinda naked without your mustache."

"Yeah," Larson answered, rubbing his smooth upper lip. "Thanks, Chuck, it won't take me long." He glanced at the items of evidence as he walked slowly to the back of the room. *Aha, there they are.* He stopped and leaned back to see if the policeman at the desk could see him. Satisfied, he sorted through a box of thin metal drums, chose two, opened his jacket, and tucked one under each armpit. *The fifty round drums will work fine. The hundred's are too heavy.* He continued to the back of the room and shuffled boxes on a shelf, making enough noise so he was sure the man at the desk would hear.

Returning to the front of the room, Larson opened the door and stepped out into the hall. "Thanks, Chuck, I didn't find the stuff. Tork must have it. See you later."

Andy Larson walked into the squad room, pulled a chair over to Torkelson's desk, and flopped down onto it. "When are they going to give you your own office?" he asked looking around the room. "A sergeant should be able to have a private conversation without everyone in the room overhearing it."

Torkelson glanced at all the empty desks. "Damn, Andy, right now I don't see anybody else in here, so I don't figure anybody's listening."

"Yeah, well, you know why I'm here," Larson said, bringing the pistol out of his shoulder holster. He dropped the cylinder, tipped the weapon up, and caught the bullets as they fell free. "Want to check it?" he asked, holding out the pistol.

Torkelson took the gun, glanced at the back of the cylinder and, with a flick of his wrist, snapped it closed. "You got another one of these?"

"Not on me," Larson answered honestly as he stood the six cartridges in a neat row on the desk.

"I'd advise you to carry one."

"That goes without question. I've got a forty-five in my

truck." He brought his wallet out of his coat pocket, pulled it open, and unhooked his shield. "I've only got one of these," he joked as he slid it onto the desk. He looked around the room again to make sure they were still alone. "I'm going to go kill somebody, Tork."

Torkelson shook a cigarette out of a pack on his desk and stuck it in the corner of his mouth. "If you are," he struck a match, lit the cigarette, and took a deep drag of smoke, "why are you telling me this?"

"I don't know. I figure I can trust you."

"Why in the hell would you tell a cop, you idiot? Trust me? Do you think I'll be easier on you when I arrest you because you told me about it beforehand? I'm a cop. I have to do what's right."

"I'm not going to kill anybody here in Bismarck."

Torkelson shook his head and blew a series of smoke rings and chuckled. "That takes a load off my mind. You're bullshitting me, right?"

"No, I'm going to kill the bastards that murdered my friend Whitney Samples. It's something I have to do. They shot him, and then they hung him up by the neck and he strangled. I don't like that. It's a damned hard way for a man to die."

"There was nothing in your report about him being strangled."

"His hands were rope burned, and he had fingernail marks on his neck from trying to save himself. It's up to the medical examiner to report that. Until then, it's just a cop's theory."

"Your report says you didn't recognize any of those men because they wore masks. Did you lie in the report?"

"No, I didn't recognize any of them, but I'll know one of those bastards when I meet him again."

"How'll you do that?"

"One of the others called him Rudy. He's a short little shit, and I know his voice and accent. Trust me, I'll find him."

"Is this gonna be like the still that blew itself up down in Dog Town a while back?"

"It works on the same principle. It speeds up the court system," Larson answered. "I know those guys that shot up Samples' place Saturday aren't locals. They're people who work by their own set of laws, and I've had about all I can take. I've got a few laws of my own I play by from time to time." Larson stood and stuck out his hand. "It's been a pleasure working with you, Tork. This suspension gives me the time I need for my search. I'll be in touch. If Wenzel wants to get hold of me, tell him I put everything I know in that report." He shook Torkelson's hand and walked to the door. "I came in and cleaned out my desk Sunday afternoon. I knew this was coming." He opened the door, turned and touched his fingertips to his brow. "See you, Tork."

"Oops, wait a minute, Andy, I forgot to mention that your buddy Bernie Maxwell is back from that school they sent him to."

"Shit." Larson paused and looked back. "Well, I won't have to see the bastard for at least thirty days." He stepped out the door, closed it quietly, moved a big house plant, picked up the metal drums, and tucked them back under his jacket.

"Take care of yourself, Andy," Torkelson shouted.

Larson raised his hand to signal he'd heard his friend, and he whistled softly as he walked toward the door.

He stopped at three gun shops and bought boxes of cartridges to load in the metal drums lying on the front seat of his truck. *No sense in calling attention to myself by buying a lot of ammo in one day.* Now that he had plenty of the correct ammunition, he was going out into the country to familiarize himself with the Thompson machine gun he'd taken during the whiskey-truck heist.

CHAPTER TWENTY-SEVEN

William Werner leaned forward across his desk, scooted the phone to him, and lifted the receiver. "This is Werner," he answered.

"This is Salvatore," a voice growled. "What do you have for me today?"

Werner took a deep breath. "I'm sorry, Guido, I don't have anything new for you." He held the phone receiver away from his ear to soften the string of curses flying from it. "I'm sorry, Guido," he repeated, trying to make his voice sound strong.

"Let me tell you something, you little pissant," Salvatore hissed. "Uncle Al has sent some of his boys over to help with this. He's not getting any happier about his missing gold, and I'm flat-assed pissed off about my whiskey! You remember the men with Bruno last week?"

Werner cleared his throat. "Yes, I remember."

"Three of them work for Al Capone. Bruno and Rudy are my men. I see in the papers that the sheriff down there in Wilton had a heart attack. Hard luck. Something like that might happen to you."

"The police tell me he was beaten before he had the heart attack," Werner volunteered, weakly.

"*Oh, no,*" Salvatore answered, mock horror in his voice. "Do you suppose that could be a lesson to certain people? Maybe a sign of something bad to come?"

"I'm trying to get information for you, Guido. One of the

cops I was paying under the table has suddenly gotten a change of heart. I've got other cops, but there's nothing new coming out. Most of the investigation is being handled by the State Highway Patrol and other state law enforcement offices. I don't have anybody that high up."

"Well, then I'd say that you'd best be getting a few of those people on your secret payroll. Remember what I told you about fires?"

"I remember." Werner dug a handkerchief from his pocket and began to wipe at the sweat that suddenly appeared on his forehead.

"Buildings like garages have terrible fire records. They're just chock full of highly flammable substances like gas, oil, and grease. Then look at those old horse barns of yours. All that hay and aged, dry wood. *Poof,* and they're all gone. I'd advise you to be checking your insurance."

"Please, Guido . . ."

"From now on you'll address me as *Mister Salvatore,*" Salvatore interrupted. "Only my friends call me Guido. You're not my friend. A friend would have gotten me the scoop on who stole my whiskey along with Uncle Alphonse's gold. When you come up with something usable for me, we'll be friends again. Understand?"

Werner's voice was almost a whisper when he answered. "I understand, Mister Salvatore." The phone clicked dead and he hung up the receiver. "Oh, God . . ." He took a swipe at his face and shuddered.

Suddenly, William Werner slammed his hands down on his desk. "Bullshit!" he shouted, jumping to his feet. He walked over to a cabinet, flung the door open, and pulled out a bottle of liquor. *This is bullshit! I didn't get to be this big a business by quaking in my boots when some wop gangster like Guido Salvatore threatens me.* He pulled the cork, took a healthy swallow, coughed, and wiped at his eyes. *You won't call me a pissant again, you wop bastard. I'll show you who's got balls. You may be a big shot in Minot, but you sure as hell don't run Bismarck.*

Werner walked back to his desk and flipped a switch on his intercom. "Lana, get hold of Bill Hall and tell him to come to my office right away." He folded his arms and sat on the corner of his desk to wait. *Salvatore won't think little pissant when he tangles with me the next time.*

Minutes later there was a firm rap on Werner's office door. "Come in."

The door opened and Bill Hall, a small, hard-eyed, balding man entered. He wore a rumpled blue jacket and pants and was in need of a shave. He clutched a shapeless sweat-stained hat in his large callused hands, and his collar-loose tie was stained from past meals. He was not a neat-looking man, but he was a good man when it came to security. Years before, heavy-handed tactics had caused his dismissal from a state law enforcement agency. "What d'ya need, Boss?" he asked, as he pushed the door shut behind him.

"How much muscle do you have down at the shops?"

"Depends on what ya need. Ya mean like lifting?"

"No, I want at least ten men willing to fight and aren't afraid to use a gun. Men with balls like coconuts. Five dollars a week bonus for anyone who wants to kick some ass."

Hall gave him a crooked smile and thumbed his gray walrus mustache. "Hell, I know of at least nine or ten men right off the bat that'll do about anything you want for an extra five bucks a week. Me included," he added. "Most of them damned veterans are tough as leather and ain't 'fraid of nothin'."

"Good. I want a man outside and a man inside each of the major garages, warehouses, and old barns at night. Tell them to bring pistols, shotguns, or rifles. Whatever they feel they're good with. I'll supply the ammunition, so make a list of what you'll need."

"Damn, Boss, what's happening?"

"I've got a punk wop from Minot who's threatening to burn me out. Put a couple of armed men roaming around the complex during the day. I want a show of power, but I figure he'll try to do his fire work under the cover of darkness."

"I'll have a crew bring out those two old fire pumper-wagons that're stored in the back of warehouse number two. We'll check 'em out and fill 'em with water."

"Good idea, Bill. I'd totally forgotten those old wagons. They're horse drawn, but we can park them between the barns. Have somebody pick up a truckload of extra fire extinguishers and get them distributed around the buildings. Make sure no large amounts of gas or anything highly flammable are left in the garages at night. I'll be damned if that little wop son-of-a-bitch is going to burn *me* out of business."

CHAPTER TWENTY-EIGHT

Andy Larson ran his thumb across his smooth upper lip. *I've gotta grow that damned thing back,* he told himself as he drove down a gravel road enjoying the scenery and the smells of the country. *I feel naked without it.* The clear blue sky was dotted with large white puffs of clouds. It had been a good year for rain, and the lush prairie grasses of North Dakota rippled and rolled in the light breeze. He returned the wave of a farmer driving a tractor pulling a mower through a rolling field of alfalfa.

Larson was going to a high, heavily wooded cut bank along the Missouri River to fire the Thompson machine gun lying beside him on the seat of his truck. He had taken this weapon from the whiskey truck robbery, but in 1923 Thompson machine guns were readily available to the American buying public for the exorbitant cost of two hundred dollars. The Thompson was known by a variety of names: Tommy gun, Persuader, Annihilator, Chopper, Street Sweeper, Heater, Chicago Typewriter, and Chicago Player Piano. It was quickly developing a legendary status with the criminal element of the day.

Larson had fired this model machine gun several times at law enforcement meetings and police training schools, but this would be the first time he could work with and test-fire the weapon at his own pace. He was looking forward to it with great anticipation.

He turned down along the river and backed his truck into a small clearing. He dropped the tailgate and laid out the machine gun, six boxes of ammunition, a twenty-round clip, and two fifty-shot drum magazines. He sat next to his array of equipment, opened two of the boxes of ammunition, and thumbed twenty cartridges into the clip. He rapped it on the tailgate to make sure all the rounds were seated and set it aside. He slid the center retainer from the first drum to free the lid and laid both pieces on the tailgate.

One by one he set fifty cartridges between the dividers on the feeder ring, replaced the lid, and pushed the center retainer back in place to lock the drum shut. He looked at the instructions stamped on the lid and turned the center mechanism for ten clicks to wind the spring that fed the cartridges to the firing chamber. He repeated the process with the second drum and slid off the tailgate to his feet.

Larson picked up the Thompson and looked it over closely before he slid the clip into it and pulled the knob on the top of the receiver to seat the first cartridge. He walked several steps toward a large dead cottonwood and slowly raised the weapon to his shoulder, getting the feel of it. *That's about twenty yards.* Most of the bark had fallen from the center of the tree trunk, leaving an expanse of pale wood with a large ragged scar at the height of a man's stomach. He felt the selector switch, pulled it to the rear, took a deep breath, and lined up the sights. As he let his breath out, he squeezed the trigger. The gun kicked against his shoulder with a sharp report and a ball of flame and smoke were expelled with the slug from the end of the barrel. A small dark hole appeared high and to the right of the scar on the trunk. "Damn, that's loud," he muttered as the smoke slowly cleared from in front of him. He raised the gun again, made an adjustment to his sight pattern, and fired another round. Another small dark hole appeared near the center of the scar. *Okay, that should do it.* He fired six quick shots and waited for the smoke to clear. All the bullet holes were now in an area the size of a dinner plate. *That's good.*

Larson flipped the selector switch forward, dropped the muzzle toward the ground, and half turned away from the tree. He spun back, swung the weapon up, and squeezed the trigger. The gun spit flame and smoke as it slammed and bucked against his shoulder.

The line of holes climbed up the tree at an angle to the left of the scar, and then suddenly the gun was silent. The last of the empty cartridge cases made soft clicking sounds as they fell against other casings in the grass to his right. *Damn, that was fast,* he told himself as he lowered the smoking muzzle of the weapon and rolled his shoulder. He reached up and pushed a finger into his ringing ear. *And loud.*

He walked forward through the smoke to the tree for a closer examination of the holes in the soft wood. *This thing climbs to the left, but the son-of-a-bitch'd be dead,* he told himself and smiled. *I'll have to use the front grip to lean into it and hold it on line for full automatic.* He gave a second look at the patterns of the holes, turned, and walked back to the truck. He dropped the magazine into his hand, laid it on the tailgate, and picked up one of the fifty-shot drum magazines. He snapped it into the slot and worked the action as he stepped back to his firing position. He raised the weapon to his shoulder, tightened his hold on the front grip, leaned forward, and gave a quick squeeze to the trigger. Again there was a fast display of fire and smoke as a line of empty casings arced away from the weapon. He raised the smoking muzzle up over his shoulder and looked at the target tree through the thinning smoke.

From here it looks like I managed to keep them pretty well centered. I don't see any high climbers in the bullet holes. That was about ten or twelve shots. Let's try it again.

Larson repeated the processes, firing single rounds and then short automatic bursts from the weapon. From time to time he would walk up to the tree and examine the damage and bullet patterns. He finished by reloading one of the drum magazines, holding the gun at his hip and firing the entire fifty rounds into the lower part of the trunk, watching holes appear and chunks of bark tear off to fly through the air and disappear in the surrounding brush. The weapon clicked on an empty chamber and he knew the magazine was finished. He lowered the hot, smoking weapon and looked down at the grass littered with an array of spent shell casings. He walked to the tree and studied the torn, shredded hole where the scared wood target had been. *Not bad,* he told himself as he reached out and moved his fingers in the chipped and broken wood. *Now I understand the gun and what I can do with it.*

Larson trudged slowly back to the truck and sat on the tailgate. He laid the machine gun across his knees and closed his eyes. The dull ache of his shoulder, the ringing in his ears, the feel of the warm weapon, the smell of gun smoke hanging in the air, and the recent chattering of gunfire brought back a flood of memories.

When Andy Larson was sixteen years old he saw the movie newsreels and articles and photos in the newspapers and magazines about *"the war to end all wars."* He wondered why Canada was fighting, but the United States was not yet in the war. He knew he must go and fight. He was tall and had shaved for over a year, so he was sure he could lie about his age and not be questioned. He hopped a freight train to Detroit, crossed the border over into Canada, and presented himself to a recruiting station. He was quickly accepted and assigned to a unit called *American Friends of the Canadian Expeditionary Forces.* He and other Americans were trained and sent off to Europe to fight. Soon the United States entered the war, but Larson chose to remain with the Canadians. When the war ended, he returned to Canada and was discharged as a decorated first lieutenant in the Canadian Army. He eventually returned to Bismarck, attended school, and joined the police force. He found police work to be unchallenging, dull, and mundane, so he constantly volunteered for special assignments in the hopes of finding something that would again give him the excitement of battle. When he was finally assigned to Sergeant Fred Torkelson, he found some of the activity he had craved. Yet he still wanted something a little more dangerous, a bit more adventuresome. Then he came up with the idea of stealing a truck of whiskey for himself and his friends. Stealing from the criminal element would be a dangerous challenge, interesting and exciting.

CHAPTER TWENTY-NINE

Bill Hall took a sip of steaming coffee as he waited for William Werner to finish his phone call and join him at the conference table. He looked at his notes and smiled slightly. *This'll work good,* he told himself, as he took another drink of coffee. *The boss should be impressed as hell. I wonder if I should hit him up for a couple of extra bucks a day over and above the five I'll be getting. Nah, I'll be sitting on my ass in the office most of the time anyway. No sense in pushing it. Five bucks is five bucks.*

Werner hung up the phone receiver, adjusted his pince-nez, picked up his cup of coffee, and joined Hall at the table. "Well, what have you put together for me, Bill?"

Hall turned the tablet, pushed it in front of Werner, and put on a stern face. "Here it is, Boss," he started. "I've got ten men, all veterans, who're more than willing to work the extra hours for the extra money. There'll be two men to each of the major buildings. One inside with a shotgun and the other outside with a pistol and a rifle. Oh, yeah, I've got the mechanics taking two-hour turns walking around and keeping an eye out for anything suspicious during the daytime."

"Are the mechanics armed?" Werner asked.

"Just like you said, Boss, they've all got rifles. Anybody sees them knows it's a show of power."

"Give those mechanics an extra dollar a day. I'll call payroll after our meeting. Tell them I expect total vigilance."

"They'll be very happy."

"Continue with your plan."

"The men at night'll be on four-hour shifts. Four in the building and four outside. I told 'em they could nap while they're inside."

Werner gave Hall a questioning look.

"The outside is the first line of action or defense. The inside man is to protect the interior and back up the outside man in case he's needed. These men are still working their regular shifts during the daytime and need a little sleep. Especially the drivers."

"Yes, you're right. Good thinking."

"These are all experienced men. Like I told you, they're all combat veterans so they understand things like suspicious or unusual sounds and activity, smoking in the dark, staying under cover in case of shooting. . . . And they're not afraid to use their guns. They'll do good, Boss."

"It sounds like you've got it all well thought out and organized."

"Oh, yeah, I'll be here too. Kinda keeping an eye over the whole operation."

"When I call payroll, I'll tell them to tack an extra two dollars a day on your pay, Bill." Werner stood and held out his hand. "You're going to earn it."

Yes! Hall stood and shook Werner's hand. "Thank you, Boss, you won't be sorry. That little wop from Minot'll be the one who's *sorry* if he messes with you."

"I'm glad to hear that," Werner said. "I'll . . ." The phone on his desk rang, interrupting his talk.

Hall raised his hand. "Take your phone call, Boss. I'll keep you posted."

Werner watched Hall leave his office, then sat down and lifted the receiver of his ringing phone. Before he could say anything, Salvatore's voice barked at him, "Werner, you better have something for me today."

Werner pulled the candlestick phone closer, squared his shoulders, and leaned forward on his elbows. "Yes, I've got something for you, *Guido*," he hissed into the phone. "How about you kiss my ass?" He reached out, hung the receiver on the hook, took a deep breath, and let it out slowly. "Damn, that felt good. I wonder why this took so long?" he asked himself as he reached down and gently squeezed his testicles. "Glad to have you back, boys."

CHAPTER THIRTY

Andy Larson and Becky Dansworth stood speaking softly as they waited for the crowd of people at Whitney Samples' funeral to finish talking to the family members and slowly move out of the cemetery. They nodded, spoke, and shook hands with several people as they stopped on their way past them.

Louie Bergavin walked up and shook Larson's hand. "I hate funerals," he said, then gave a slight smile. "I still don't know how you rate a woman this pretty." He winked at the lady standing close to Larson. "How are you, Becky?"

"I'm doing fine, Louie," she answered. "Considering this is such a sad occasion."

Bergavin nodded. "Yes, it is."

Becky patted Larson's arm. "I'm going to walk over to the school for a while, Andy. Call me tonight?"

Larson smiled. "About seven. Okay?"

"I'll be waiting by the phone. Bye, Andy." She gave him a quick kiss on the cheek. She walked several steps, turned, and smiled. "See you, Louie."

Larson grinned and shook his head. "I wonder how I got such a cute gal myself sometimes. I'd appreciate it if you'd catch Billy and Mike before they leave and we can have a quick meeting."

"That'll be easy enough. They're standing over there by my car," Bergavin said, and pointed behind them.

Larson turned to look, and they raised their hands. He

returned their wave. "Okay, I'll see you in a few minutes. I've got to go have a quick talk with Julian."

Andy Larson walked over to the Samples family and waited until they were alone. "Again, I want to express my condolences to all of you," he said softly.

Mrs. Samples stepped forward, smiled weakly, and gave Andy a hug. "Thank you, Andy," she said and dabbed at her eyes with a wadded handkerchief.

"I want you to know I'm going to do everything in my power to bring these bas . . . these criminals to justice," he assured them. "Julian, can I talk to you alone for a minute?"

The two men walked back toward the grave where two men were shoveling dirt into the hole.

"Who do you buy your booze from, Julian?" Larson asked.

"Is this official police business?" Samples asked.

"No," Larson answered. "In case you haven't heard, I've been suspended for thirty days because I was out at your place when all that shit happened last weekend."

"I'm sorry, Andy."

"Don't be. It gives me a chance to do a few things on my own in the way of investigating. I don't have to follow so many rules."

"I get it from Ernie Bush. Bush's Plumbing is his cover and he uses his business-marked trucks for delivery."

"Who does Ernie get it from? I know he makes a little in that still he has hidden upstairs in his garage, but I've tasted that goat piss he makes, and you serve better stuff than that out at your blind pig."

Julian chuckled. "Is there any local-made hooch that you haven't tasted?"

"Oh, I know of a few. There's a couple I wouldn't taste with *your* tongue."

"You mean like booze from the still that blew up down in

Dog Town a couple of weeks ago?"

"Hey, making moonshine can be dangerous if you don't know what you're doing. If the stuff was all that potent, think what it'd have done to your guts. Now tell me, where does Ernie Bush get his liquor?"

"I'm told it comes from a man named Salvatore up in Minot," Samples answered.

"You got any idea how he gets the stuff down here?"

"Every once in a while we get a few cases with a lot of coal dust on them."

"Like maybe it was shipped in a coal gondola?"

"That'd be my guess. Either that or a coal truck. I never ask how it gets here. There are some things that are better off unknown to me. You know what I mean?"

Larson stopped and stared up at the sky as if looking for something. "Coal . . . hmm . . ." He dropped his eyes to his shoes, nodded and smiled slightly. "Yeah, I guess I'll have to go down to the railroad yards later and take a look around. Thanks, Julian. Give your family my condolences again."

"They know how you feel, Andy."

"Is your place open again?"

"Why, you looking for a drink?"

"Don't be a smart-ass. I was just curious."

"Sorry. Yeah, we're gonna open tonight. I don't expect too many people'll be coming out after that little fracas the other night. But then again, maybe the curiosity factor will bring 'em out. We just finished hauling away the last of the burned cars yesterday. Lots of insurance people have been out looking over that mess. Surprisingly, not too many people are really pissed off about it."

"What the hell could they have done anyway? They're probably happy to be alive."

"Yeah," Julian agreed. "Stop by and I'll buy you your first drink."

"That sounds good to me, Julian. I'll probably see you later." Larson turned and walked across the grass to where his friends were waiting.

"How's Julian doing?" Mike Garske asked.

"He's hanging in there," Larson answered. "He's opening his place again tonight and we're all invited out for a drink or two."

"We'll drop by," Louie Bergavin agreed.

"All right," Andy Larson began. "I'm going to be out of town for a few days. If anything should happen to me, I want you to ramrod the whiskey operation, Louie."

Bergavin gave him a searching look. "Where are you going?"

"That doesn't really matter. The less you all know about what I'm up to, the better off you are."

"Now that's bullshit, Andy," Billy Nestoss argued.

"No, it's not," Larson said. "I'm a cop. . . . Make that a suspended cop. And I've got some things to do. You'd just be in the way." He held up his hand. "Don't argue with me. I don't plan on having anything happen to me, but there's always a chance. Now, like I said, I've got things to do. I'll see you out at Samples' about eight. That's it." Larson turned and without looking back walked to his truck.

CHAPTER THIRTY-ONE

Bill Hall sat at the conference table in William Werner's office waiting for him to finish talking on the phone. *I wonder what in the hell he wants this early in the morning?* He glanced up at the clock on the far wall. *Shit, it's only ten after eight. He usually doesn't even come in until nine these days.* Hall rubbed at his itchy eyes. He'd been up most of the night playing poker. The game was set up so the men who were supposed to be on inside guard duty were coming over to his office and playing cards in four-hour shifts. He knew if anything started outside, the men could be out in a matter of less than a minute, and besides they all had extra money these days. *What if he knows about the damned poker game?* Hall was letting his mind become his enemy. *It's only been one night since we started the guards and nothing's happened, so he must know about the damned poker game. Why in the hell else would he want to see me this early?*

Werner hung up the telephone receiver and slammed his hands down on his desk.

The sound startled Hall, who had been concentrating on how he was going to talk his way out of his poker game problem.

Werner stood, walked over to the conference table, and sat down facing Hall. "Well, Bill . . . ," he began.

Oh, shit, here it comes, Hall told himself.

"Things were pretty quiet last night, weren't they?"

"Yes, Boss. Quiet as a tomb," Hall agreed.

"Do the men you chose seem to be working out okay?"

133

Hall nodded. "Yes, Boss."

"Do you suppose one of them could take over your duties at night? Maybe a couple of them split it up?"

Hall looked down at his hands rolling the brim of his hat. *Shit, here it comes. I was right, he knows about the damned cards and the bastard's gonna play games with me before he gives me the axe.* He raised his eyes and looked at Werner's smiling face.

"Well?" Werner asked, impatiently.

Shit, the poker game was your idea. Face it like a man. He's gettin' enjoyment out of your misery. Hall cleared his throat. "Yes, Mister Werner, I think Brad Maylo could handle the job of supervisor," he answered, trying to keep his voice strong.

"Good," Werner said loudly and slammed his hands down on the conference table.

Again, the slamming of Werner's hands on wood made Hall jump slightly.

"I'm making you my personal bodyguard."

Hall felt like someone had let all of the air out of him. *Son-of-a-bitch!*

"Aren't you going to say anything?" Werner asked.

Hall again cleared his throat. "Um . . . , ah . . . , er . . . , yah, Boss . . . , you really caught me off guard with that one."

Werner laughed and slammed his hands on the table again.

I wish the hell he'd quit doing that, Hall thought as he smiled weakly at Werner.

"I want you to go down to Stern's and buy yourself a couple of good suits, half a dozen shirts and ties and some new shoes. And get a decent hat while you're at it."

Hall looked at Werner questioningly. "That's gonna be a little expensive, isn't it?"

Werner raised his hands.

Don't slam 'em on that damned table.

Werner clapped his hands and laughed. "It's all set up. I

talked to Mel Stern at the club last night and told him to deck you out in the best. If you're going to be my personal bodyguard, I want you to look respectful. I'm paying for all of it."

"Damn, I don't know what to say, Boss."

"Don't say anything, Bill. I feel good today. I made some big decisions yesterday and I feel good."

"Yes, Boss."

"And then, after you get those clothes, go get a shave and a haircut at the Patterson Barber Shop. It's all on me."

Bill Hall stood up. "Thanks, Boss."

"One last thing, Bill, go over to the Sioux Gun Shop and order yourself a Thompson machine gun. I've got a feeling this little wop bastard, Salvatore, is well armed and I think it's best that we be ready for him and his people."

Hall started to open the door.

"Oh, one last thing, Bill."

"Yes, Boss?"

"Tell Maylo if I find out he's running that poker game of yours, I'll fire his ass."

Hall looked down at his scuffed shoes and nodded. "Yeah, Boss."

Chapter Thirty-Two

"Mister Werner, Sergeant Andy Larson, of the . . ."

"I know who he is, Lana," Werner interrupted. "Send him in." He flipped the switch on the intercom, stood up and, stepped around to the front of his desk.

Larson opened the door, walked in, and closed it behind him. "Morning, Mister Werner," he said, pushing his hat back.

Werner tilted his head and smiled beguilingly. "Ah, Sergeant Larson, or should I say Mister Larson? I know this isn't official police business, because I'm informed you've been suspended from the police department. If I'm not mistaken, it was for frequenting an establishment that serves alcoholic beverages."

"Yeah, I'm the only one on the force who drinks, so they've taken away my sainthood status," Larson agreed and smiled. "It looks like there're no secrets in this town."

"Let me guess. You're here seeking employment," Werner bantered.

"In a pig's ass," Larson countered. "I'm here to ask you some questions, unofficially. You don't have to answer them, but I can pass them on to Sergeant Torkelson, and he can come down here and ask them. Since you're not paying him anything under the table anymore, he can be meaner than I am. Talking to me cuts out a middleman. The man who was murdered the other night, Whitney Samples, was a friend of mine. I want the man or men who killed him brought to justice."

Werner walked back around to his desk chair and sat down.

"What can I expect in exchange for these answers?" he asked as he reached up and adjusted his glasses on the bridge of his nose.

Larson dragged a chair from under the conference table, spun it around, and sat down astraddle it, facing Werner across his desk. *This is turning into some sort of a damned bartering contest.* "What are you looking for in the way of a trade?" Larson asked.

"Well, for a starter, how much more do you know about the truck full of whiskey . . . ?" Werner's voice trailed off when he realized he wasn't supposed to know what was in the missing truck. *Damn! How much am I supposed to know about that missing truck?*

Larson smiled. "Truck full of whiskey?"

Werner took a deep breath and squared his shoulders. "It's common knowledge that the missing truck of hay was full of whiskey," he bluffed.

"What missing truck of hay is that?" *You've stepped in it now, Werner.*

"The one that was with the two trucks of hay that were burned up north of Wilton," Werner answered, exasperation showing in his voice. "The incident where three of my drivers were killed."

"Hmm, I didn't know there *was* a third truck. I thought that was just a rumor."

"That old sheriff up in Wilton told the highway patrol there was a third truck."

Larson tipped the chair forward on two legs. "How'd you get confidential police information?"

Wanting time to organize his thoughts, Werner opened a humidor on his desk, lifted out a cigar, and rolled it under his nose. "I recall you made the statement a few minutes ago about no secrets in this town."

Larson shrugged. "You got somebody on the force on your payroll?"

"What makes you think that?"

"I'm just asking." Larson grinned, leaned forward, flipped open the top of the humidor, and helped himself to a cigar. He ran it back and forth under his nose and slipped it into a shirt pocket. "Thanks. I'll smoke this later."

Werner opened a drawer and rummaged around until he brought out a cigar cutter and snipped off the end of the cigar in his hand.

He's stalling. "All right," Larson began. "I'll get this thing rolling by asking you a few questions."

Werner snapped a flame onto a fancy silver lighter and moved the flame back and forth under the end of the cigar. "Okay, what do you want to know?" He put the cigar into the corner of his mouth and sucked a glow onto the end of it.

"We were here the other day when that big guy Bruno and those thugs left. Did any of those black-suiters talk with an accent?"

"Bruno was the only one who talked, so I can't tell you."

Larson stood and spun the chair back toward the table. "I'll give you some advice, Werner. Salvatore is not a man to be fooled with. We've done some checking on him and it appears he's got connections high in the Chicago crime family. He must have most of the police force up in Minot paid off, but he'll find it's a hell of a lot different down here. He won't get established in Bismarck. We've got too many good cops. Maybe not *saints,* but damned good *cops.*"

Werner blew a large cloud of smoke over his shoulder. "I'm glad to hear that, *Sergeant.*"

Larson pulled his hat back down close to his eyes. "One more bit of advice. Stay away from the booze business. It's not healthy." He raised his hand. "Enjoy your cigar. I know my way out."

CHAPTER THIRTY-THREE

Andy Larson sat on a folding metal chair on the rear platform of a parked vacant railroad passenger car in the Bismarck rail yards. It was almost a full moon, and the yard was awash in soft blue light. Scattered throughout the yard, high on wooden poles, electric lights with porcelain shades added to the light and helped deepen the shadows. Larson stretched, yawned, pulled his pocket watch out, and tipped it so he could see the time. *Almost three o'clock. Maybe there isn't any booze to be picked up tonight. It's funny though, I haven't seen any railroad bulls patrolling in here since midnight. I know for sure they stay on all night. But no guards, and it's easier to make a pickup. At least I was able to get down off that roof and make myself comfortable.* He swung his feet up onto the platform rail, nestled down onto the chair, and yawned. *Oh, well, it was just a hunch.*

Larson's head snapped up from his chest, and he looked around foolishly. *Shit, I must've fallen asleep.* He dropped his feet to the floor, yawned, and ran his tongue around the inside of his dry mouth. *I wonder how long I was out?* he asked himself as he reached for the chain to pull his watch out and check it. Suddenly, he realized what had awakened him. A large flatbed truck with no headlights was bumping along the ties and gravel toward the row of coal cars he had been watching. "I *was* right," he muttered. "There is somebody picking up some booze to-night."

The round beam of a flashlight appeared on the side of a

coal car and flashed from car to car as a man on foot preceded the truck down the line. "Here it is," the man with the flashlight called and slapped the side of a gondola.

"Hey, hold it down," someone on the truck warned, and the brake lights flashed as the vehicle came to a stop.

"Hell, the guards were paid off to disappear at midnight," someone said. "All we gotta do is git the stuff unloaded and outta here."

Larson climbed down the steps from the platform and reached back between the rails to grab a canvas sack. As he walked quietly along the tracks, he rummaged in the sack and brought out a large flashlight. He squatted in the shadows of a boxcar a short distance from where the men had started to work in the piled coal of a gondola.

"Don't dump too much of that damned coal on the ground," someone warned. "Remember how pissed off they were the last time when they had to clean it up."

"Yeah, yeah."

Larson opened the bag again and brought out a short-barreled shotgun. *Just in case,* he told himself as he carefully laid the bag down. *I'm not sure how many are over there.*

"Here it is," one of the diggers announced. "For a change, they didn't bury it very deep. This shouldn't take too long tonight."

Larson stood up and switched on the flashlight, catching two men on the gondola in the beam. "What the hell?" one of them shouted, putting a shielding hand up in front of his face.

"Put that damned light out," a man standing on the back of the truck ordered.

Another man stepped from behind the truck and shone a flashlight at Larson, who quickly stepped back behind the corner of the boxcar. "Didn't Billings tell you assholes to disappear at midnight?" he demanded. "Bush pays him damned good money to stay away while we're working."

"You haven't paid *me* anything," Larson called and extended the flashlight back around the corner of the boxcar.

"I told you to put out that damned light," the man on the truck shouted. "Either you put it out or I'm gonna shoot it out." The man put his hand to his waist as if reaching for a gun.

Larson switched off the flashlight and jammed it in a pocket as he swung up the shotgun and dropped to his knees.

"We don't want any gunplay," the man with the flashlight said. "Just talk to Bush in the morning and tell him to give you more money."

"Yeah," the man on the truck agreed. "Bush ain't gonna like it when we tell him one of his men is working on his own."

"What makes you think I work for Bush?" Larson heard a slight noise to his left at the front of the boxcar. He crouched lower and saw the legs of a man sneaking around to get behind him. He lowered the shotgun, cocked one hammer, and fired it at the man's legs.

The blast of the gun briefly lit up the area and echoed off the boxcars. The man screamed when the load of buckshot tore through his legs, dropping him onto the rocks.

Larson cocked the second hammer, switched the shotgun to his left hand, and yanked the big automatic pistol from his shoulder holster. "Here we go," he muttered.

The man lying at the front of the boxcar continued to scream curses as he rolled onto his side, raised an automatic pistol in both hands, and began firing at Larson. Each shot was a roar and a flash and Larson heard the slugs snap past him as he hid behind the heavy steel boxcar wheel.

A slug ricocheted off the wheel, and Larson heard the engine of the truck start.

"Let's git the hell outta here!" someone shouted as the front of the boxcar lit up from another pistol shot.

Larson leaned around the wheel, took quick aim, and fired a single round from his pistol at the man lying at the front of the boxcar.

The slug caught the man in the center of his face, snapping his head back, spraying the air behind him with blood, bones, and brains. The man jerked in death convulsions and was still.

The driver put the truck in gear, and it rattled and bumped down the ties and into the yard, where it swerved as it skidded onto the asphalt. One of the men from the gondola ran and finally managed to jump aboard the back of the truck as it gathered speed across the parking area and crashed through the large metal gates into the street. The second man, shouting curses, chased the truck as it sped down the street.

Larson holstered his pistol, lowered the hammer on the shotgun, walked back to the burlap bag, and pulled out a half-gallon jug of liquid. He threw the jug up into the gondola and heard it break. He lifted the bag, swung it up over the side of the coal car, and again heard breaking glass. He smiled as he tucked the shotgun under his arm and dug a box of matches from a pocket. He extracted one match, lit it, held it to the box, and watched as the matches inside flared. He stepped up closer to the coal car and tossed the burning box up over the side.

There was a sudden *whoosh* and flash of bright flame as the gasoline ignited. "That's gonna piss off Salvatore and Bush and leave some really pissed off, thirsty people around here," Larson told himself as he walked toward the back of the rail yard. Minutes later he opened the door, shoved his shotgun under the seat, and climbed into his truck. The sky over the rail yard was now well lit by the growing fire in the coal car and it was suddenly punctuated by a second ball of flame as the cases of whiskey began to explode.

Larson smiled. *This is just like an early Fourth of July.*

CHAPTER THIRTY-FOUR

Sergeant Fred Torkelson pulled his pocket watch out and checked the time. *Six-fifteen.* Eight uniformed policemen were on duty with him, poking around the railroad yard and directing traffic in the streets. One of them stood guard over the tarp-covered body lying between the rails in front of a boxcar.

The sun was breaking over the horizon to the east creating a beautiful orange North Dakota sunrise. The multicolored beams of sunlight seemed to magnify the thinning column of black smoke and heavy white steam rising like a funeral pyre from the coal gondola a short distance away. Firemen slopped through puddles of water and mud, pulling and rolling hoses over the tracks while yelling and talking to each other.

Torkelson shook a cigarette out of a pack, lit it, and blew dragon-like plumes of smoke from his nose as he waited for Chief Pearce to join him.

"What can you tell me, Tork?" the Chief asked, shaking his head when Torkelson held the pack of cigarettes out to him.

"One body over there," Torkelson answered, pointing to the policeman guarding the shroud. He pointed at a white-helmeted fireman walking toward them. "Here comes Chief Raveling. Let's see what he has to tell us. I can tell you one thing though, this is a helluva mess."

"No shit," Pearce responded.

Raveling stopped and talked to a fireman rolling up a hose, nodded, patted him on the shoulder, and continued toward them. He pulled off his white leather Chief's helmet and wiped at his forehead with the back of his hand. "Hell of a way to start the day," he said and pointed to the steaming coal car. "We're damned lucky the fire was confined to that one gondola. We sprayed a hell of a lot of water in it and now we're just standing by. We saw most of the water was running out the bottom about as fast as we put it in, so now we're letting it go. It'll probably burn out within the hour. It's just smoldering now. Not much of a problem."

"What about the whiskey?" Pearce asked.

"Yeah," Torkelson said. "For some reason this place smells like a distillery."

"That's an interesting point," Raveling responded. "We don't know how much booze was in there, but it was a lot, and some of it definitely blew up. You've no doubt noticed all the busted glass from broken bottles around the area. Between the burning coal and the wooden cases that stuff was in, it got mighty hot. When the bottles started to blow, they must've thrown those others up and out of the car. I haven't seen any yet that survived the landing." Chief Raveling laughed at his own humor. "What about the body over there under the tarp?"

Chief Pearce looked at Torkelson for an answer.

"There's been a lot of water damage to any evidence, but that couldn't be helped. There was enough light when we got here to do a primary investigation. The dead man was shot in the legs with a shotgun and took a single large-caliber slug in the face. He had an empty pistol in his hand and a pile of empty casings around him. We found a couple of bullet holes in the bottom of the rail car and some slug splatter marks on one rear wheel. I'd say he put up a hell of a fight with somebody at the other end of that boxcar before he took that slug through his face."

Chief Pearce nodded. "The front gate's been busted out into

the street, so it looks like somebody was in a hell of a hurry to get out of here."

"Yeah, I put the word out to be looking for a busted-up truck," Torkelson said. "But I doubt if we'll find it."

"I wonder how big the gun battle was?" Chief Pearce questioned. "There had to be a fair-sized crew to unload all that whiskey. We know at least one man had a shotgun, and he could have used the pistol, too. I'd say the man over there was killed by a pistol slug. We found one forty-five casing at this end of the boxcar."

"I'd guess there must have been a bigger force," Chief Raveling interjected. "I don't see how one man could have driven off at least . . . What would you guess for a loading crew? Four or five men?"

"There should be guards on duty here at night," Raveling said. "Do you suppose the dead man was a guard?"

"He wasn't wearing a uniform, so I doubt it," Torkelson answered.

"Now that you mention it, where the hell's the head of security for the yard? He should have been here by now," Pearce noted. "Where's his office?"

Torkelson pointed over his shoulder. "Guy's name's Brian Jeffors and I've already been to his office. It's locked up tight. It looks like he's flown the coop."

A short man in a suit with strained buttons came ambling toward them, holding an unbroken whiskey bottle triumphantly above his head. "Hey, Chief," Detective Bernie Maxwell called, in a high squeaky voice. "Here's a bottle that managed to survive a flight," he said with a grating laugh as he handed the bottle to Pearce.

Looks like the department ass-kisser is back from his school, Torkelson told himself. *And he's starting right where he left off. Kiss, kiss, kiss. I think I'm gonna puke.*

"It has a good clear label on it." Maxwell's jowls rode on the collar of his shirt and he had small, dark, narrow-set eyes and big ears. He wore a constant five o'clock shadow and had a persistent, disgusting habit of sniffing and rubbing his nose with the back of his hand. His fellow officers didn't trust him because he'd still stab anybody in the back to make points with people higher than him in the chain of command. He was known to be free with the use of a thin shot-lined leather sap when it came to questioning people, but no one had ever turned him in because of his upper level pull. He still searched for the person or persons who had made him the brunt of their practical jokes. Things like dog turds in his shoes, dead fish on his car engine, and assorted dead birds and animals under the seats of his car. Maxwell had recently returned from an eastern police academy and this was his first day back on duty.

Pearce looked at the label and handed the bottle to Torkelson. "Okay, Tork, you're the booze expert. What can you tell me?"

Torkelson looked at the label carefully and nodded. "The Bronfman Brothers up in Yorkton, Saskatchewan, made this. The 'Superior' label makes it their top of the line rye. Their lower grade yak piss rye is labeled as 'Black Night'. Their best Scotch is 'Prince of Wales' and the bottom of the Scotch line is 'Glen Levitt'."

"What's a bottle of that rye sell for?" Chief Raveling asked.

Torkelson looked at Raveling and grinned. "C'mon, Chief, are you telling me you've never bought a bottle of whiskey?"

Raveling tapped his helmet against his leg, scratched his chin, and looked at each of the others. "Okay," he said, with a soft laugh. "It's about five bucks a bottle."

Torkelson swung the bottle in his hand. "Damn, Chief, for a minute there I thought I was gonna have to put you in for some sort of a good citizen award. But I know now you get a courtesy discount when you buy your booze."

The other two men laughed and Raveling nodded foolishly. "Okay, okay."

"Well, I've got work to do," Torkelson said. "Since my number-one man is on a thirty-day unpaid vacation, I'm gonna have to hustle. First thing is, we've got to see if we can find Brian Jeffors."

"I'll walk with you, Tork," Maxwell volunteered. "There's a number of things I'd like to discuss with you, now that I'm back."

"Suit yourself."

Maxwell looked over his shoulder until he was sure the two chiefs couldn't hear him. "I want you to know that if I had been here, I would have done every damn thing in my power to keep your asshole buddy, Larson, from getting that promotion."

Torkelson glanced at him out of the corner of his eye. "It looks like a lot of time at the academy was spent on personality development, Bernie. Once a prick, always a prick."

Maxwell swung around in front of Torkelson and put up his hand to stop him. "I was delighted when I heard they'd suspended the bastard for thirty days."

"Yeah, I bet you were."

"I want you to know that I'm after him, and you can tell him that. I know he's the one with all the practical jokes. I will get him, trust me, I will get him."

"That oughta make him really nervous," Torkelson taunted. "Now get the hell out of my way before I have to knock you on your ass. Your rank doesn't mean diddly to me. Larson's a good cop and won't put up with any shit from you. I got work to do. See you later." Torkelson stepped around Maxwell and was soon out in the street. "Shithead," he muttered. "Andy'll have him for lunch."

CHAPTER THIRTY-FIVE

Guido Salvatore reached forward and lifted the receiver from the hook on the side of his phone. "This is Salvatore."

"Guido, this is Ernie Bush."

"What can I do for you, Ernie?"

"How about you start by replacing my forty cases of whiskey that got burned up this morning?" Bush shouted. "Forty cases of paid-for whiskey."

"Wait a minute, calm down," Salvatore growled. "What do you mean, burned up?"

"My men went to unload the whiskey from that damned coal car this morning and got into a gun battle with some asshole."

"What about the burned up whiskey?"

"After he killed one of my men, he set fire to the gondola and my whiskey." Bush's voice was growing louder and angrier.

"Slow down and quit shouting for a goddamn minute," Salvatore warned. "How many men did you send to pick up the whiskey?"

"Four, like always."

"And one man ran them all off?"

"Near as they can tell, it was one man."

"I don't know what to tell you, Ernie. I delivered the whiskey. You people screwed up when it got there."

"Now don't hand me that shit, Guido. I paid you twenty-five dollars a case, delivered, for that whiskey. You owe me a thousand bucks!"

"Tough shit. Like I told you, I delivered. It looks to me like you're just out a lousy grand."

"Wait a goddamn minute, Guido. . . ."

"Be a big boy, lick your wounds, and get over it," Salvatore said. "It's one of the chances you take in this game."

"Like hell I will," Bush shouted. "How do I know there were forty cases of whiskey in there in the first place? Maybe there was only twenty, and you staged this whole thing to cover the difference."

"Shit! I told you there were forty cases. I'm a man of my word. There were forty cases of whiskey in that damned coal car."

"How do I know this wasn't something you'd planned?"

"Do you think I'd go to all that trouble for a lousy thousand dollars?" Salvatore snarled. "That's a drop of piss in the ocean to me. I spend more than that a month on cigars. If you want more whiskey, just send me more money."

Bush sputtered and slammed the receiver back in the hook of his phone. "Asshole," he muttered. *God, what am I going to do now? I've got to try to find somebody else with some readily available whiskey at a decent price. I've got ten or twelve cases in my warehouse, but that's not gonna last me long. Shit!*

Ernie Bush spent the rest of the morning and most of the afternoon in his office trying to find a new source for whiskey. None of his customers had any extra they were willing to sell when they found out he couldn't resupply them for the next few days. He looked up when he heard the front door of his showroom open and saw a man walk to the counter. "Can I help you?" he shouted.

"I'm here to talk to Ernie Bush," the man called back.

Bush muttered a string of curses as he stood up and walked

out into the show room. "I'm Bush and I'm busy. What do you need?"

"I understand you're looking for some whiskey," the man replied.

Bush cocked his head and looked at the man. "You must be mistaken. I'm a plumber, not a bootlegger."

"Okay, my mistake," the man said and started to turn back to the door.

"Wait a minute, wait a minute," Bush said. "Where'd you hear I was looking for whiskey?"

"Word on the street," the man answered, turning back.

"So if I *was* needing whiskey, you'd have some?"

The man grinned. "I've got fifty extra cases."

"And how much are you asking for a case?"

"Thirty dollars. You pick it up."

Bush shook his head. "That's five bucks a case too much."

"Suit yourself. I'm sure there are plenty of others who'd be interested. They're more than willing to cut out the middleman." The man laughed as he started to the door. "That'd be you."

"When can I get it?" Bush asked.

"First thing in the morning. I'd deliver it, but I'm working alone on this one. You pay me when you pick it up. Cash only," the man said and stepped back to the counter.

"Where do I pick it up?"

"I'll call you tonight. Right at seven."

"You got a name?" Bush asked.

The man smiled and slid a card onto the counter. "See you in the morning," he said, walked to the door and disappeared outside.

Bush picked up the card and smiled. *I might make out on this thing after all.* He walked back to his desk, lifted the receiver and dialed his phone.

"This is Salvatore," a voice answered.

"Guido, this is Ernie Bush. How much was the reward for information on your stolen whiskey? From that truck job a couple of weeks ago?" There was no response. "Guido, are you there?"

"Yes, I'm here. The reward is ten thousand dollars."

"Well, Guido, I think I may have your man."

"I'm listening."

Ernie Bush grinned as he lifted the card and read from it. "The man's name is Bernard Maxwell and he's a detective with the Bismarck Police Department."

CHAPTER THIRTY-SIX

Detective Bernard Maxwell belched softly, wiped his mouth, stood, straightened his coat, and signaled the waiter for the bill.

"That was very good, Charles," he told the cashier at the counter by the door. "As usual."

"Thank you, Mister Maxwell, we always appreciate your business. Please come back and see us."

Maxwell laughed. "Next Thursday, at seven. My usual corner table, Charles." He shook the man's hand and left a dollar bill in it.

Charles put his hand in his pocket and nodded. "We'll see you next Thursday, Mister Maxwell. It's good to have you back in town."

The detective whistled tunelessly as he ambled across the dark parking lot to his car. *It's good to be home again. I like the respect I get here.* He opened the door, slid under the wheel of his four-door Ford, and reached forward to put the key in the ignition. Before he could close the door and turn the key, he felt something cold and hard pressed against his neck.

"Put yer hans on da vheel un' don' try to turn around," a raspy voice commanded from the back seat. "Somevun vants to hafe a little talk mit you." A strip of cloth was quickly wrapped around his face and pulled tight over his eyes. He felt handcuffs click shut on his wrists. "Don' move." He heard the rear door open and was pushed over to the passenger side of the seat. The car swayed when another person climbed into the back seat.

Hands began to pat over his coat, and he felt his pistol pulled from his shoulder holster. "I want you to know that I'm a detective on the Bismarck pol . . ." A hard rap above his ear made him bite his tongue, and stars swam before his blindfolded eyes.

"Keep yer damned mouth shut," a deep voice ordered. "We know who ya are. Next time I'll hurt ya."

The car was started and driven out of the parking lot and into the street. Maxwell tried to tell by the sounds where they were traveling and soon knew they were on the highway. He fought the urge to say something, but realized it would be a waste and probably lead to another whack on the head. He felt the car turn onto a gravel road and stop. His door opened, and he was grabbed under the arm and lifted out of the car.

"That isn't him," someone said. "That's not *him.*"

"What?" a second voice shouted. "Are you sure?"

"The man who came into my place was taller and thinner."

"Son-of-a-bitch! I should just shoot both of you," the second voice ranted. "I didn't drive all the way down here to . . . to . . ." the voice sputtered searching for words. "You, with the blindfold, are you Lieutenant Bernard Maxwell?"

Maxwell's head bobbed up and down. "Yes, yes."

"Do you know anything about some whiskey for sale?"

Maxwell shook his head. "I . . . I don't know anything about any whiskey."

"Bush here tells me someone came into his place this morning and offered to sell him fifty cases of whiskey. He gave him your business card, *Lieutenant* Maxwell."

"I have no idea what you're talking about," Maxwell whined. "This must be some kind of a joke. . . ." Maxwell's voice trailed off. "Was he tall, hard looking, with a heavy black mustache and dark eyes? Kinda cocky?"

Ernie Bush nodded his head. "That sounds like him, but he didn't have a mustache."

"Listen, please," Maxwell pleaded. "Believe me, it was a damned cop named Larson. He's always playing practical jokes on me. At least I think it was him."

"Getting you killed is a practical joke?" Salvatore asked incredulously. "Am I missing the humor in this?"

"What was I supposed to have done?" Maxwell pleaded.

"A man came in today and offered to sell me fifty cases of whiskey," Bush answered. "He gave me your business card."

Maxwell shook his head. "I wouldn't even know where to get fifty cases of whiskey."

"Somebody stole a truckload of whiskey from me about two weeks ago," Salvatore answered. "I'm looking for my whiskey and some other things that were stolen. I want the heads of the bastards who did it."

"Two weeks ago I was at a police academy in Bethesda, Maryland," Maxwell said, relief showing in his voice. "There's no way I could've done it. You can check with the department. It was a month-long school. I was in Maryland two weeks ago."

"All right, who was this guy passing himself off as you?" Salvatore asked.

"I told you, it's got to be that damned Andy Larson," Maxwell answered.

Salvatore pointed at Bush. "The guy knew you were looking for whiskey?"

"Yes," Bush answered softly.

"How'd he know that?"

"He said he'd heard it on the street and I'd been calling people all day looking for whiskey. I figured he'd probably overheard people talking in a bar or something."

"I want to know if this bastard you've been talking about is Larson," Salvatore growled.

"So do I," Maxwell said.

"*You,* shut the hell up!" Salvatore shouted. "I might forget this was a hoax and have Rudy put a slug in you, just for the pure fun of it."

Maxwell's head bobbed up and down furiously.

"Bush, in the anticipation you had some good information for me, I brought you down twenty-five cases of whiskey. I still haven't worked all this out in my mind, but I've got some ideas. I was going to give the whiskey to you as part of the reward, but since this isn't the right man here, I can't do that with a clear businessman's conscience. *But* I am willing to sell them to you for fifteen dollars a case. It saves me the trouble of hauling it back. It's in that little truck parked over there. I'll add six seventy-five to your next order. Unless you've got the cash and want to pay me now."

Bush fumbled in his coat. "I just happen to have enough cash on me, Guido."

"Yeah. You see, Bush, I'm not that bad a person," Salvatore said, as he smiled and stuck out his hand.

Bush pulled a wad of money from a pocket and counted a stack of bills into the hand of the smiling man. "Thank, you, Guido. Thank you very much."

Salvatore nodded as he slipped the money into a coat pocket. "Bruno, have the driver take you, Rudy, and Mister Bush to his place, and the three of you help him get his merchandise unloaded and stored. I'm going to have a little talk with Detective Maxwell here."

Maxwell was a bit nervous when he heard the doors of the truck slam, the motor start, and the tires crunch away on the gravel. *Would he shoot me while the others are gone?* He felt the knot at the back of his head being untied and blinked in the waning light at the small, nattily dressed man standing across from him.

"Here you are, Detective," Salvatore said, handing him a small key. "Take those bracelets off so you can be comfortable while we're talking."

Maxwell quickly unlocked the handcuffs and held them questioningly toward Salvatore.

"Oh, just lay them on the hood," Salvatore instructed, pointing at the long, black Buick Roadster beside them. "It's a beautiful summer evening, so let's take a little walk while we discuss a few things. The subject of which, I'm sure, will be most beneficial to the both of us."

Maxwell quickly matched his pace and trod alongside him.

"Maxwell, do you mind if I call you Bernie?"

"No, no, of course not. What should I call you?"

"My friends call me Guido, and I believe you and I will become friends. Good friends. Could you use a little extra money, Bernie?"

"A man can always use a little extra money," Maxwell answered.

"Good. Now tell me what you know about this man Larson."

CHAPTER THIRTY-SEVEN

Guido Salvatore looked up at the large clock on his wall. *Let's see how prompt my new stoolie is,* he thought, as he took a sip from his steaming cup of coffee. *It's almost eight-thirty.* As if on command, the phone suddenly rang. Guido leaned forward, pulled it to him, and lifted the receiver from the hook. "This is Salvatore."

"Guido, this is Bernie Maxwell. I had to get out of the station and use a pay phone to call you. Even with a private office, you can never tell who might listen in."

"I understand, Bernie. What have you got for me?"

"According to the official report, someone was at the rail yard obviously unloading the whiskey in the burned coal gondola. For some reason there was a gun battle, and one man is dead. He works for a plumber here in town, and they're checking into it as we speak. The reasoning behind the idea that whiskey was being unloaded is a smashed gate. The gate is hanging out toward the street, so it indicates a large vehicle hit it from the inside at a high rate of speed. They guess the people in the vehicle unlocked the gate when they came in and then locked it behind them so no one would notice it."

I know all this shit. "What about yard security?" Salvatore interrupted.

"They can't find the man who's the head of security. They figure he'd been paid to look the other way and then when the shoot-out started, he got the hell out of there."

158

"What about the burned coal car?"

"Someone set fire to it, after or during the gun battle, maybe even before. At this point, without any witnesses, it's all a matter of conjecture."

Well, no shit. Salvatore frowned. *Who in the hell's doing this? Kidd Cann? Is he trying to muscle in on my territory? It can't be one man doing this. It has to be Cann. The bastard will learn not to fool with me.* "What did you find out about Sergeant Larson?"

"He's kept a pretty low profile since he was suspended a couple of weeks back. Nobody seems to know much about what he's been up to. I'll keep an eye out and let you know if I find out anything new about him. The more I think about it, the more I believe he'd be the type of person to steal a truckload of whiskey," Maxwell said and smiled to himself. *I'll show that bastard what a practical joke can lead to.*

"Thanks, Bernie. Keep me posted. It looks like that cash I gave you last night is paying off already." *Dumb asshole, I knew all that before he did, but I've got to be nice to him for a while. At least until he turns up something I don't already know. This Andy Larson is someone I'm going to have to look into.*

"I'm doing what I can, Guido," Maxwell answered and heard the line click dead. *Now I've got to find out who the bastard is that's passing himself off as me, but I bet it's Larson.*

Salvatore pushed the phone back and scribbled on a pad in front of him. *KIDD CANN—ISADORE BLUMFELD.* Kidd Cann was Isadore Blumfeld's nickname in the crime world.

Salvatore swore a string of curses, slammed the pencil down, stood and began to pace. He stopped to light a cigar and continued to walk, leaving a trail of pungent smoke in his wake. Finally, he sat back down, riffled through a small directory, found a number, pulled the phone to him, and dialed it.

"This is Guido Salvatore. Let me talk to Mister Blumfeld, please." He rolled the ash from his cigar as he waited.

A voice came on the line. "Guido, my old friend, how are you?"

"Don't give me that *old friend* shit," Salvatore snarled.

"Guido, you sound a little tense. Something wrong over there in North Dakota?"

"I know what you're trying to pull; you're trying to muscle in over here."

"I'm sorry, but I have no idea what you're talking about," Kidd Cann said.

"You're coming after my business, aren't you, you prick?"

"Let me tell you a few things, Guido. I know for a fact that you owe a large amount of money to Big Al Capone. It seems you were moving some gold coins for him and they were stolen. He doesn't really believe you and it's a matter of time before he sends his people over to collect. Meyer Lanksy down in Florida keeps me posted on these things. I might someday decide to take over your business, Guido, but right now I've got bigger fish to fry. When Big Al takes you out for the missing gold, your business goes up for grabs, and since I'm the big dog over here, I figure it'll automatically go to me. I'm not trying to take your *fucking* business; I'm going to wait for it to be handed to me!"

Before Salvatore could respond, the phone clicked and began to hum in his ear. He shakily reached over and hung up the receiver. *God, I've got to come up with sixty-thousand dollars quick. Shit, no doubt there'll be interest added.*

Chapter Thirty-Eight

William Werner blew a large cloud of pungent cigar smoke across his desk as he looked up a number and dialed the phone. He leaned forward on his elbows and listened when he heard it start ringing.

"This is Salvatore," a voice growled from the other end.

"Ah, Guido, this is William Werner."

"What do you want?"

"It seems we had a fire down here in a railroad coal car full of whiskey the other night."

"I heard about it," Salvatore said. "So, what do you want? I'm a busy man."

"Was this little blaze an attempt on your part to show me your fire-starting abilities?"

"What?"

"You heard me. Was that . . ."

"Let me tell *you* something, you asshole," Salvatore interrupted. "I had nothing to do with that damned fire. I lost *my* money replacing that whiskey. I don't like things that cost me money. And I'm beginning to really not like you!"

"Is this one of the ways you bragged about bringing your whiskey into Bismarck? You said I was handling less than a quarter of your liquor transportation business. Isn't delivering your merchandise in coal cars a tad messy? Now it seems it's a bit unreliable. At least my trucks are good and clean." The phone clicked and began to hum.

Werner hung the receiver back in the hook, blew a smoke ring, and smiled. *Well, so much for that. I'm sure that got under the bastard's skin a bit.*

As Werner reached again for the telephone, his intercom buzzed. "Mister Werner, there's a Lieutenant Maxwell from the Bismarck Police Department here to see you."

"Send him in, Lana." *I've never met the lieutenant, but I've read about him and seen his picture in the paper.*

Werner stood, adjusted his coat and vest, checked his tie, squared his glasses on the bridge of his nose, and raised the corners of his mouth into a smile. *First impressions.*

The door opened, and the lower half seemed to be filled by the man coming through it.

Werner proffered his hand. "Lieutenant Maxwell, nice to meet you."

Maxwell gripped Werner's hand firmly and pumped it several times. "Likewise, Mister Werner. Please call me Bernie." He removed his hat and laid it on the table.

"Bernie, please call me William. I detest the names Bill or Willy and have always preferred William. Bill and Willy sound like little boys' names." He made a sweeping motion toward his conference table. "Have a seat, please."

"Thank you," Maxwell said, pulling out a chair and settling his bulk onto it.

"Coffee, Bernie?"

"Yes, please, black."

Werner walked to his desk, pushed the button on his intercom and spoke. "Lana, two black coffees, please."

"Now," Werner said, pulling up a chair across the table from Maxwell. "What can I do for you, Bernie."

"I've just returned from the police academy in Maryland, and I'm going to begin working a few of Sergeant Torkelson's cases. I found yours to be very interesting and decided to make it a priority on my list."

The secretary brought two steaming cups of coffee and set them on the table in front of the men. "Anything else, Mister Werner?"

"No, thank you, Lana. No phone calls, please, while the lieutenant and I are talking."

"Yes, Mister, Werner." The secretary left the room, quietly closing the door behind her.

"That police academy must have been interesting," Werner said, and took a sip of his coffee.

"Yes, but that's not why I'm here," Maxwell answered. "According to Sergeant Torkelson's notes, you're suspected of shipping liquor. Possibly a wholesaler in that illegal substance."

"I can assure you, Bernie, that I do not deal in alcoholic beverages of any kind. I may, from time to time, imbibe a little, I mean we all do." Werner gave a knowing chuckle. "But I do not deal in it. Does it mention in their report how they brought a number of policemen and searched my buildings for liquor and found nothing?"

Maxwell nodded.

"Does it mention that Sergeant Torkelson manhandled my attorney, Cyril Shark, when he attempted to intercede? Or how Sergeant Larson threatened to *slap me around* if he didn't get the answers he wanted?"

Maxwell suddenly had a stern look on his face. "Of course, there's no mention of any of that in the reports. It's the kind of behavior I would expect from those two . . . loose cannons."

"They are a disgrace to the entire law enforcement community," Werner said.

Maxwell nodded in agreement. "By the way, does Larson still have that big black mustache?"

"No, he was smooth shaven both times I saw him. Why do you ask?"

Maxwell shook his head. "It's nothing of importance. I see by the report you had three of your drivers killed in what may possibly be the theft of a truckload of liquor."

"It was their day off, and I have no control over what my people do on their own time. Besides, I understand there is only conjecture as to the third truck anyway."

"Yes, that's what I read." Maxwell reached into a jacket pocket, brought out a small notebook, and briefly leafed through it. "Do you know Guido Salvatore from Minot?"

"Yes, I was supposed to ship a load of doors for him to Minneapolis."

"You didn't ship them?"

"No, the deal fell through, why do you ask?"

"No particular reason. I was just curious." Maxwell brought an expensive fountain pen from his shirt pocket, unscrewed the cap, and scratched some words in his notebook.

"That's a beautiful pen, Bernie," Werner noted. "I have several like it myself."

Maxwell held the pen up and looked at it. "Yes, it was a gift. This type of pen is much too expensive for a man on a policeman's salary to be able to afford."

"I can see you're a man of taste," Werner said. "It really is a shame the pay for your chosen profession is so inadequate that you can't often obtain the sort of things you obviously enjoy."

"Yes, that's what I'm burdened with," Maxwell paused and chuckled. "Champagne tastes and beer income."

"Bernie, how would like to be able to afford a few of the finer things in life?"

"How do you mean?"

"Well, like a second job, a second income."

Maxwell smiled. "Thank you, but I'm not the truck driver type."

"Nothing as physical as that, Bernie. I was thinking possibly I could pay you for any information useful to me, that you may happen upon in the line of your duties."

Maxwell tilted his head and looked at Werner with hooded eyes. "How much would we be talking about?"

"I don't think fifty dollars a week is out of line," Werner answered and smiled.

"What sort of information?"

"Things that don't make the papers. Details on what really happened at the rail yard the other night. Items such as that. The inside track on things such as that could be helpful to me in the transportation business."

Maxwell rubbed his chin as he looked into Werner's eyes. "You would be willing to pay me *fifty dollars* for things such as that?"

"Of course," Werner answered as he drew a large wallet from an inside suit pocket and began counting out bills.

Maxwell glanced at the growing stack of money and tried to suppress a smile. *It would appear this police business is beginning to pay off well for me.*

Werner smiled as he pushed the stack of bills across the table. *Lose one cop and buy another. It's amazing what some men will do for such a piddling amount of money.* "My secretary will have an envelope for you every Monday with a like amount in it, Bernie."

CHAPTER THIRTY-NINE

The sun was getting close to the western horizon and crimson and gold were beginning to tint the clouds. Billy Nestoss wiped at his face with a faded red bandana as he handed the water jug to Louie Bergavin. "Here you go, Louie, wet your whistle."

Bergavin stuck his hayfork into the ground, swung the jug up and took a long drink. He pushed his hat back and wiped the cool wet surface of the jug across his forehead. "Good stuff," he commented, swinging the water vessel over to Andy Larson.

Larson tipped it up and took several deep swallows. "This'll do for now, but I've got a surprise in my truck, back up at the farm." He took his hayfork and stuck it into the loaded hay.

Mike Garske, head hanging, sat in the evening shadow of a large rack, piled high with fresh hay. "I need a drink of whiskey," he muttered. "Not that damned water."

"There's nothing like the smell of new cut hay, is there?" Nestoss asked, ignoring Garske's comment. "It really has a definite smell of its own."

"So does fresh cow shit," Garske said, and giggled at his own humor. "There's a lotta things out here on the farm got their own peculiar smells, and it's getting to the point I don't like any of 'em much."

"Damn," Bergavin said. "Mike, you got a horse's ass attitude for a man who just about worked three of his good friends to death. This has been one hell of a long, hard day. This'll be the fourth rack of hay we've loaded and moved. Buck up, boy."

CHAPTER FORTY

The three men stood silently staring at their dead friend. Tears streamed down the faces of Louie Bergavin and Billy Nestoss. From time to time Andy Larson would sniff and run a finger under his nose.

"What're we gonna do?" Nestoss asked.

Larson raised his hand. "Let me think on this a bit more. First we need to get something to carry Mike down to the barn. Then I've got to go find a chicken and a jar or a can." He turned and started back toward the farm.

Nestoss and Bergavin blinked at each other unbelievingly and ran to catch up with him.

"What'n the hell are you gonna do with a chicken, Andy," Nestoss asked.

"Here's my plan," Larson answered. "You call the sheriff's office in a couple of hours or so and report Mike's suicide. Tell him you came out to see how the harvest was going and drink a few *illegal* beers. You drove up and found him dead in the barn. In the meantime, we've got to get a lot of things to set up."

"What about the chicken?" Nestoss asked again.

"I'm coming to that," Larson answered. "These are the few things we have to do. Sheriff Krauss is a smart man, so we have to get ahead of him. First, we want him to think Mike was in the barn when he shot himself."

"Why the barn?" Bergavin asked.

"Because it's a long ways from the family graveyard on the

hill," Larson said. "There's a fresh grave up there with no stone and no explanation of who's in it. He'll want to know more if he notices it."

"Damn, that's right," Bergavin agreed. "But what if he *does* see it while he's looking around and goes up there to investigate."

"When you get Mike moved down here, you'll go back up and dig the grave again down about five feet. The first one for Bert was at least six feet deep, and that'll leave about a foot of dirt on top of his coffin. The sheriff'll find an open, fresh-dug grave."

"What're we doing that for?" Nestoss asked.

"I'm betting the sheriff will think Mike was digging a grave for himself. After all, he'll be investigating a suicide."

"Damn, you're thinking all the time," Bergavin said.

"What about smell?" Nestoss asked. "Won't Bert's decomposing body stink? I don't think a foot of dirt'll stop that smell."

"Remember why we put all that rock salt in his coffin?" Larson asked. "Besides, a body needs air to decompose. No air gets through six feet of dirt. It won't be decomposing."

"Damn! That's right," Bergavin agreed. He turned and gave Larson a searching look. "How in the hell . . . ?" He shook his head. "Never mind."

"Billy, don't you and Mike wear about the same size shoe?" Larson asked.

"Yeah, I think we both wear about a size ten," Nestoss answered, looking down at his work boots. "What difference does that make?"

"I only want size ten boot tracks up there. Billy, you put on Mike's boots for now. They've got very distinctive soles. Hopefully the sheriff will make the conclusion it was all his work. You can both dig it, but I want Louie's big footprints well covered. I'll go up and check it before I leave."

"Where are you going?" Bergavin asked.

"It's best the sheriff doesn't find a suspended cop out here. He'd know I'd have been looking things over and might wonder if I'd made some changes to help protect a dead friend's reputation."

"I'm not sure I understand, but we'll go along with anything you say," Nestoss said. "I'm gonna ask you one more time, what's the chicken for?"

"You saw all the blood on the ground around Mike's head."

"Yeah," Nestoss agreed.

"When the body's moved, there won't be any blood around his head. The Sheriff'll be suspicious he's been moved. I'll cut the head off a chicken, put the blood in a jar, bring it down, and pour it beside Mike's head. Blood's blood to them. They won't be checking samples from something so obvious. It'll look like it came out of Mike's wound."

Bergavin shook his head. "Son-of-a-bitch. You think of everything, don't you?"

"I'm trying to set a simple suicide scene for the sheriff and his men to investigate. I want it to be smooth and quick. Answers to all the questions before they're asked. Now, you get Mike hauled down here while I go find a chicken."

Two hours later the three friends stood inside the barn door, sipping beers and sadly looking down at Mike Garske's body.

"Did either of you touch the gun?" Larson asked.

"No," Nestoss answered. "It's tight in his hand, so I just lifted his wrist and laid it on his chest while we carried him down here."

"Shit," Larson said, handed his bottle to Nestoss and quickly knelt beside the body to examine the dead man's shirt. He looked up at the two men and smiled. "I was afraid there'd be blood on his shirt that somebody might notice and ask questions about it. Luckily, there isn't." He stood and took his beer back. "I checked the hill and saw only one size boot track with that distinctive tread."

"That was the shits, putting the boots back on Mikey," Nestoss mumbled, looking down at his own feet.

"Mike's body looks like it did when we first saw it," Larson said. "The blood is splattered and pooled like it should be. The slug would have gone out into the farmyard, so they probably won't even look for it. I'm taking off. Give me about a half hour and then call the sheriff. It'll be good and dark by then, so there probably won't be too much of an investigation tonight. All my bottles are in the back of the truck, so there's no fingerprints, just in case they check."

Andy Larson squatted and tapped his fingertips on the chest of Mike Garske's body. "I'm sorry I brought all this on you, my friend. Really, truly, sorry." He quickly stood and walked out the door, keeping his head turned so the others couldn't see the tears streaming down his cheeks.

CHAPTER FORTY-ONE

Andy Larson sat on the top rail of the corral beside the barn and watched the cloud of dust marking the convoy of cars and trucks leaving the Garske farm. They had buried Mike Garske in the freshly dug grave on the hill in the family plot and eaten a grand feast, as was customarily put together by family, friends, and neighbors of the Garske family. After the meal, people talked as they cleaned up and packed remnants of food to take home, since there were no family members to leave it with on the farm. He could see Louie Bergavin and Billy Nestoss had finished filling in the grave, shovels over their shoulders, as they walked back down to the buildings. He caught the glint of a badge out of the corner of his eye and turned to see Burleigh County Sheriff, Oley Krauss, walking toward him. He sighed, pushed off the fence to his feet and held out his hand.

"How are you, Oley?" Larson asked.

"I'm makin' do, Andy," the sheriff answered and gave Larson's hand a single, firm pump. "What about you, now you've got all this spare time on your hands?"

"Oh, I've kept busy. Working around my house, helping Mike out here. I wish I'd been here the other day. I might have been able to prevent him from doing himself in. There've been too damned many funerals around here lately."

"Yeah," Sheriff Krauss agreed. "I'm really sorry about your friend."

"Thanks, so are we. Have you been able to locate Bert or

find any relatives to come and take over the place?"

"We're still looking. Odd thing, Mike told the neighbors Bert was working for an uncle over in Montana, but we can't seem to find that uncle."

"Yeah, that's what he told us when we asked him where Bert was. Said he was helping an old uncle somewhere over near Helena. We've been helping out here whenever we could 'til Bert got back. That's how they found him the other night."

Nestoss and Bergavin leaned their shovels against the corral rails and joined Larson and Sheriff Krauss.

"Damn, I hated that job," Bergavin said. "It's tough to bury a friend."

Billy Nestoss nodded and ran a finger under his nose.

"I was just talking to Oley about finding a relative of the Garskes to come out and take over the farm. Seems that old uncle over in Montana might not even exist," Larson explained.

"Son-of-a-bitch," Bergavin said softly. "What's gonna happen to the place if they can't find Bert or some relative to take it over?"

"If worse comes to worse, the county'll have an estate sale and put the money in escrow for the relegated amount of time," Sheriff Krauss answered. "When was the last time any of you saw Bert?"

Larson glanced at his friends. "Oh, I'd say . . . three weeks or more. What about you guys?"

Bergavin and Nestoss both shrugged and nodded.

Sheriff Krauss studied each of their faces. "Okay. You've turned all the cows and horses out to pasture?"

"We did that the other night," Bergavin answered. "The chickens can feed themselves for a few days. One of us'll stop out and check the place every couple of days or so."

"Okay," Krauss said. "Make sure everything's locked up when you leave. Again, I'm sorry about Mike. Keep me posted if you hear anything at all about Bert. I've got to hurry if I'm gonna make it back to town by dark."

"We will, Oley," Larson answered and held out his hand. "Thanks for all you've done."

Sheriff Krauss shook hands with the three men, walked to his car, and drove off down the road, his trail of dust glowing in the golden light from the setting sun.

"The rest of that beer over in the root cellar?" Larson asked. "Let's have a drink while we talk some of these things over."

Minutes later the three friends sat on a bench in front of the barn, sipping beer. "Oley seems to have made up his mind it was a suicide," Bergavin said. "I wonder if he's gonna let it stay that way or make it an ongoing investigation?"

"He really doesn't have any reason to keep it open," Larson said. "I'd guess the biggest thing to concern him about Mike's death now will be to find a relative or sell this place."

"Hell, if I had the money, I'd buy it," Billy Nestoss said, waving a hand in front of him. "This'd be a helluva lot better than working down at the damned lumberyard for old man Herman. I wonder how much the farm'll go for?"

Louie Bergavin chuckled. "I bet I know where you can get some money. What *are* we going to do with all that gold, Andy?"

Larson leaned forward, rested his elbows on his knees and stared out across the farmyard. "Buying a farm *would* be a good investment. I guess all that gold goes into a three-way split now, so I'm sure you could afford to buy this place. Do you want to be a farmer, Billy?"

"It'd be a lot of hard work, but slaving for old man Herman ain't exactly like a long weekend off," Nestoss answered. "I think I'd kinda enjoy it. At least I'd have something that was mine."

"Well, let's see what happens a few months, maybe even a year, down the road, and then we can decide. I don't have any problem with splitting up the money, Billy," Larson said. "But if it attracts attention, it'll be deadly. It's too soon to take a chance on trying to move it. For some reason, I don't think the Saint-Gaudens belonged to Salvatore, but there's word on the street about a big reward for information leading to the recovery of the coins, and he's the man to contact."

"You mentioned something once about taking it to Minneapolis or Sioux Falls or someplace like that to cash it in," Nestoss said.

"The person who owns the gold has power, and that means he's probably got connections with the big banks and they control the small banks. I'm sure there's word out by now to every banker in the country to be on the lookout for those twenty-dollar coins. These days there aren't many of them in the hands of the average person, and more than one or two would be sure to attract attention. We have no choice but to leave it where it is until things settle down."

"Yeah, you're right," Bergavin agreed with a sigh. "Billy coming up with that much money on the wages he gets from the lumberyard would be sure to get some unwanted attention."

Nestoss nodded. "I guess I won't be a farmer for a while. Damn."

"I do have one more thing to bring up," Larson said. "Have either of you been out to the whiskey lately?"

Both Billy Nestoss and Louie Bergavin shook their heads.

"I don't like to speak badly of the dead, but then Mike was stealing it. I don't think I should call it stealing. After all he was entitled to his share. But he was being sloppy and leaving tracks off the road out there when he took it."

"Are you sure it was Mike?" Nestoss asked.

"I saw the tracks running off to the gate the day before Mike killed himself. I was going to ask you all about it after we got done with the work that night. I parked on the road and walked down to the dugout. The lock was still locked, and we all knew where the key was, so it had to be one of us down there. There were two cases of whiskey missing off the top row. I'll tell you I was pissed, but I was relieved it was one of us, not someone else stumbling on the cache. I did my best to straighten up the grass and cover the tracks on my way out."

"Do you think it's covered well enough?" Bergavin asked.

"I'm sure it'll be okay. I'll drive by again tomorrow and take another look. I found the missing cases hidden up in the root cellar behind the house today before the funeral. As near as I can tell, there's about eight bottles gone. That makes no matter anyway. If you want to take some of it, go ahead."

"I'll take a couple of bottles," Bergavin said. "I'll never turn down free whiskey."

"Me neither," Nestoss said.

Larson slapped his knees and stood up. "I've got a lot of things to think over. I'll be in touch." He shook hands with his friends and walked slowly across the darkening farmyard to his truck. It looked like someone was slumped in the corner of the passenger side of the seat. Larson went into a crouch and moved cautiously toward the vehicle. He peered into the dimly lit interior and stood up laughing. He smiled and rapped his knuckles lightly on the roof. "Becky, Becky, wake up."

The young lady stirred, stretched, rubbed her eyes, and smiled sleepily. "Hi, Andy," she said softly. "I need a ride."

Larson got in the truck, closed the door, and started the engine. "Why didn't you tell me you were still out here?"

"I figured you had some things to talk over with your friends, so I just waited. I'm not in a big hurry."

What a sweetheart, Larson told himself as he pulled on the headlights and put the truck in gear. "I guess Mrs. Daniels gives all you gals your own keys to the front door."

Becky smiled at him coyly. "She never locks the doors, but what difference does that make, Andy? I'm staying at your house tonight."

CHAPTER FORTY-TWO

Julian Samples thought he heard a car drive up out front of the converted barn where he was sweeping the floor. He waved his way through a cloud of settling dust, leaned the push broom against a table, walked to the partially open sliding door, and peered outside. A squat man in a dark suit extracted himself from the car, pulled on a hat, and adjusted his clothing as he looked around. He dug a notebook out of a pocket and thumbed through it.

Samples pushed the door open farther and stepped out into the sunlight. "Can I help you?" he asked with a cautious smile.

The man looked up from the notebook. "Is this the Samples Saloon?"

"It's not a saloon, sir, it's only a dance hall," Samples answered, suspiciously. *He looks like a revenue agent.*

"Are you Julian Samples?"

"Yes, I'm Julian."

The man slowly looked around the area. "Did you have a fire out here?" he asked, pointing at the large blackened area in front of the barn.

Samples nodded. "We did." *Where do you suppose all that burned grass came from?* "Are you a fire inspector? The insurance people have already been here."

Bernie Maxwell shook his head as he pulled his coat back to expose his badge and pistol. "I'm Detective Lieutenant Bernard Maxwell of the Bismarck Police Department. I'm here to investigate a recent murder at this location."

Pompous bastard, I've heard Andy talk about him. "That was my brother, Whitney, who was murdered. I'm sure the Mandan sheriff's office will appreciate the help, but they've been here a lot of times, and I don't believe you have any jurisdiction on this side of the river."

Maxwell tipped his head back and narrowed his eyes. "I assure you, I am well aware of the boundaries of my official jurisdiction, Mister Samples," he said, through tight lips.

"So, what can I do for you?" Samples asked.

"I see in the reports that Sergeant Andrew Larson of the Bismarck Police Department was on the premises when the murder took place."

"If that's in the official reports, then it must be true."

"Are you a friend of Sergeant Larson?"

Samples nodded. "I know who he is."

Maxwell raised his notebook and seemed to be reading. "How many times have you been raided?"

Samples shrugged. "Two or three, I guess."

"Has Sergeant Larson ever warned you about an upcoming raid?"

"I thought you said you were here investigating my brother's murder," Samples said, exasperation beginning to show in his voice. "Why all these questions about An . . . Sergeant Larson?"

"Was he drinking when he was here that night?"

"I told you this isn't a saloon."

Maxwell nodded and smiled. "Was Larson wearing a sidearm the night of the incident?"

"No, he was carrying a damned elephant gun over his shoulder."

"Are you getting smart with me, Samples?"

Samples shook his head. "No, that was a stupid question, so I gave you a stupid answer. How in the hell would I know if he had a gun? Don't all off-duty policemen carry guns?"

"Not if they're in an illegal establishment, participating in illegal activities. And right now he's suspended from duty, so I'd best not find out he's carrying one at all. If I do, I'll hang his ass."

Maxwell crossed the burned grass and pushed past Julian Samples into the dance hall. He slowly walked around the room looking intently at the layout and contents of the room. He stopped at the beer keg and rapped it several times with his knuckles. "Sell much beer?"

"As a matter of fact, we give it away."

Maxwell turned and pointed at Samples. "You're getting smart with me again."

"No, that's the truth. Free beer is covered by the price of admission."

"Giving away piss-warm beer. That must be one hell of a drawing card." Maxwell continued his circuit of the room. "What do you serve at these bars?" he asked, tapping his fingers on one of the bars.

"Sarsaparilla, soda pop, water, and milk. And *that* was a smart answer. Excuse me, I have work to do." Samples picked up the broom and began to sweep, long, hard strokes, raising clouds of dust into the air.

Maxwell walked through the airborne pall of fine dirt to the door and coughed several times before turning and pointing at the man pushing the broom. "If I were you, I'd be expecting a few more raids over here," he shouted.

Samples leaned on his broom and watched the man amble through the burned grass to his car. "Blow it out your ass," he grumbled to himself and began to push the broom again.

A short time later Samples heard a vehicle drive up to the front of the building. *I wonder what that asshole wants this time?*

he asked himself as he leaned the broom against the wall and walked to the front door. He was surprised to see Andy Larson striding toward him. "Hey, Andy, your boss just left," he called.

"What do you mean by that?" Larson asked as he shook his hand.

"*Detective Lieutenant Bernard Maxwell* was just here," Samples answered, emphasizing the man's title and name.

"What the hell did he want?"

"He's investigating my brother's murder."

"He doesn't have any jurisdiction over here."

"That's what I told him, and he told me it wasn't any of my business. He asked me more questions about you than he did about Whitney."

"I wonder what the bastard's after?" Larson said. "What'd he ask about me?"

"Were you drinking? Were you carrying a gun? Things like that. He told me you're suspended and if he finds out you're packing, he's gonna hang your ass."

"My hands are shaking so bad I won't be able to button my fly the next time I take a leak."

"He told me to expect more raids out here."

"Well, that's enough," Larson said with a sigh. "It's time to put a few dents in that little turtle's shell. I don't like him threatening my friends with all that power he thinks he has. My father always told me to never write a check with my mouth that my ass couldn't cover. I think *Detective Lieutenant Bernard Maxwell* just overdrew his account."

Samples grinned. "You want a beer?"

"Not out of that piss-warm keg."

"That must be cop talk. Maxwell called it the same thing. I've got some on ice out in back."

"Let's go."

CHAPTER FORTY-THREE

Guido Salvatore was not his usual natty self as he paced his office, trailing a cloud of cigar smoke. He stopped, ground out the butt in the overflowing ashtray on his desk, and went into a coughing spasm. His pants were wrinkled from sleeping in them on his office couch for two nights. His tie hung loose from the open, dirty collar of his expensive white shirt. His eyes were puffy, and he was in bad need of a shave. He hadn't left his office and had been beating himself up mentally for three days. *How does that asshole Kidd Cann know about Capone coming after me for the stolen gold? Should I call Uncle Al and talk to him about it? I should be able to work something out to repay the money. I can come up with half of it right now. Who in the hell will loan me the rest? I've got too much tied up in inventory. Possibly he'll work with me for a chunk of my inventory. Booze is as good as cash. I haven't seen those goons of his lately. Where the hell are they? Did they go back to Chicago?* He was afraid to go home because they might be waiting for him there. *God, what am I going to do?* He glanced at his calendar and saw it was Sunday. *I'll have to call Uncle Al tomorrow and try to work something out. He's not an understanding man, so I'd better have some damned good answers for him.*

A loud knocking on Salvatore's office door startled him. He moved quickly to his desk, picked up the large, automatic pistol, and held it behind his back. He cleared his throat. "Come in," he called, and his hand tightened around the handle of the pistol.

The door opened and Bruno Campagna filled the space. He quickly looked Salvatore up and down. "Damn, Boss, you look like shit."

"Where in the hell have you been?" Salvatore shouted as a visible look of relief swept across his face. "Close that damned door."

"I told you I was going over to Grand Forks and play poker this weekend," Bruno answered and pushed the door shut behind him. "I just got back in town, and when I saw your car out front, I came in to see what you were up to. It ain't like you to be here on Sunday. You sick or something?"

Salvatore shook his head as he walked over and flopped down in his desk chair. He pulled open a drawer and slid his pistol into it. "No, I'm not sick," he answered. "I got word Friday that Capone is after me for his stolen gold, and I've been hiding out here."

Bruno laughed. "That fancy Buick Roadster of yours out front is kind of a giveaway to where you might be, Boss."

"Shut up, damnit," Salvatore ordered. "How much heat have you got with you?"

Bruno opened his jacket, revealing an automatic pistol under both arms. "I've got a Tommy gun and a couple of shotguns in my car. Are we expecting a war?"

"I don't know. Where are those three men from Chicago?"

"They went home Wednesday. Capone called them and they left."

"Do you know why he called them?"

"They didn't say. Pooch told me Capone wanted them back there, so they loaded up and took off."

"Did they say anything about when they'd be back?"

Bruno shook his head. "Nope, he just said they were goin' back to Chicago."

Salvatore stood up, stretched, and yawned. "Let's drive over to my place so I can clean up, eat, and get some sleep. I've got a lot to do tomorrow."

"Yeah, like I said, Boss, you look like shit. I ain't seen you like this in years. Way back when we were still operating out of Detroit."

"Shut up."

The next morning Guido Salvatore, neatly dressed, shaved, and looking his usual suave self, sat at his desk sipping from a steaming mug of coffee and scratching words and numbers on a pad in front of him. The buzzing of his intercom broke his chain of thought, and he swore softly as he reached up and flipped the lever. "Yes?"

"Mister Campagna and three other gentlemen are here to see you, Mister Salvatore."

"Send Bruno in first."

"Yes, Mister Salvatore."

The door opened. Bruno walked in and closed the door behind him. "Hey, Boss, guess who's back?" he asked as he crossed the room. "Pooch and the guys from Chicago."

Salvatore sat up straighter and pulled open the drawer where he kept his pistol. "I was afraid that was who was with you."

"Pooch says he's got a letter for you from Mister Capone."

Salvatore's eyes squinted as he looked at Bruno. "Okay. What else did they tell you?"

Bruno shook his head. "That's all, Boss. He just said he's got a letter for . . ."

"Tell him to bring it in," Salvatore interrupted. "Just Pooch, and you stay in here."

Bruno walked back to the door, opened it, and waved his hand. "Pooch, bring the letter in. The rest of you boys, sit tight."

The man known as Pooch entered the office, eyed Salvatore coldly, then walked to his desk and laid an envelope on it. "I deliver this *personally* to you from Alphonse Capone," he said as he stepped back and folded his hands in front of him.

Salvatore picked up the envelope, held it up to the light, tapped one end of it on the desk, and deftly sliced it open with a silver letter opener. He slid the sheet of paper out, unfolded it, and quickly read it. He looked up at the man standing across the desk. "All right, Pooch, what's your full real name? Yours and the other two from Chicago. I'd like to know that."

"My legal name is Alexander Puccini. The short man is M.D. Rowell, and he's called Doc. The third man is Patsy Roach and he's known as . . ."

"The Bug," Salvatore interrupted.

Pooch smiled. "Yeah, that's right. He's a mean one."

"Mister Capone says you three are here to help me find who stole his gold and recover it. No holds barred."

"Yes, Mister Salvatore."

"You'll do anything to accomplish this."

"Yes, Mister Salvatore."

"Are you still driving that big black Packard?"

"Yes, Mister Salvatore."

"Bruno, get an older, less conspicuous vehicle for the trip to Bismarck. You'll take Pooch and the others down there and pay a visit to Mister Werner and his transportation company tonight. Send Rudy in to see me. He'll be in charge of the visit."

CHAPTER FORTY-FOUR

Andy Larson sat in his truck a block north of the Bismarck Police Station, watching people coming and going from the building. He poured himself a cup of coffee and pushed the cork back in the thermos bottle. *C'mon, Maxwell, I want to see who you throw your weight around at today and how long it takes you to find your little present. It's nice that you always insist on driving your own car. The half a cent a mile you get must really fatten your wallet, you cheap bastard.* He pulled his watch out and checked the time. *You've been in the station for over an hour now; it's about time for you to get out on the streets and act important.*

Lieutenant Maxwell sauntered from the police station, squared his hat, and looked both ways up and down the street.

Larson pulled his hat down and slouched so he could barely see over the dashboard. *Ask and ye shall receive.*

Satisfied, Maxwell stepped to his car and looked in the windows before walking around behind the vehicle, opening the door, squeezing in, and rolling down the window. A small cloud of smoke signaled the start of his engine, a hand reached out to adjust the rearview mirror and the car drove away from the curb.

Larson started his truck and pulled into the street, keeping a block distance behind him.

Maxwell turned the corner and drove several blocks before edging to the curb, sliding out and walking to a pay phone booth.

Larson found a space, quickly parked, and took a pair of binoculars from under the seat. He brought them to his eyes and focused on Maxwell squeezing into the phone booth and bringing a handful of coins from a pocket. He removed a notebook from a coat pocket, flipped it open, thumbed through several pages, dialed the phone, and waited. He nodded and began to pick up coins and drop them into the slots.

That much silver means he's calling long distance, Larson told himself. *There must be a good reason for him not using the phone in his office.*

After a short conversation, Maxwell hung up the phone, scooped the remaining coins into a pocket, returned to his car, and drove to Werner Transportation. He got out of his car and looked around before entering the building.

Larson found a parking place and slouched down to wait. *I wonder if he's on the take from Werner like Tork was? I'll bet a dollar to a dog's butt he isn't there to gather evidence.*

Maxwell spent a few minutes in the building, came out the door, and stood nonchalantly studying the parking lot and street from under the brim of his hat. *The man seems to have a worry about someone following him.*

Maxwell walked to his car, opened the door, stopped and appeared to be sniffing the air.

Larson smiled. *That engine of his must be getting nice and warm by now.*

Maxwell shook his head, wedged himself into the front seat, pulled the door shut, started the engine, and drove into the street. He had driven several blocks when he suddenly swerved the car to the curb, jumped out, and yanked the side of the hood open.

A cloud of smoke rose into the air, and he began to scream curses and kick the tire. *Looks like he found his surprise,* Larson told himself and began to laugh as he made a U-turn and sped away. He glanced in his rearview mirror in time to see Maxwell reach into the cloud of smoke and yank a large, smoking fish from under the hood. *That one's nearly as funny as the dog turd in his shoe. I'd best keep away from him for a while. Maybe I'll go fishing.*

Larson glanced at a car going the opposite direction, suddenly put his truck in neutral, and hit the brakes. *That was Bruno riding in there!* He put his truck back in gear, made a U-turn, and pulled up behind the car he thought he had seen Bruno in. As he got closer he could make out the bulk of the huge man in the front passenger seat. *There's no doubt that's Bruno. I wonder if Salvatore's with him?* He pulled his hat down and stepped on the gas to pass the car with the questionable passenger. He glanced at the passengers as he sped around it. The driver honked and gave him the finger as he swerved back in front. *That's Bruno, all right, but I didn't see Salvatore. But what the hell are they doing in town?* He studied the passengers in his rearview mirror before he turned a corner and drove around the block to get behind them. *I'll tail them and see if I can figure out what they're up to.*

The car with Bruno in it seemed to drive aimlessly around Bismarck for the remainder of the morning, but Larson noted they had passed Werner Transportation several times. *They're casing Werner's joint, that's for sure.*

At a little before noon the car stopped at the curb. The five passengers climbed out and walked toward the McKenzie Hotel. Larson drove slowly past the men as they ambled along the sidewalk, talking, looking, and pointing at things in the windows. *I wonder if the small guy's . . . ? No, I'm not that lucky.* He found a space, parked his truck, and trotted to catch up with the five men as they pushed through the doors of the hotel. He waited in the lobby and watched as they were seated at a large table in the back of Peacock Alley.

I've got to hear the little guy talk. If he's Rudy, I'll know the bastard from his voice and accent.

Larson pulled off his hat, stopped at the door of the restaurant, and waited for the maitre d' to greet him.

"Good morning, sir," the tall graying man with the mechanical smile said as he approached. "Will you be dining alone this noon?"

"No, I'll be having four others joining me in a few minutes," Larson answered, returning his smile. "Could we have one of those big tables in back?"

"Certainly, sir, table for five. There's one back there near those other gentlemen. Would that suffice?"

"Perfect."

The headwaiter led Larson back to the table, pulled out a chair, and handed him a menu after he was seated. He adroitly placed four more menus around the table, folded his hands, and stepped back. "Would you care for a cup of coffee while you wait?"

"Yes, that'd be fine." Larson picked up his menu and appeared to begin studying it. Out of the corner of his eye he watched the men at the nearby table as they chatted and looked at their menus. The short man had not spoken.

A waiter brought Larson a steaming cup of coffee. "My name is Dwayne, and I'll be your waiter when the rest of your party arrives."

"Good." *Now get away from me so I can listen.*

As the waiter walked away, Larson heard the small man finally speak.

"Ve vill haf to stop und git more petrol for tonight."

Larson lowered his menu and looked squarely at the little man. *Rudy, you little bastard, now I know what you look like without your black mask!* He stood, dug a handful of change from his pocket, dropped it on the table, and pulled on his hat as he strode toward the door.

"Sir, sir . . . ," Dwayne called, waving his hand as Larson disappeared into the lobby.

CHAPTER FORTY-FIVE

Pooch watched Andy Larson hurry out of the dining room. "That guy's sure going someplace in a hurry," he said and pointed at the man turning the corner.

"It might tell us something about da food in here," Rudy said, and laughed. "Vhat'd he hafe?"

"No, the food here's good," Bruno said, holding up his menu. "Mister Salvatore and I always eat here. The meals are real tasty, and they serve big portions. I like that."

"Exactly why are we down here this time, Rudy?" Pooch asked.

"I vill tell ya da plan after da vaiter gits our orders und nobody can hear me," Rudy answered, glancing around the room to make sure there was no one nearby.

Minutes later the waiter carried their orders back to the kitchen, and Rudy signaled for everyone to lean in and listen to him.

"Da main reason ve're down here is to burn out Verner Transportation tonight," Rudy started.

"I thought we were back from Chicago to get Al Capone's gold," Doc interrupted.

Rudy raised his hand. "Dis is the first part of Mister Salvatore's plan to git da big man's gold back."

"How's burnin' down this transportation company gonna help with that?" Pooch asked.

"Salvatore thinks Verner knows who's got da gold und burning his place vill make him decide to cooperate."

"I don't understand," Pooch said.

"Do you think Salvatore got to where he is by being stupid?" Bruno asked.

"Tank ya, Bruno," Rudy said, and smiled. "Ve're here to do his dirty vork for him. If he says torch da place, ve torch da place."

"You got another blind pig for us to hit while we're here this time?" Doc asked.

"Yah, I gotta couple places in mind," Rudy answered. "Ve'll see how da time goes. Ve did pretty good on dat last vun across da river."

"Do I have to wait in the car again?" Bruno asked.

"Like I told ya before," Rudy said. "Dey got a damned hard time identifying regular-sized guys in black suits, hats, und masks. Somebody as big as you, Bruno, is easy to spot later. Ya'll drive agin. Ya git da same money as ve do."

Bruno nodded. "Okay, okay."

"I wasn't too crazy about you killin' that guy last time," Pooch said.

"He vas pissing me uff," Rudy growled.

"There's been a time or two, you've pissed *me* off, but I didn't shoot *you* and hang you up to die slow like that," Pooch said.

Rudy patted the lump under his arm and shrugged. "Chust 'cause ya're from Chicago, don't mean ya scare me, *Pooch.*"

Pooch tilted his head, narrowed his eyes, smiled knowingly, and nodded. "I'm beginning to believe those stories about you fighting for the Kaiser in *The War,* you little, hard core bastard. Maybe the day will come when we see who's scared of who."

Rudy grinned. "Ya chust never can tell, *Pooch,* old man."

"All right, you two," Doc interjected. "You can continue this pissing contest some other time."

"Ya, vhen da verk is done, ve can discuss dis again," Rudy agreed.

Doc turned to the little man next to him, who seemed to be carefully studying his menu. "Something wrong, Bug? You seem awfully quiet today."

Bug laughed. "No, I'm just getting a kick out of these two boys, standing up on their hind legs an' growling at each other. I ain't seen either one of 'em do anything in a fair fight. I wanna be there when they finally stop growling an' get 'round to biting."

"That may be sooner than you expect," Pooch said, glaring at Rudy.

Andy Larson drove to his house, walked into his bedroom, and slid the dresser away from the wall. Dropping to his knees, he pushed down on the end of a board by the wall, and the other end rose enough for him to get his fingers under it. He lifted a hidden door in the floor, pulled out a guitar case, dropped the door closed, and pushed the board back down. He stood, swung the guitar case onto the bed, and shoved the dresser into its original position. Satisfied, he opened the guitar case to reveal several small wooden partitions built into the wide section of it. Two of them contained fifty-shot drum magazines, and another held four twenty-shot box magazines. All were fully loaded. He lifted a blanket-wrapped bundle free from the center, laid it on the bed, pulled the end of the blanket, and it unrolled to reveal a Thompson machine gun. *This might be the day I get to test this thing for real,* he thought as he lifted it and worked the action several times. He picked out one of the drum magazines, snapped it into place in the weapon, and hefted it. *Feels good.* He pushed the button to release the drum, slid it back into the case, closed the lid, and snapped the locks shut. *If I can't get the job done with a hundred and eighty rounds, I'm in deep shit. It's time to go back and see if those hoods are finally done with their lunch and what they've got planned for the rest of the day.*

Chapter Forty-Six

Salvatore's men came out of the dining room rubbing their stomachs, picking at their teeth, and making small talk.

"I'm gonna use this pay phone to call Mister Salvatore," Bruno said, pulling the door to the booth open.

"Vat do ya haf to call him fer?" Rudy asked.

"He told me to call him after lunch," Bruno answered. "This is after lunch."

"He put me in charch dis morning," Rudy argued. "Vhy didn't he tell *me* to call him?"

"Maybe he was afraid he couldn't understand you," Pooch answered, and the others echoed his chuckle.

Rudy spun and glared at Pooch, who tilted his head and grinned.

"Back off," Bug ordered, stepping between the two men. "Make the call, Bruno."

Bruno dug a handful of change from his pocket, dumped it on the counter under the phone, squeezed into the booth, and managed to push the door shut.

Rudy began to pace back and forth in front of the booth as Doc and Bug walked over to the news rack and scanned the magazines and papers.

In a matter of minutes Bruno pulled the door open and pushed out into the lobby. "It's a good thing I made that call," he announced, motioning for the others to join him.

"Mister Salvatore has someone on the police force down here

on his payroll," Bruno said, his voice almost a whisper. "He told him Werner has a bunch of guards armed to the teeth all around his buildings during the day and more at night. We coulda walked into a hell of an ambush tonight."

"That is damned lucky," Doc agreed. "Now what?"

"He says come home and he'll work out something else."

"Vell, as long as ve're here," Rudy said. "Vhy don't ve knock ofer a blind peeg?"

"What have you got picked out?" Bug asked.

"Der is vun down by the train yard," Rudy answered. "Der is a shift chanch at four. Der's a lot uf dem railroad boys go der und drink. Ve go in about four-tirty und git der cash."

Bruno looked at the large wall clock across the lobby. "Let's go for a ride, see the town or something. We've got over three hours to kill."

Andy Larson slouched down and watched the five men come out of the hotel and walk casually back to their car. *They don't seem to be in too much of a hurry, now that they've eaten,* he told himself as they climbed into the car.

He let another car get between them as they pulled away from the curb and drove down Main Street. He followed them as they crossed the Memorial Bridge and drove the short distance to Mandan, where they seemed to wander aimlessly through the streets before returning to Bismarck. *They're killing time for some reason.*

Bug drove the car into a small city park, pulled onto the grass, and turned off the engine. "Let's get out and get some fresh air," he said, opening his door and stepping out. "We've still got a couple of hours before the hit."

The others opened their doors, got out of the car, and walked to a wooden picnic table.

Doc brought a box of playing cards from a jacket pocket, shook them out, and began to shuffle. "How about a little penny ante poker?"

The others dug change from their pockets and stacked the coins in front of them on the table.

Bruno brought a large silver flask from an inside coat pocket, unscrewed the cap, and took a drink. "Anybody care for a bump?" he asked, offering the flask.

Bug took the container of liquor and smiled. "I thought you'd never ask," he said as he lifted it in a toast and took a quick drink. "That's good stuff. Where do you get your booze?" The others laughed, and Bug passed the flask to Pooch, who took a drink and handed it to Doc.

Doc took a swallow. "Are we letting Rudy drink?" he asked.

Rudy grabbed for the flask, but Doc jerked it up and he missed it. Rudy's eyes narrowed, and he unbuttoned his coat.

"Oh, oh, look out, he's going for his guns, Doc," Pooch said, with a laugh. "He gets mean when he drinks, but he gets meaner when he doesn't. Better give it to him."

"Yeah," Bruno agreed. "Gunshots in the park this time of day are sure to bring the cops."

Doc shrugged and handed Rudy the flask. "Keep your iron under your coat," he said, with a grin.

Andy Larson sat on the running board of his truck atop a small hill at the far end of the park and watched the antics of the men at the picnic table through a pair of binoculars. *I wonder how much longer they're gonna screw around like this. They're waiting for something.* He pulled out his watch. *Ten to four.* He leaned back and felt the warmth of the sun-heated door on his back. *Boy, that feels good.* He tipped his hat forward and closed his eyes to rest a minute.

When Larson's head snapped up, he blinked at the brightness and realized the men and the car he had been watching were gone. "Son-of-a-bitch," he muttered as he jumped to his feet and raised the binoculars hanging around his neck. The car was just turning onto the street, and it quickly disappeared. He yanked open the door to his truck and started the engine. The rear wheels threw grass and dirt into the air as he jammed it into gear and tromped the gas pedal to the floor. When he reached the street, he looked in the direction he had last seen the car. The street was empty. "I'll be go to hell," he shouted, and banged his hands on the steering wheel. "Now I'll have to try to find them. The first place is back to Werner's."

Larson drove immediately to the yards of Werner Transportation and circled it several times. *Where in the hell would they have gone? Maybe they went back to Minot? No, they were here in town for some reason.*

"Turn here," Rudy ordered, pointing to a rundown garage with rows of vehicles in various stages of disrepair parked around it. "Dat garage der is da front for Blaine's blind peeg. Dey vill hafe da cash from all day und da new buncha boys vill have ders in der pockets. Der is a doorman."

"I'll take care of him," Pooch said. "You others just stay back where he can't see you until the door is open."

There was no sign of life until a man tumbled out the side door of the building and fell to his knees. He finally managed to get to his feet and began cursing and making obscene gestures at the closed door. He staggered to one of the nearby car bodies, leaned on it, and threw up. He wiped his mouth with the back of his sleeve, shook his head, retched several times, and staggered on down the alley.

"This must be the place," Doc said and chuckled.

"All right, I'll take it from here," Pooch said. "I'll fire my shotgun into the ceiling as we go in, and that'll get their attention. Doc, you carry that little shotgun of yours and get the cash drawers. Bug, you wave your Tommy gun around so everyone can see it. Rudy, you'll pass the bag. Bruno, keep the

201

motor running and the doors open out front. Have the Tommy gun on the seat and hit the horn twice if anything looks like trouble. We should be in and out of there in five minutes or less. Put your masks on and let's go."

CHAPTER FORTY-SEVEN

Andy Larson was furious at himself as he drove looking down streets and alleys, in search of the car with the five men from Minot. *How in the hell did I ever let myself fall asleep?* he chastised himself again and again. As he neared the train yards, he glanced down a street and saw a small group of men crossing it two blocks away. The men were all dressed in black. He hit the brakes, yanked the truck into reverse, and backed up to look down the street. There was no one in sight. *Damn, it has to be them.*

He turned down the street and sped toward where he had seen the men walking. As he approached, the car he was looking for made a U-turn in front of him and stopped in front of a ramshackle brick building. *It is them.* He slowed his truck as Bruno got out of the car and opened the door behind the driver's side. *That's odd.* Larson went into a coughing spasm and put his hand up over his mouth as he drove past. He watched in his rearview mirror as Bruno opened both doors on the passenger side of the car, walked around, and crammed himself back behind the steering wheel.

Larson turned his truck out of sight at the corner, shut off the engine, and snapped open his guitar case. He pulled on a pair of thin leather gloves, lifted out the Thompson, grabbed a drum magazine, slammed it into place, and worked the action to seat a round in the chamber. He picked up the other drum and dropped it into a coat pocket. He pulled his hat down to shadow his eyes, opened the door, stepped out of the truck and pushed the door shut. He hung the machine gun back behind his leg to conceal it, and started for the corner. *Now I'm heeled enough to handle what's going on.*

Pooch and his gang of men in black walked down the alley, stopped outside the door of Blaine's blind pig, and adjusted their masks. Pooch pumped the action of his shotgun and chambered a round. The outside hammers of Doc's sawed-off shotgun clicked loudly as Rudy shook out his canvas bag. Bug pulled back the knob on the top of the machine gun action and let it slam forward to seat a round.

Pooch signaled them to get back to the walls. He ran his hand over the door. "He must be paying off the cops. This door'll go in easy," he whispered as he pulled his hat down and rapped his knuckles on the old wood. At the sound of the small window in the door opening, he lowered his shoulder and smashed through it.

The doorman flew back from the impact of the door, sprawling over a table and tumbling to the floor. The crash of the door was followed immediately by the deafening blast of the shotgun and a shower of plaster pouring from the ceiling. The room was momentarily silent as a few pellets rattled to the floor and the cloud of plaster dust and smoke settled.

"Anybody moves is dead!" Pooch barked, his voice slightly muffled by the mask. "Get your hands in the air."

Everyone in the room quickly raised their hands, the look of fear in their eyes.

"When he passes by you with the bag," Pooch continued. "Just pretend this is church and be most generous with your donations."

Larson ducked behind a rusty car body at the muffled sound of the shotgun blast. *They're not playing games.* He raised his head enough to see Bruno intently watching the alley. He leaped to his feet and dashed to the open rear door of the car.

Out of the corner of his eye, Bruno saw the movement in the rearview mirror and started to turn. The impact of the machine gun barrel on the side of his head made stars burst in front of his eyes. He fought to remain conscious and felt the cold steel pressed into his ear.

"If you move, Big Man, your brains'll splatter all over the steering wheel," Larson snarled. "Put your hands up where I can see them."

Bruno raised his hands and grasped the steering wheel.

Larson leaned forward, lifted Bruno's machine gun from the front seat, and laid it on the floor in the back. "Out of the car," he ordered, prodding the big man with the barrel of his gun and stepping out. "Bring the keys and keep your hands where I can see them."

Bruno pulled himself out of the car and stood in the street, one hand holding the keys up by his shoulder and the other holding the side of his head. He lowered his hand from his head, looked at the blood on it, and glared at Larson. "You're a dead man," he threatened.

Larson waved the machine gun and shook his head. "Not yet. Unlock the trunk."

"What?"

"You heard me. Unlock the damned trunk. Either that or I'll just shoot you now. Come on, *Lard Ass,* move!"

Bruno looked at Larson as if he might challenge him, but thought different, moved to the back of the car and unlocked the trunk.

"Open it and crawl in," Larson ordered. "This might just save your life."

Bruno lifted the trunk door and looked back at Larson.

"You don't wanna try," Larson warned him. "Get in the damned trunk."

Bruno glared at him and crawled into the opening. "I'll remember you," he warned.

"I'm worried. Now pull it shut," Larson ordered.

Bruno reached up and tugged the door down until it was almost closed.

Larson stepped up, spun around, and dropped his butt against the door, slamming it tight. He pulled the keys free and threw them in among the rusty car bodies. He lifted Bruno's machine gun from the back seat, dropped the clip from it, stuck it in his pocket, worked the action to clear the chamber, and tossed it back into the car. He walked around the vehicle, closed all the doors, stepped to the far side, and laid his machine gun on the hood. He hefted the drum of ammunition in his pocket, patted the clip in another pocket, then loosened the automatic pistol in his shoulder holster.

Larson took several deep breaths and looked down at his trembling hand as he reached for the machine gun while chilling memories of combat action ran through his mind.

CHAPTER FORTY-EIGHT

"We want it all, boys," Pooch cajoled. "Dig deep. You don't want to piss off those two little guys. They're meaner'n hell when they're riled. After you've made your contribution, get on your belly on the floor and put your hands behind your heads. Start collecting, Rudy."

Rudy stepped to the first man and waggled the bag in front of him.

The man dug his hand down into a pants pocket, brought out a handful of coins, and dropped them into the bag.

"Ya got a vallet?" Rudy snarled.

The man shook his head vigorously. "N . . . no," he finally managed to croak.

Rudy began moving quickly through the small crowd as the men emptied their pockets and quickly got down on the floor.

Doc laughed softly as he pulled a small drawstring, canvas bag out of his pocket and handed it to the bartender. "I can be kinda nasty myself. Dump your cash drawer in this. You got a safe in here?"

The trembling wide-eyed bartender nodded and pointed at a door in the corner. "In there," he croaked. "It's in there."

"Is it open?" Doc asked.

"I don't think so. Blaine usually locks it when he leaves."

"You dump that drawer and we'll go take a look," Doc said. "Hurry up!"

The man quickly dumped the drawer and set it back under the bar.

"Now," Doc said. "Put *your* take for the day in the bag."

"What do you mean?"

"I used to be a bartender, so I know you steal from the till. All good bartenders steal. It's part of the job. Where is it?"

The man could see Doc's hard eyes through the holes in his mask and knew he wasn't bluffing. He dug into a pocket and brought out a small wad of bills.

Doc leaned closer to the man. "Did you steal all of that today?" he asked softly.

"No, that's for the whole week. I had it hidden and was taking it out of here when I get off in an hour."

Doc quickly looked around to see if any of the men in black were paying any attention to them. Satisfied they weren't being observed, he smiled under his mask. "I'm impressed. Put it back in your pocket."

The bartender was surprised, but he didn't argue and quickly stuffed it in his pocket.

"Let's go look at the safe," Doc said. "I got the loot from the cash drawer," he announced and waved the canvas bag. "We're going to go look at the safe in the back room."

Pooch waved to signal he had heard as the two men opened the door and disappeared.

"Stand over there," Doc instructed and the man quickly obeyed. Doc tried to move the handle on the safe door. "You sure you don't have the combination to this?"

"Blaine don't trust anybody, but hisself," the bartender answered. "Nobody."

"If I were to shoot your foot off, would you know the combination?" Doc asked, dropping the barrels of his shotgun to point at the man's feet.

"No, really, honest, I don't know it. Please, don't shoot me," the man begged, waving his hands and shuffling his feet.

"I believe you," Doc said, raising the shotgun and pointing it at the door. "Let's go back out front." He stopped at the desk and yanked the phone cord from the wall. "No phone calls when we leave."

The man was visibly relieved as he opened the door and walked back into the main room.

"There's a helluva big safe back there," Doc announced. "But it's locked, and only the guy who owns the place has the combination."

"You sure of that?" Pooch asked.

"I told him I'd blow his foot off, and he still didn't know it," Doc answered. "I believe him. He knows I'm not the kind to be tested."

"All right," Pooch agreed. "We've got everything we can get. Let's head back to Fargo."

As the four men in black backed toward the door, Rudy grabbed a bottle of whiskey from the bar and dropped it into the bag. "We'll need a drink on the way home," he said with a laugh.

Pooch stopped, grabbed the receiver of the pay phone, jerked the wire free, and tossed it to the bartender. "Don't come out of this place for at least five minutes," he ordered, pulling the door free of the shattered frame and stepping out into the alley, quickly followed by the others.

CHAPTER FORTY-NINE

Out the corner of his eye Andy Larson saw a car cross the intersection to his right but gave it no real thought. He heard the squeal of brakes and the grinding of gears and turned to see the car come backing around the corner. *What the hell?*

The car skidded to a stop, and a scowling Lieutenant Bernard Maxwell leaped from it. "There you are, Larson, you son-of-a-bitch!" he shouted as he rounded the front of his car. "I've been looking for you, you bastard."

Larson motioned toward Maxwell. "Get back in your damned car and get the hell out of here," he called.

Maxwell grimaced as he continued forward. "You don't be giving me orders," he shouted. "What's that in your hands? A machine gun?"

"Yes, now be smart for once in your life and get your ass down."

"You're on suspension. You're not allowed to have any weapons in your possession."

Pooch, Rudy, Doc, and Bug backed out the alley door of Blaine's. Bug pushed the door shut, raised his machine gun, and fired a short burst through the top of the door, swinging it partially inward on the loosened top hinge. "Nobody'll be coming out that door for a while," he said as they turned and trotted toward the street, pulling off their masks and laughing.

★ ★ ★ ★ ★

"What the hell was that?" Maxwell asked, stretching to see around the car Larson was standing behind.

"That was a machine gun, you idiot, now get down!"

Maxwell fumbled for the fancy engraved silver pistol on his belt as he ambled forward.

"Get down!" Larson ordered.

Maxwell stepped to the back of the car and saw four men moving toward them down the alley. "They're armed."

"No shit. Now *get down,* you damned idiot."

Maxwell opened his coat to expose his badge and waved his pistol at the approaching men. "Halt, police!" he screamed.

The machine gun in Bug's hands belched fire and smoke, and the slugs lifted Maxwell up and back to bounce off his car. His eyes were wide with surprise and pain as he died, leaving a wide smear of blood when he slid slowly down the door and crumpled onto the street. The sound of the shots echoed off nearby buildings.

Larson leaped up and fired a short burst from his machine gun over the hood of the car. A slug caught Pooch in the throat, flopping him backward over onto the pavement. Three slugs punched across Bug's chest, throwing him back among the rusted car bodies.

Larson immediately dropped from sight. *I know I hit at least two of them,* he told himself as he quickly checked his weapon and fought to control his breathing.

Rudy instinctively dropped to his stomach when he saw Larson pop up from behind the car. The weapon in Larson's hands erupted in fire, smoke, and death. Rudy heard the slugs slap into flesh, snap through the air, ricochet off the building, and punch holes in metal. Then it was suddenly, eerily silent, and he looked up at the clouds of thinning smoke drifting in the air. Bug's machine gun lay a short distance away. Rudy scrambled to it, rose to his knees, and fired a short burst into the car Larson was hiding behind.

Larson cringed from the sounds of gunfire and tearing metal as glass rained down onto the brim of his hat. *Stay behind the engine block,* he told himself. *I wonder how much ammo he's got for the Tommy gun? I'm sure I hit the man carrying it with my first shots.*

Doc raised up from between two car bodies and watched Rudy fire at the car. "How many are there?" he called.

"I know der is vun behin' da auto," Rudy answered, keeping his weapon pointed at the car and slowly getting to his feet. "Und der is a dead vun in da street over der."

"It's that bastard Rudy," Larson said softly.

Rudy gave Doc a hand signal to try to circle around behind the car where Larson was hiding.

Doc nodded and disappeared among the cars.

Larson lifted the machine gun above the top of the hood and blindly fired a short burst in the general direction of Rudy's voice. The sound of the shots echoed off the buildings and the empty cartridges made clinking sounds as they dropped to the street.

Rudy cringed and ran back to duck out of sight behind the brick wall. He raised the machine gun, aimed it at the car by the curb, and fired until it clicked on an empty chamber. *Shit, dat vus stupid!* He dropped the machine gun to the pavement, worked his automatic pistol free of the holster, and pointed it at the car.

Larson heard the chatter of Rudy's weapon and saw a line of holes appear in the door as the slugs tore through the car body. He moved swiftly around to the front of the car and took a quick glance at the building before ducking back. *I can see his shadow so I know where that one is, but there's another goon around here someplace. It's time for me to move.* He quickly peeked around the front of the car again, crouched for a running start, pointed the machine gun at the corner of the building, and fired a quick barrage of slugs to tear at the bricks as he ran to the wall. As he stood pressing against the wall, he looked for movement in the junkyard of cars. *Nothing moving.* He could see Rudy's shadow as he moved back up closer to the corner.

Rudy looked carefully at the shot-up car by the curb and slowly raised his pistol.

Larson saw the barrel of Rudy's pistol suddenly poke around the corner. He lowered the machine gun and leaned it against the wall. He pulled his automatic from its holster, tucked it under his arm to muffle the sound of the hammer, and cocked it. He leaned tight against the wall and grasped the pistol in his gloved hands.

The barrel of Rudy's pistol extended a bit more and then stopped.

He must have fired all the ammo for the machine gun and now he's waiting for me to make some kind of a move. He has to think I'm still behind the car. Larson took a deep breath and began to release it as he squeezed the trigger. The flash of the shot obscured Larson's view of the pistol barrel, and the sound of the report reverberated off the wall.

Rudy screamed when the pistol was torn from his grip to fly off into the junkyard, and chunks of brick ripped into his fingers. He grabbed his hand and mistakenly stepped forward only to have a pistol slug punch a neat hole in the side of his head when it entered, blowing blood, brains, and bone from the crater as it exited. He spun in a wavering half circle before he crumbled to the alley floor where he twitched and lay still.

Doc knew what had happened when he heard the two shots. He shook his head as he looked at what he had in his hands; a sawed-off shotgun and a bag of money. He quickly tossed the shotgun into a broken car window, opened the top of the bag, and brought out a handful of paper money. He stuffed the bills into an inside coat pocket, hefted the bag of coins, shook his head, and dropped it in beside the shotgun. He quickly glanced around, then straightened his suit coat, squared his hat, and stepped out onto the street at the opposite end of the block from where the shooting was taking place. He forced a weak smile onto his face, puckered his trembling lips and tried to whistle as he walked away on unsteady legs.

Andy Larson holstered his pistol, picked up his machine gun, and stood on the sidewalk surveying the carnage around him. There was no one in sight. *Nobody'll come out with all that gunfire going on.* He knew what he had to do, and he had to do it quickly. He leaned through the shattered window into the back-seat, grabbed up the machine gun, dug the clip out of his pocket, and snapped it into the weapon. He looked around again to make sure no one was in the street, worked the action of the weapon, pointed it into the air, and felt it buck and roar as he emptied the clip. He dashed into the street and pressed the still smoking gun into Lieutenant Maxwell's lifeless hands. He picked up Maxwell's fancy silver pistol and pushed it back into its holster. "I think I just made you a *hero*, Bernie, you miserable idiot," he said as he stepped over to the shot-up car and knocked on the trunk lid.

"Are you still alive in there, Bruno?"

Bruno's muffled, frightened voice answered, "Yes, what's happening out there?"

"You tell Mister Salvatore to keep the hell out of my town," Larson answered. "This is just a sample of the trouble my people and I'll give him if he comes back down here." He rapped the butt of the machine gun sharply on the trunk for emphasis, glanced about the area, trotted around the corner, and nonchalantly climbed into his truck. He started it and drove away from the scene of the afternoon battle. Not another living soul had summoned the courage to come out and see what the commotion was about.

CHAPTER FIFTY

The scene of the afternoon shootings was roped off with a number of policemen working around the area. Two plainclothes officers were talking to the men from inside Blaine's, asking questions and taking notes. The scene was briefly lit by flashes as a policeman lifted the tarp and the photographer snapped pictures of the bodies. A trail of burned flash bulbs marked his path. Dark red stains soaked through the canvas shrouds, and rivulets of blood ran from under them to pool and congeal in low spots in the pavement. Another photographer was taking pictures of the shot-up car. One man lifted empty shell casings with a pencil, examined them, and tried to put them back on the exact spot from where he had originally lifted them, while another was dusting Rudy's machine gun for fingerprints.

Chief Pearce stood over Bruno, who was sitting on a wooden box, holding a bloody cloth on the side of his head and staring down at his feet. Pearce said something. Bruno grunted and shook his head. Pearce spoke and again Bruno shook his head.

Sergeant Fred Torkelson glanced at the crowd and saw Andy Larson standing among the spectators. "Hey, Andy," he called and waved.

Larson returned the wave.

Torkelson motioned for Larson to join him. "C'mon in here. I wanna talk to you."

Larson lifted the rope, ducked under it, and walked to join Torkelson.

They shook hands. "It's good to see you, Andy," Torkelson said.

"It's good to see you too, Tork. Looks like you're staying busy."

"Yeah. What've you been up to?"

"I've been catching up on my sleep, doing some fishing, working out at Garske's farm, drinking illegal beverages. Stuff like that. What's going on here?" He pointed at the scurry of activity around them. "Looks like some sort of gang warfare."

Torkelson studied Larson's face and nodded. "Something like that," he agreed and motioned to the covered body in the street. "That's your buddy, Lieutenant Maxwell out there."

Larson glanced over his shoulder. "No shit?"

"No shit. That's Maxwell."

"What happened?"

"We're not really sure," Torkelson answered. "You see Bruno over there, getting grilled by the Chief? They found him in the trunk of that shot-up car."

"He been shot?" Larson asked, making a point to keep his back to Bruno.

"Small nick on the side of his head. Nothing serious."

Larson smiled inwardly. *Bullshit, that's from my rap with the gun barrel.* "If Bruno's here, his boss, Guido Salvatore, can't be far away."

"There's no sign of Salvatore, but we're one short of the robbery team, so it might be him."

"What's that mean?" Larson asked.

"According to the men from the bar, there were four thugs that stuck the place up. We've only got three bodies. Somebody got away."

"What about Bruno? He'd make it four. Maybe he got out and locked himself in that trunk."

"He's too big. Besides he's wearing a brown suit, and all the holdup men were wearing black," Torkelson said.

"What's the story on Maxwell?" Larson asked, hooking a thumb over his shoulder.

"Well, right now it looks like he might be a hero."

Larson fought to keep a straight face. "Old *shit-in-the-shoe* Maxwell's a hero? C'mon, be serious."

"Maxwell's got a Tommy gun clutched in his hands, and two of these dead men were shot by a machine gun."

Just the way I wanted it. "Which proves?" Larson asked.

Torkelson shook his head. "Nothing, really. Maxwell was killed by a machine gun, too. Probably the one they're dusting for prints over there."

"What about the third guy over there in the alley? How'd he die?"

"A shot in the side of the head and he's got a bloody hand they're trying to figure out. It's got some good-sized brick chips in it."

"Maybe he got shot with a brick," Larson joked.

"I can see you haven't lost that shitty sense of humor while you've been off."

Larson shrugged. "It took a long time to develop. I won't lose it overnight."

"It looks like the Chief's had enough of Bruno," Torkelson commented.

Larson glanced over his shoulder to see three policemen walking Bruno toward a paddy wagon. "Sure does," he agreed.

Chief Pearce walked up and stuck out his hand. "Good to see you, Larson. Don't tell me you were in there for the robbery."

Larson shook the Chief's hand, grinned, and shook his head. "I'm sorry, Chief, but I can't make all of 'em."

"These damn blind-pig hold-ups cause a lot of problems," Torkelson said.

"Because now you'll have to recognize the fact it's here and close it up?" Larson finished.

Chief Pearce looked at both the men and shook his head. "Yeah, we'll shut him down, and he'll be closed for a few days. Blaine'll probably find another abandoned building and set up another pig. Hell, he might already have another one. He'll pay a fine, get a slap on the wrist, and continue to march."

"I know it's been said at least once a day, but this damned prohibition is making criminals out of a lot of honest men," Larson said. "He had a nice legal saloon before prohibition came in. I wonder how long it'll be before the politicians in Washington pull their heads out of their asses and realize how stupid all of this is. It's making the gangsters, booze-runners and bootleggers rich. And criminals out of honest men," Larson added.

A ruckus started among the group of men from inside who were being questioned by the policemen.

"Looks like Lieutenant Weaver's got problems," Chief Pearce said. "I'd best go see what's happening." He started to the group of shouting men, trailed closely by Torkelson and Larson.

"What's the problem, Weaver?" Pearce asked.

Weaver shook his head. "Shut up!" he shouted at the men from the bar. "We've got the bag of money from the blind pig here, Chief," he said, and one of the uniformed policemen handed it to him. "It's the money those thugs took from these guys. We found it in the alley when we got here. One of the dead guys was lying on it. That's blood. . . ."

"I can see what that is," Pearce interrupted.

The men from the bar began to talk and gesture.

"Shut up!" Weaver shouted. "Just keep quiet while I explain this to the Chief."

"So what's the problem?" the Chief asked.

"We don't have any way to identify the money from these men."

Pearce looked questioningly at Weaver. "So what?"

"They're all demanding their money back, but how do we know how much to give 'em? Hell, every one of them says he dropped twenty bucks in the bag, and I can tell you there isn't that much cash in here," Weaver said, swinging the bag in front of him.

"Their money back, my ass," Pearce said, pulling the bag from Weaver. "Was there a cash register or something like that behind the bar?"

One of the men pointed at a man in their midst. "He's the bartender, ask him."

The man stepped forward and nodded. "They dumped the cash drawer in a small bag with a string tie. They had two bags when they left, but that ain't the one from the drawer." He unconsciously slid his hand into his pocket and felt the small roll of bills in it. "There was a lot in it, but I couldn't tell you how much." He shook his head. "That ain't the bag from the cash drawer."

Pearce held up the bag. "Are you sure?"

"Yeah, I'm sure."

"This is evidence, and we're impounding it," Pearce said, handing the bag to one of the uniformed policemen. "Take it to the station and tag it. Now that was easy, wasn't it?"

The men in the group began to shout curses and threats.

Pearce waved his hands. "Be quiet, damnit, shut up!" he shouted.

The men quieted somewhat, but there was still muttering and mumbling among them.

"You realize I can have you all arrested, jailed, and fined for being in an establishment selling and serving illegal liquor, don't you?" Pearce asked, glaring at the men.

All of the men nodded and whispered among themselves.

"We've got your names and addresses, so we can call you for

witnesses if necessary. If I arrest you, you'll have to make bail and pay a fine. You'll probably lose time from work and maybe get fired. That all adds up to money. You might get the money back later, but I doubt it. If I tell the lieutenant here to let you go, you come out ahead on the whole deal, don't you?"

The men were silent, but several of them nodded.

"Okay," Weaver began, fighting to keep the grin off his face. "All those who want to be arrested stay around. Those who don't had best get the hell out of here." He made a scattering motion with his hands. "*Scram!* Get outta here."

The men turned and ran up the alley away from the shrouded bodies.

"That takes care of that," Pearce said. "For now at least. You men get back to work. I want a very thorough job done on this investigation."

Larson raised his hands. "I think I'm going fishing."

CHAPTER FIFTY-ONE

The ringing of the phone in the kitchen woke Andy Larson. He blinked sleep from his eyes as he listened to the sequence of rings. A short ring, two longs, and another short ring. *Yeah, that's mine,* he thought as he slid out of the bed trying not to wake Becky. He glanced at the clock as he shuffled across the cold floor. *Five-twenty. Who in the hell's calling me at this hour?* He cleared his throat as he lifted the receiver and leaned toward the mouthpiece. "This is Larson."

"Andy, Torkelson here. We're down at Herman's Lumberyard. Your friend Billy Nestoss's been hurt. You'd better get right over. He's asking for you."

"I'm on my way," Larson said. He hung up the phone and ran into the bedroom to get dressed.

Becky rose up on an elbow and rubbed at her eyes. "Who was on the phone?"

"It was Tork," Larson answered as he pulled on a pair of pants and grabbed a shirt from the closet. "Billy's been hurt, and he wants to talk to me." He leaned down and put a quick kiss on her forehead. "Go back to sleep."

"Let me go with you," Becky pleaded.

"No, you stay here. I'll be home when I can." Larson trotted out to his truck, started it, and drove to Herman's Lumberyard. He leaped from his truck and surveyed the area, then ran toward the flashing red lights reflecting off the walls.

Torkelson met him and held up his hand. "He's over there,

Andy," he said and grabbed Larson's arm. "Slow down and walk with me. They were starting to unload a flatcar of timbers when a chain snapped. Most of the big beams rolled over him and busted him up pretty bad. The medical crew doesn't think he's gonna make it."

Larson stopped and faced Torkelson. "What in the hell are they doing unloading lumber at this hour of the morning? And what the hell are you doing here?"

Torkelson looked at him and shook his head. "I was on my way in early to get some paperwork done when it was still quiet. I saw the ambulance so I followed it." He reached out and grabbed Larson's arm. "Brace yourself, Andy. There's a lot of blood."

Larson shook his arm free. "I'll be okay. He's a friend." He walked around the corner of the warehouse to the rail siding and saw the flashing lights of the ambulance and two police cars. Five uniformed policemen, Mister Webster, and several other men stood beside a tumbled pile of heavy beams.

Two men in white coats knelt beside an inert form. One of them wiped a red stained cloth gently on the bloody face of Billy Nestoss.

Larson dropped to his knees and looked closely at his friend. "Billy, can you hear me?" he asked.

Nestoss' eyes fluttered open. He smiled weakly and gave a rasping cough. A small rivulet of blood ran from the corner of his mouth. "Andy . . ." was a weak whisper, and then he closed his eyes.

"He can hear you, Mister," the man with the cloth said softly. "But he can't talk anymore. I'm afraid his broken ribs have punctured his lungs, and they're filling up with blood. There's a couple of nasty cuts on his head, and his arms are broken. Probably his back too." He motioned at the jumble of lumber. "That's a lot of weight rolled over him. I gave him a shot of morphine so he's not feeling any pain. He ain't gonna last much longer. You must be Andy Larson."

"I'm Larson."

"He was muttering something about you and whiskey and gold when we first pulled him out from under all that lumber. It didn't make any sense. He said something about letting him buy the farm."

Andy Larson's eyes filled, and tears rolled down his cheeks. He reached out and gently touched Billy Nestoss' shoulder. "I'm sorry, my friend," he sobbed. "I'm really sorry for all the hurt I've caused you and the others."

Nestoss' eyes fluttered open, and he smiled again. Suddenly his chest heaved. A gusher of blood ran from his mouth, his eyes closed, and his body went limp.

"He's dead," the man in the white coat said and spread the cloth over Nestoss' face.

"No!" Larson screamed as he leaped to his feet and looked down at his dead friend. He grabbed a four by four from a rack beside him and swung it to break on the ground. He beat the remains of the board on the rack, and it broke again. He screamed and threw it, spinning off into the darkness. He grabbed another piece of wood and began to beat it on anything in his reach.

Sergeant Torkelson, the ambulance attendants, Mister Webster, and the other men drew back to let Larson vent his anger and frustration. After several minutes he threw the shattered remains of another board to the ground and fell to his knees beside his dead friend.

Torkelson put his hand on Larson's shoulder and firmly patted him. "C'mon, Andy," he said. "I've got a bottle in my trunk."

Chapter Fifty-Two

The sun was beginning to bring color to the sky in the east as Andy Larson walked on wobbly legs into the large front doors of the Bergavin Blacksmith shop and flopped onto a bench just inside. He raised a bottle, took a short drink, and stuck the bottle between his knees.

Louie Bergavin looked up from the anvil where he was making sparks fly off the chunk of red-hot steel he was slamming with a large hammer. He dunked the piece of steel into a barrel of water and watched it hiss and steam while it cooled. He shoved it back into the fire and wiped his shirtsleeve across his soot-blackened face as he walked over to join Larson. "Little early in the day to get drunk, isn't it," he asked as he sat down and reached for the bottle.

"Where's your dad?" Larson asked as he watched Bergavin wipe his hand over the mouth of the bottle and take a drink.

"He went out to Wentz's place to do some work on a cutter. Why?"

"He'd have a real case of the red-ass if he saw you drinking here in the shop," Larson answered and reached for the bottle.

"That's true. So why are you drinking this early?"

"Billy's dead," Larson answered flatly.

"What?" Bergavin asked in a shocked voice.

"He was killed by a damn load of lumber."

"Okay, the joke's over."

"No, I'm not joking. I was there when he died about an hour

ago." Wet-eyed, they shared the bottle as Larson told the story of Billy Nestoss' death. "One of the ambulance people told me that Billy'd said something about letting him buy a farm."

"You can't let this eat you up, Andy. We agreed we couldn't spend any of that gold."

"I know, Louie, but it *is* eating at me. All that damned gold . . ." Larson took another sip from the bottle. "That damned gold is *cursed.*"

"You don't believe in things like that, do you?" Bergavin asked, taking the bottle and tipping it up.

"Look at what's happened to us since we stole it. Bert, Mike, and Billy are dead. We've got five bags of Saint-Gaudens twenty-dollar gold pieces buried out there and we can't do a thing with them. Six hundred coins to a bag."

"How do you know there's six hundred in a bag?" Bergavin asked.

"I was out there a while back and counted one of the bags. They all seemed to weigh about the same when we buried them, so I figure they've got equal amounts in them."

"That means there's . . . ," Bergavin paused as he did mental figuring. "Three thousand Saint-Gaudens is . . . That means there's sixty-thousand dollars buried out there!"

"That's my guess," Larson agreed. "Have you got any molds here in your shop?"

"What kind of molds?"

"The kind you melt lead in."

"Yeah, we've got some back there someplace. A couple years back we made a bunch of ten-pound lead slugs to be used as some kind of counterweights for a grain elevator over in Mandan."

"What do they look like?"

"Like small bread pans. They made a lead weight about the size of a small brick."

Larson looked up at the beams across the ceiling as if in deep thought. "All right, I've got an idea. How many do you have?"

"They're in a block of six forms."

"We can make six bars at a time, then."

"What kind of bars are we making?" Bergavin asked.

"We're going to melt the coins down into gold bars."

"You *really* are drunk. Do you think gold bars are easier to get rid of than gold coins?"

"Let's go in the office for a few minutes. I've gotta do some figuring."

"That's a good idea," Bergavin said. "I've got a pot of good strong coffee back there."

Minutes later the two men sat at a table as Larson wrote a series of numbers. "Gold is worth twenty dollars and sixty-seven cents a Troy ounce on today's market. A Saint-Gaudens twenty-dollar gold piece weighs an ounce." He took a sip of coffee and scratched another set of figures.

"You think pretty good for a drunk man," Bergavin said, looking at the figures. "How do you know all this shit, or are you making it up as you go along?"

"A while back I was trying to figure out how rich we'd be when we could spend our cache," Larson answered. "There are twelve Troy ounces to a pound. That means twelve coins to a pound, times ten is . . ." He licked the tip of the pencil and wrote more numbers. "Twenty-four hundred dollars in a ten-pound gold brick. Let's see, we have three thousand gold coins at an ounce each. That's . . ." He scribbled more numbers and lines. "Damn, I wish I wasn't . . . , I hadn't had . . ."

"Too much to drink," Bergavin interrupted. "Here, gimme the paper and pencil. Drink your coffee." He turned the paper and looked at the numbers. "What're you trying to figure? How many ten pound bars we can make with three thousand coins?"

"Yup, that's what I was looking for."

"Ten pounds is one hundred and twenty coins. Right?"

Larson nodded. "Okay."

"We divide three thousand by one hundred and twenty." Bergavin did some quick figuring, wrote a number, and turned it to Larson. "Twenty-five ten-pound gold bars."

"We're not going to melt all the coins," Larson said.

"What?"

"We're not going . . ."

"I heard you," Bergavin interrupted. "Let me ask you something very important. Who in the hell are you planning on selling the gold bars to?"

"Guido Salvatore."

Bergavin looked at Larson and shook his head. "You're too damned drunk to make any sense. Why don't you go home and sleep it off. We'll talk again when you're sober. I'll call Billy's mother and see if we can do anything to help."

"I'm not that drunk," Larson argued. "You wanna hear my plan or preach to me?"

"I wasn't preaching."

"Okay, now listen. We'll have to melt the gold at night when your father's not here."

"I figured that. You're not really gonna sell the gold bricks to Salvatore, are you?"

"Do you wanna listen? I thought this thing out very carefully a few days ago and was gonna tell you about it when the time was right. The time is right. Can you make me heavy metal Iron Crosses if I draw them to size for you?"

"You mean the German hero medal?"

"Exactly."

Bergavin looked at him incredulously. "Is this something left over from the war, Andy?"

Larson shook his head and smiled. "No, just one hell of a plan that popped into my head last week when I was driving out to Garske's farm to check on things."

"Were you sober?"

Larson laughed. "Stone cold sober. You wanna hear the plan?"

CHAPTER FIFTY-THREE

Andy Larson turned the tablet, wrote the number eighteen, and spun it back toward Louie Bergavin. "We'll make eighteen bars of gold."

"Why eighteen?"

"Because you've got the molds to make them six at a time. We'll make three batches of bars. Eighteen is a good number to sell to Salvatore, and I've got a use for a few of the coins later."

"More coffee?" Bergavin asked, pouring himself another cup and holding out the pot.

Larson nodded and pushed his cup across the table. "I'll need six Iron Crosses to use in the molds."

"Why?"

"Because we're going to sell these to Salvatore as *war booty*. Something I picked up over in Germany and smuggled back to the States after the war."

Bergavin looked at Larson over the rim of his cup. He set the cup down and began to chuckle. He leaped to his feet and slammed his hands down on the table. "Yes!" he shouted. "By damn, yes! *Now* I understand what you're up to."

Larson sat back in his chair, grinned, took a sip of coffee, and set the cup on the table. "When the bars come out of the molds with the Iron Cross impression in them, we'll use your steel punches and put nineteen-eighteen for a date and a few meaningless numbers on them. They'll look official as hell to Salvatore's greedy, untrained eye. The bright shine of the gold should overcome his common sense and caution."

"We can weigh them and stamp the weight into them in kilograms," Bergavin suggested. "We've got conversion charts around here someplace."

"Great idea. We'll make them look as official as possible," Larson agreed. "Can we start tonight?"

"You have the gold here at nine, and we'll get the job done. It shouldn't take too long. I'll have the furnace stoked and ready to melt. How are you going to let Salvatore know about the gold?"

"I'll phone him and tell him what we have to sell. I'll work out a meeting at some neutral location and show him one or two of the bars. Maybe up in Minot or one of the small towns around here. I'll let him take a couple of them to run tests. Suggest that he bore into them to make sure we're not trying to dump some gold-wrapped lead on him. I'll offer them to him at a good price, but not so good as to make him suspicious. I'm just a battle-weary veteran who wants to get rid of some war plunder and make a little money."

Bergavin nodded and smiled. "And we'll be getting paid for something we stole from him in the first place."

"You've got it," Larson agreed. "We're passing the curse back to him and he's paying us for it. Hell, that could be part of the curse, him buying back his own gold. I'll drive out and dig up the coins and see you here at nine. My wife's not gonna be happy about my being out tonight, but I'll make it up to her."

"Your what?" Bergavin asked, sitting up straighter in his chair and giving Larson an open-mouthed stare.

"Oh, yeah, Becky and I went to the courthouse and got married two days ago."

"Well, you sneaky old son-of-a-bitch!" Bergavin shouted, leaping to his feet and sticking out his hand. "Why didn't you tell me? Did you tell anybody?"

Larson grinned as he shook his friend's hand. "Not yet. Things have been moving pretty fast the past few days. I've got a week left of my suspension, but it doesn't matter because I've accepted a deputy sheriff job over in Wolf Point, Montana. Becky found a teaching job in a school over there, so we're going to pack up and move in a couple of weeks."

Bergavin shook his head. "Damn, you sure are full of surprises."

"Yeah, I know too much about the illegal booze business here in Bismarck and feel I couldn't do a fair job if I stayed on here as a cop. I like working for the law, but I have to do it right. I want to put all this whiskey and gold thing behind me. There're too many hard memories for me here in Bismarck. Becky's been a strong influence with my decisions. You understand, Louie?"

"I understand, my friend, and you're a lucky dog to find someone as sweet as Becky. Tell her congratulations and ask her when we're going to have the party?"

"In a day or two. Let me draw the Iron Crosses for you so you can have them ready for tonight."

"They're all straight lines, so it'll be snap. Married to Miss Becky, huh? You are a lucky man, Andy."

The intercom on Guido Salvatore's desk buzzed and he flipped the switch. "Yes?"

"I have a call for you, Mister Salvatore. A Mister Tompkins is on line one."

Salvatore flipped the intercom off, pulled his phone closer, and lifted the receiver. "This is Salvatore."

"Mister Salvatore, my name is Roger Tompkins, and I have something you might be interested in purchasing," Andy Larson said, as he riffled the small stacks of coins on the shelf in the phone booth.

"Do I know you, Mister Tompkins?"

"No."

"Then why would you have anything I'd be interested in buying?"

"Gold?"

Salvatore sat up and pulled the phone closer. "Gold? What makes you think I'm interested in gold?"

"Word on the street is that you're looking for a lot of Saint-Gaudens."

Salvatore took a deep breath. "Do you know where they are?"

"No, I don't, but I do have some gold bars for sale. Eighteen to be exact."

Salvatore pondered the man's answer. "Tell me more."

"These are German bars I smuggled back from the war."

German gold? There's no way to trace that, and I can pay Capone back. "How much do they weigh?" Salvatore asked.

"They're marked in kilograms, so I don't know for sure," Larson answered, smiling. *He's hooked.* "I'd say they're about ten pounds each."

Salvatore pulled a tablet and pencil over and began to write. "You said eighteen ten-pound bars?"

"Yes."

Salvatore scribbled more numbers. "How much do you want for them?"

"I've been studying this for a couple of years now, and I know gold is worth twenty dollars and sixty cents a Troy ounce on the open market. I just can't get up the nerve to try to sell them because of the way they're marked and everything. I could end up going to prison or something."

"How are they marked?"

"They have an imprinted Iron Cross, the weight in kilograms, the date nineteen-eighteen, and some other numbers."

"How do I know these are real?" Salvatore asked.

An operator came on the line. "Please deposit another seventy-five cents for an additional five minutes."

Larson dropped a quarter in the slot and heard it ding.

Salvatore also heard the sound of all three coins. *He's calling long distance.*

"Oh, they're real all right," Larson answered. "Two of my friends and I found a cache of gold in a bunker near Ypres. Eighteen bars were all we could carry, or we'd have taken more. We went back a few days later, but somebody else had gotten to them first."

"All right, let's say I'm interested. I'll want to have them tested and assayed, things like that. I want to make sure of what I'm buying."

Larson smiled. *Gotcha.* "I'll call you tomorrow at exactly nine o'clock and make arrangements to meet you someplace so you can check them out." He hung up the phone, scooped up his coins, and pushed out of the booth into the quiet of the hotel lobby.

CHAPTER FIFTY-FOUR

Shadows swayed and danced eerily around the walls where the two sweaty, shirtless men worked. A row of large dirty single bulbs hung down the center of the smoky room, casting a myriad of shadows that radiated from the open flames of the forge where they toiled.

"How many coins are in there now?" Louie Bergavin asked, pointing at the heavy crucible of melted gold resting in the white-hot fire. He gave the handle of the bellows several quick strokes so the fire rose and sparks danced in the air above it.

Andy Larson reached a gloved hand into the cut top of the canvas and leather bag and brought out a small pile of Saint-Gaudens twenty-dollar gold pieces. "We've put three hundred and fifty of 'em in there now. Ten more should be exactly right for weight." His lips moved as he pushed ten coins aside and dumped the rest back into the bag. He held his gloved hand close over the crucible and swiftly tipped it to let the coins plop down and disappear into the steaming molten gold liquid. "That's it," he said, wiping the back of the leather glove across his forehead.

Bergavin nodded. "The level of melted gold's right about at the marker ridge, so I think the first set of ingots is ready to be poured." He reached into one of the molds and squared the crude steel Iron Cross into the center. "Those should be heavy enough to stay in place while we pour the gold." He lifted a pair of special open-centered tongs and closed them in the groove around the middle of the crucible. "Now we'll do just like we practiced. On the count of three, you lift from your side; we take it up from the fire and pour slowly into each section of the mold up to the inside marker ridge. Ready?"

Larson nodded and grasped his end of the tongs. "One, two, three."

Both men lifted and slowly centered the crucible over the first mold in the set.

"This isn't too bad," Larson commented.

"Now tip and pour slowly," Bergavin instructed.

A fall of steaming molten gold ran from the crucible and slowly filled the first mold to the indicator ridge.

"That's it," Bergavin said as they tipped the crucible up, moved to the next mold, and repeated the process. "Nice work, Andy, nice work."

They filled the first three molds, looked at each other, and grinned as they lifted the crucible and returned it to the fire.

"Hell, that looks like it was about perfect," Larson said, pointing to the droplets of liquid gold still in the bottom of the melting pot. "Those must have run off the sides when we finished."

"That looks like a mighty sweet job of pouring," Bergavin said. "Start filling up for the next run while these cool." He pulled a watch from his pocket. "Just about a half an hour. I'd say, with cleanup and all, we'll be done around two and that's good because my dad comes to work at five. It'd be a little tough explaining what we're doing."

Larson walked back to the table and reached into the canvas bag. "I'll start counting the next batch."

They repeated the process and stood drinking water while impatiently waiting for the last set of molds to cool.

Bergavin licked his finger and tapped it down on the last mold to be filled. He tapped it again, nodded and smiled. "Let's tip this and see what we've created. We can just lift and spin the molds and the bars should fall right out. Watch your feet."

They lifted the set of molds and stepped back from the sawhorses where they rested.

"On three?" Larson asked.

"On three," Bergavin agreed. "One, two, three."

They quickly turned the rack of molds, and the six gold bars fell heavily to the dirt floor, serving up small puffs of dust when they landed.

Larson and Bergavin set the molds back on the sawhorses and fell to their knees beside the shiny new ingots.

Larson lifted one, tossed it from hand to hand, and quickly dropped it. "Damn, these are still hot," he muttered.

Bergavin looked at him and laughed. "You didn't see *me* picking one up, did you? Besides, that's the last one we filled, so it's got to be the hottest."

Larson nodded and blew on his hands. "Okay, I'm learning." He lifted the far gold bar, stood and hefted it. "Ten pounds, huh? It sure feels heavier than that." He turned it over. "Damn, the Iron Cross is still in it."

Bergavin got to his feet, took it from him and looked at it. "Not a problem. Some of the gold got under it and fused it in. That's easy to fix." He carried the ingot to a workbench, stuck a small pointed tool under the Iron Cross, and popped it free with a flip of his wrist. "Let's check the rest of them and get to work. Five o'clock'll come mighty fast."

"You go start counting coins into the crucible and I'll start putting the numbers on these things," Bergavin said, picking up two ingots with each hand. "I looked up the conversion, and ten pounds is a little over four and a half kilograms. I'll stamp 'em four point six KG, the date, and then a few random numbers."

"The meanings of which are known only to the Germans I stole them from," Larson added, as he laughed and held up one of the canvas-and-leather bags. "All right with you if I throw these things in the fire when they're empty?"

CHAPTER FIFTY-FIVE

Andy Larson and Louie Bergavin stood admiring the rows of gold bars on a metal worktable in front of them.

"It's not quite three-thirty, and we're about done," Larson said and smiled. "It's been a good night's work."

"Yeah," Bergavin agreed, pulling on his shirt. "And ain't they pretty?"

"I think we oughta ding them up a little," Larson said. "They should look like they've been hauled around for a few years."

"We can do that." Bergavin picked up a small hammer and began rapping the sharp edges of one of the bars.

Larson picked one of the ingots up and randomly dropped it onto others on the table.

"This shouldn't take too long," Larson said. "Pure gold is pretty soft."

A half hour later they dumped them roughly, three at a time, into six canvas sacks.

"We're ready for the next step," Larson said, hefting one of the sacks. "Let's put these into my truck and I'll go catch a short nap."

Bergavin elbowed Larson aside, easily picked up two bags in each hand, and leered at him. "Short honeymoon, huh? Save your strength, I'll carry these out to your truck. You take the other two."

"Hell, as strong as you are, I figured you want to show off and carry all six," Larson said, with a laugh and hefted the other two bags off the table. "Let's go, Big Boy."

Larson looked at the clock on the far wall of the hotel lobby and pushed into the phone booth. He dropped a handful of coins on the shelf, glanced at the numbers on a sheet of paper, dialed, gave the operator the long-distance number and, on her command, began to deposit coins.

"Mister Salvatore," his secretary announced over the intercom. "A Mister Tompkins is on line one."

Salvatore snatched the receiver from the hook and leaned forward to his phone. "This is Salvatore. I like a man who's punctual, Mister Tompkins. What do you have to say for yourself?"

"I'm sure you know where Coal Harbor is," Larson said.

"Of course. It's a little town about forty-five, fifty miles south of here on the main highway to Bismarck," Salvatore answered.

"I'll be waiting at the little park by the river outside town at ten-thirty. Come alone."

"I never travel anyplace outside of Minot without my driver and bodyguard."

That means he's gonna have Bruno with him, and that goon will know me the minute he sees me. "Are you talking about Bruno?" Larson asked. "I understand you got him out of jail."

"It seems you know many things about me, but you said we'd never met."

"Not formally, but I know who you are when I see you and I also know Bruno."

"Those are my terms. I bring Bruno or no deal. Just how bad do you want to sell that gold, Mister Tompkins?"

"All right, let me think for a minute," Larson said. He shuffled through the coins as he thought. "Okay, here's how we'll work it. The man traveling with me and Bruno will wait in your car across the park while we transact our business."

"How do I know this isn't some sort of a set-up?" Salvatore asked, suspicion creeping into his voice.

"A set up for what? I didn't ask you to bring any money with you this time. I just want to sell you some damn German gold, not put a hit on you or steal your fricking clothes or something like that . . . geez."

Salvatore waited, thinking over the situation carefully. "You'll have one person with you?"

"Yes. I'll tell you what I'll do. There's a little hill about a mile south of town. No trees or anything anybody can hide behind. I'll be parked off the road a short distance. You have your driver drop you off, and the man with me gets in your car and they park fifty yards away. All I want to do is sell you this gold. I'm in bad need of money. You'll be able to see from the beat up piece of shit I drive how broke I am."

"How much am I expected to pay you for this gold?"

An operator broke into the call and requested more money. Larson quickly complied.

"I know that gold is worth over twenty and a half bucks an ounce. I'll sell it to you for eighteen."

"I won't go anything over fifteen dollars an ounce for hot gold," Salvatore said.

Larson smiled as he waited before answering. "I don't have a pencil with me. How much then will you pay me for 180 pounds of *hot* gold?" He could hear the adding machine on Salvatore's desk working.

"Thirty-two thousand, four hundred dollars," Salvatore said. "And to show you I'm a generous person, I'll round it off to thirty-two, five. Of course, like I said before, I'll want to do some tests. Weighing the bars, drilling the centers, assaying the gold for purity, you know, things like that."

"I understand. How many bars do you want to test?"

"Oh, three will do. Of course, I'll choose the bars."

"In other words, you want me to bring all eighteen of them with me. I need to think this over. I'll call you back in a half hour," Larson hung up the phone, picked up his change, and pushed out of the booth. He walked to the hotel café, sat down at the counter and ordered a cup of coffee. *I didn't put enough into the planning of this thing. It isn't going to work. I've got to come up with a better plan. Maybe he'll come up with one, once the greed factor takes over his thinking. One we can both work with. Hell, he's trying to steal the gold from me that I stole from him in the first place. It's so ironic, it's actually funny.*

Half an hour later, Andy Larson returned to the phone booth, dumped the coins on the shelf, dialed the operator again, gave her the Minot number, nodded and began to deposit the coins he knew she would request. "This is Tompkins again. Let me talk to Mister Salvatore, please."

"This is Salvatore."

"I'm afraid this isn't going to be worked out," Larson said, pushing shut the phone booth door. "You're worried about me tricking you, and I don't trust you, even though I do need the money. I've got the name and number of a man in Grand Forks who'll be easier to work with. Sorry."

"Wait a minute!" Salvatore shouted. "Don't hang up. I'm sure we can work out something to the satisfaction of both of us."

"Then let me hear it," Larson said.

"What if we worked this through neutral parties?" Salvatore asked.

"How do you mean?"

"Do you have anyone you can trust enough to meet with Bruno, and let him pick out three of the bars for testing?"

"Where?"

"I'll let you pick the place," Salvatore answered.

Larson thought briefly and smiled. "Okay, here's how we do

it. You have Bruno drive down to Coal Harbor at ten o'clock tonight. Do you still have that big Packard Touring Salon with the Illinois license plates?"

"Damn, you do know a lot about me, don't you?" Salvatore growled. "Yeah, the boys that were driving it aren't around anymore, so for the time being it's mine."

Larson laughed. "I've been planning this for a while. I know all of the things that might be important. That car would be hard to miss."

"Okay, I'll send Bruno in the Packard down to Coal Harbor at ten o'clock. Then what?"

"A truck will drive up behind him and flash the headlights. He's to pull off the road and stop. Leave the headlights on and the motor running. He'll be given instructions to go to the back of the truck. There'll be eighteen bars of gold laid out. He picks three of them, gets back in his car, turns around and brings them back to you. If my man sees another car, the whole thing's called off, and Bruno won't be guarding your body anymore, understand? You've got until nine o'clock tomorrow morning to have them tested and the money ready to go. I'll call you at nine."

"How do you know I won't just keep the three gold bricks?" Salvatore asked.

"I'm told you're a smart man, Salvatore," Larson said. "If I thought you were stupid enough to steal eighty-six hundred bucks' worth of gold when you could steal over forty-four thousand, I wouldn't waste my time with you. I'd go right to the man in Grand Forks. Hell, he might even make me a better offer. Besides, if you *are* stupid enough to try anything, I'll kill you. And that's not an idle threat. Remember, I know a lot about you and you know nothing about me or my abilities in that area. I learned a lot about killing in the war, and I'm good at it."

"Don't get hasty now," Salvatore cautioned. "Think it over before you do anything drastic."

"I said you're stealing it, because that's what you're doing when you're buying it at this price. You're just lucky I need my money right away. I'm told the man in Grand Forks would have to have a week to get it. Although he'd probably pay me more, I need the money now. I'll expect cash in old bills from you tomorrow."

"If the gold turns out to be okay, I'll have your money for you by then."

"Good, I'll call you in the morning for the next stage of this transaction." Larson hung up the phone and smiled. *Now this plan'll work.*

Chapter Fifty-Six

Bruno Campagna liked driving the heavy Packard Touring Salon. He grinned and rubbed his large, paw-like hand over his burr-cut hair. His other hand gripped the polished ebony wood steering wheel, and his arm resting on the open window frame deflected wind into the car. The sun had disappeared behind the horizon to his right, and the large fluffy clouds reflected a myriad of gold, yellows, and reds.

"Tonight you'll take the Packard and drive south until someone flashes their headlights behind you," Salvatore had instructed him. "Pull off the road and wait. They'll walk you to the back of a truck and show you eighteen gold bars. You pick out three and bring them back to me as fast as you can. Got it?"

"Got it, Boss," he had answered.

This's easy enough, he told himself as he reached down, pulled on the headlights, loosened his tie, and began to sing to himself.

It was now dark, and in the rearview mirror Bruno saw a pair of headlights appear on the road behind him. He eased up the gas pedal and tapped his foot on the brakes several times to slow the big car. The headlights gained quickly, then changed lanes as a large car roared past him to become glowing red taillights as it disappeared ahead of him. *Asshole must think he owns the road just because he drives a damned Buick,* Bruno told himself and stomped on the gas pedal. *I'll show him a thing or two about big cars.* The Packard began to gain on the taillights of the Buick when Bruno glanced at the speedometer and suddenly realized he wasn't being very smart. *Somebody's supposed to get behind me and flash their lights. Ain't nobody gonna catch me at this speed.* Again he took his foot off the gas and let the vehicle slow to a reasonable speed. *Mister Salvatore wouldn't take kindly to my screwing this thing up.*

"Okay, let's go over it one last time," Andy Larson said, looking across the table at Louie Bergavin.

Bergavin nodded. "It's all very simple. When we come up behind Bruno and he parks, I keep the bright lights on, and you get back a ways in the ditch to watch for anyone beside Bruno coming out of the car. Then you get across the highway to the far ditch so you can watch the road in both directions."

Larson held up his hand. "Wait a minute. We'll take a flashlight, and you tell Bruno to stay in the car, hands out the window, while you shine the light inside and check for hidden passengers. That'll give me plenty of time to get in the ditch to cover you. Make sure he sees you've got a gun. Walk around the car, flashlight in one hand, forty-five in the other. Tell him you want to make sure he's alone. If he balks or stalls, get back in the truck and tell him the deal's off." Larson patted the Thompson machine gun lying on the table. "I'll have him covered with this if anything happens.

"When you're satisfied, have him get out and check him for guns. Any you find are yours to keep. Have him stay up in front of the truck, in the lights, with some small talk until you're sure I'm in the far ditch. With the engines running he won't be able to hear me, and the bright lights will keep him from seeing me get across. From over there I can watch and cover the road in both directions," Larson said. "Take him to the back of the truck, drop the tailgate, unwrap the bars, and let him pick three. Put them in the canvas bag that's there and send him back to

Minot. I still don't trust Salvatore. If he's got somebody in the back seat or the trunk, I'll be able to handle them from the dark. You've got the forty-five, and if the shit hits the fan, fall down into the ditch and stay flat. I'll make life miserable for anyone who tries to screw up this plan. I don't want any mistakes tonight."

"This'll work okay, Andy, unless Salvatore throws in something we aren't expecting," Bergavin said, and stood up. "It's sunset, let's get going up the road and watch for Bruno."

"Here comes a big car or a truck," Larson said, pointing at the high pair of headlights coming toward them on the dark highway.

Bergavin eased up on the gas as the vehicle approached and roared past them. "Big Buick." He stepped down on the gas again and brought the truck up to speed.

"Yeah, we're watching for that big black Packard Touring Salon."

Minutes later another set of headlights appeared ahead of them. "Here comes another big one," Bergavin commented, easing up on the gas.

As the big car flew past them, they both glanced at it and nodded.

"That's Bruno," Larson said. "Let's turn around and catch him."

Bergavin tapped the brakes, downshifted, and made a wide turn into the ditch and pulled back up on the road.

Larson opened his door, lifted the machine gun and stepped out onto the running board. "I'll be in back."

As Bergavin gained on the Packard, he began to flash his headlights and saw the brake lights go on. "He knows I'm here," he shouted out the window. "Get ready."

The big Packard cruised to a stop, and Bergavin pulled the truck up behind it. He put the transmission in neutral, pulled on the parking brake, and stepped out of the truck.

Bruno started to open his door.

"Stay in there and put your hands out the window so I can see 'em," Bergavin ordered, snapping on the flashlight and walking cautiously up to the back door of the car.

Bruno shoved his big hands out the window and waved them. "I'm alone."

Bergavin flashed the beam of light into the backseat and saw it was empty.

"You got a gun on you?" Bergavin asked.

"Of course," Bruno answered, looking at him in the rearview mirror on the door.

Bergavin raised his pistol and flashed the light on it. "I've got you covered. How many guns do you have?"

"One."

"Get it with your left hand and hold it out the window by the barrel," Bergavin ordered and cocked the forty-five.

Bruno's left hand disappeared inside the car and immediately reappeared, holding a long-barreled revolver by the barrel.

Bergavin stepped up, snatched it from his hand, briefly shined his light on it, and stuck it in his belt. "Now get out of the car and walk ahead of me to the back of the truck. You'll get to do what to some people is the dream of a lifetime, pick up three bars of solid gold. Too bad you don't get to keep 'em though. They're for your boss."

Bruno opened the door and stepped out of the car.

"Lean your hands up against the car and spread your legs," Bergavin ordered. "I'm a cautious person."

Bruno chuckled as he obeyed. "I got my orders. I'm here to pick up some gold, not get in a fight," he grunted as Bergavin patted him down.

Satisfied, Bergavin poked him in the back with the barrel of his pistol. "Here's the flashlight," he said, tapping it on his shoulder.

Bruno reached up, took the flashlight, and shone the beam down the length of the truck as they began to walk to the back of it. Suddenly, he flipped the beam across the road to the far ditch.

"What the hell did you do that for?" Bergavin demanded. "Put it back on the truck."

"I thought I saw something move over there," Bruno answered, as they continued to the rear of the vehicle.

Andy Larson slowly rose to his knees in the ditch. *Damn, that was close,* he told himself as he ran his hands over the machine gun to make sure he hadn't jammed it into the dirt when he dived to the ground.

"Drop the tailgate and open that roll of canvas in there," Bergavin instructed when they reached the back of the truck.

Bruno tucked the flashlight under his arm, unhooked the tailgate, and let it drop. He reached in, took the edge of the canvas, and tugged it to unroll and reveal a jumble of bright, shiny ingots. "Damn," he muttered as he brought up the flashlight and ran the beam of light over them. "They sure as hell're nice looking."

Andy Larson watched the two men standing in the small circle of light at the rear of the truck and relaxed. *It looks like I may have misjudged Salvatore,* he told himself. He thought he heard something unusual and turned to search the highway in both directions.

Suddenly he made out a dark shape and heard the roar of a car engine bearing down on the two vehicles parked along side the road.

"Louie!" he screamed and raised his machine gun.

Ribbons of flames tore from the approaching vehicle and he heard the staccato burst of automatic weapon fire. One weapon was being fired from the back seat behind the driver and the other by a man hanging out the front passenger window firing across the hood.

Larson swung the barrel of his weapon to bear on the speeding car and squeezed the trigger to put a long burst of destruction into the vehicle.

Bergavin dived for the ditch, and Bruno leaned out to look at the source of the noise and flame. A line of holes punched down the side of the Packard, moved on to Larson's truck, and tore through the chest of the big man standing behind it.

Bruno screamed and crumpled backward to the roadway.

The slugs from Larson's weapon punched holes in the windshield and ripped across the man firing from the front seat of the speeding car as it bore down on them. Larson lowered the barrel of the weapon and ran another line of holes through the hood and across the doors and fenders of the Buick. The car suddenly swerved from a blown tire, spun sideways, flipped onto its side, rolled several times, and began to skid down the highway, trailed by a massive shower of sparks. The sparks became a ball of flame that engulfed the vehicle as the bullet-riddled gas tank exploded and the vehicle shuddered to a dusty, fiery rest in the ditch.

"Louie, are you all right?" Larson shouted.

"Scared shitless, but I'm not hurt," Bergavin answered, climbing up from the ditch. "I'm coming up."

The two men met in the middle of the road and Larson cleared his machine gun as they looked at the damaged and burning vehicles.

"I was dead wrong about Salvatore," Larson admitted, kneeling and looking at Bruno's body. "So was he, poor fool." He stood and looked at Bergavin in the growing firelight. "You sure you're okay, Louie?"

Bergavin nodded and held up his trembling hands. "I'm okay, but I need a drink. Bad."

"There's a bottle under the seat in my truck," Larson said. "You can have it on the way home. It looks like my truck is a little shot up, but it's still running. There's gas dripping out from under the Packard. I'll shut off the engine, but I'm sure it'll go up once the fire gets to it." He pointed at the burning Buick and the little fingers of flame moving through the grass in the ditch. "There's no way we'll be able to put that out."

"Let's get the hell outta here, Andy," Bergavin pleaded. "Somebody'll spot the fire and send people out to fight it. I'll wrap the gold and close the tailgate."

"Yeah. I'll drive," Larson answered, looking around again and shaking his head. "It looks like that cold-blooded bastard Salvatore was willing to sacrifice Bruno to get his gold." He walked over as close to the burning vehicle as the heat would allow and held his hand in front of his face as he tried to see inside the mass of flame. "I can't see anything but fire. Let's head for town while my truck's still running."

Minutes later Larson could see the glow of the fire in his rearview mirror as they sped toward Bismarck. He glanced at Bergavin as he tipped the bottle up and took another long drink. "You sure you're okay?"

"Yep, I'm getting better," he answered, and waved the bottle. "You sure that was Salvatore's work?"

"Of course it was," Larson snarled. "I was plain stupid and too trusting when I told him we'd bring all eighteen bars out for Bruno to choose from. That Buick is the one we met coming toward us a while ago. I'd bet they were supposed to stay in front of Bruno, but keep an eye on him. When they saw the headlights stop, they turned around and made a gun run at us. They just weren't expecting the firepower we had. That Salvatore is one cold-hearted son-of-a-bitch. He didn't give a shit who died." He held his hand toward Bergavin. "Give me a drink."

CHAPTER FIFTY-SEVEN

Guido Salvatore's intercom buzzed. He reached over and flipped the switch. "Mister Salvatore, Mister Tompkins is on line one."

"Thank you." He flipped the switch, pulled the phone closer, and slowly reached for the receiver. *This should have been a very simple operation last night. How in the hell did it get so badly screwed up? I'm surprised Tompkins is even calling me. Was he there last night? I know he's not in a good mood, and I'd best have some answers for him.* Salvatore looked at the headlines of the newspaper on his desk and his hand stopped: MURDER ON THE PRAIRIE.

Salvatore had read the story three times. There were two badly shot-up, burned automobiles, a Packard and a Buick. His bodyguard, Bruno, was found dead in the road. Obviously all the shooting had been done with automatic weapons. Four bodies in the Buick were burned beyond recognition, and the remains of a Thompson machine gun was also found in it. A farmer had spotted the fire in the night and called the sheriff's office to report it.

One of Salvatore's police informants had called a few minutes earlier and told him the highway patrol investigators had found the ditch on the far side of the road littered with forty-five caliber shell casings. There were no tire tracks to indicate a vehicle, so someone had to have been standing in the ditch and used a Thompson machine gun to ambush the cars. The tire tracks and skid marks on the highway indicated the Buick had been speeding when it crashed. The Packard, although riddled with bullet holes, had been parked when it burned. A second badly damaged Thompson had been found in the ditch not far from the burned Buick. Investigators surmised it had been under the car when it had skidded down the highway. The police had many unanswered questions.

Salvatore took a deep breath. *Be calm,* he told himself as he lifted the receiver and put it to his ear. "Salvatore, here," he answered.

"I'm sorry my man didn't make it to the meeting last night," Larson said. "He was using that old truck of mine, and the damned thing broke down on him. He was headed for Coal Harbor, but he only got about ten miles out of town before it died. He waited for a while and finally hid the bars in the ditch and walked back in. It was pretty late, and he was damned mad, so he went to a speakeasy and got drunk. I didn't even know about it until he called me about an hour ago. He told me what happened and said he was borrowing a car to go out and retrieve the gold. I hope you're not too pissed off about his not making it. I should have handled the whole thing myself. I'm really sorry."

What? Salvatore cleared his throat. "Yes, I'm a little upset. My man Bruno drove that road all night waiting to make contact and get the gold." *Now I've got him on the defense. This could work out well after all.*

"Have you seen the papers this morning, Salvatore?" Larson asked.

"Ah . . . yes, I have," Salvatore answered, slowly.

"It looks like a good thing that old truck of mine didn't make it last night, doesn't it? I wonder how something like that could have happened? Do you know anything about it?"

"Only what I've read in the paper," Salvatore answered. "Have you got any ideas?"

"None. I wonder how Bruno got into that incident?" Larson asked.

"What do you mean by that?"

"Well, he was driving that road waiting for my friend to show up and got into the middle of some sort of a gangster-type shootout. The paper down here in Bismarck says there were two burned and shot-up cars and poor Bruno was found dead in the road. Maybe somebody thought you were with Bruno and was trying to make a hit on you."

"Damn, why didn't I think of that?" Salvatore said. *This is working out better by the second.* "I'll bet you're right. They were after me and killed poor Bruno."

"You said Bruno was your bodyguard, and that would probably be the reason for the incident. They were out to kill you."

"Yes, I do believe you're right, Tompkins."

"Does what happened last night bother you?" Larson asked.

"Of course it bothers me. I'm very upset about losing the man who protected me all these years. It'll be hard to replace a good man like him."

"I called to find out if you're still interested in buying my gold. Are you still interested or do I call the guy in Grand Forks?"

"Wait, just wait," Salvatore answered. "Of course, I still want the gold."

Okay, now we'll play the game my way. "I don't have the time to wait around," Larson said. "I need this money right away. I have a place where we can meet down here in Mandan tomorrow. You bring two people who can do the drilling and assaying and all that shit you need to do to make sure the gold is good. You bring thirty-five thousand dollars in cash. I'd prefer old bills. Nothing bigger than hundreds. Now, you're sure you can have the money by tomorrow?"

"I'll have the money," Salvatore answered.

"I need money, but that doesn't mean I'm stupid," Larson said. "I'm about to go into a consortium that's going to set up at least a dozen blind pigs across the state. I need another thirty thousand to have the fifty thousand dollars buy-in money for my part. Five of us are putting up a quarter-million dollars for a series of top-of-the-line clubs. We've already arranged the protection payoff on the law. We're going to have booze, gambling, women, and all the other things to make life good for high rollers. Your name's on the top of the list to supply the booze. A man from Fargo will be contacting you within a month with our opening orders. I've probably told you more than I should, so don't let on you know anything about the size of the operation, things like that. Just make him good offers and you'll reap the rewards."

Salvatore smiled. "What's this fellow's name?"

"I don't think I'll tell you," Larson teased. "I've already talked too much. But let me think about it. I'll call you later this afternoon about the meeting tomorrow. You get your people and the money lined up. I want this to be a fast, smooth operation. Good-bye." Larson hung up the phone. *Now it's been planted in his mind that working with me will put more money in his pockets. He won't want to do anything at this point that'll cost him money. I've got a lot to do before tomorrow.*

Chapter Fifty-Eight

Guido Salvatore leaned forward, pulled the phone to him, and lifted the receiver. "Mister Tompkins, how are you this afternoon?" he asked, smiling.

We've certainly become friends, haven't we? Especially when he can see the dollars from our friendship rolling in. "I'm fine, Mister Salvatore," Andy Larson answered.

"Please, Mister Tompkins, call me Guido."

"Well, Guido, why don't you call me Roger?" Larson asked.

"That's fine, Roger. Now what do you have for me?"

"Do you have your assay people ready to go first thing tomorrow morning, Guido?"

"Yes. We'll have a van with us to do all the work on the spot. It'll be like you want, fast and smooth. The sooner you get your money to join with the others, the quicker we'll be doing even more business with each other," Salvatore said.

You have no idea, Guido. "I'll leave a map for you at the front desk of the McKenzie Hotel. We'll do all this out in the open so there's no chance of anything . . . ah, *strange* happening. You know, something like last night. Oh, and don't forget to bring my money."

Salvatore laughed. "I have a small leather suitcase here on my desk packed full of old bills. Just as you wanted."

"Great! Follow the map and I'll see you about three o'clock. Goodbye, Guido."

"Goodbye, Roger, and I look forward to finally meeting you."

Salvatore hung up his phone and looked at the three men sitting at his conference table. "He's leaving a map for us at the McKenzie Hotel. He wants this whole thing to be done in the country. That major screw-up last night made him nervous."

"Everything was done in the country last night, Mister Salvatore," one of the men said, as he stood up. "Didn't he learn anything from that?"

The other two men laughed as they got to their feet.

"It looks like a good day to be working outside," one of them commented and adjusted the pistol under his arm.

"If we're all ready, we'd best be heading down to Bismarck," Salvatore said, pushing back from his desk, opening a drawer and bringing out a holstered automatic pistol.

Andy Larson sat on the front bumper of his truck watching the road leading out from Mandan. He had parked his truck back in the trees so the line of bullet holes down the door was not visible from the road. He pulled out his watch. *It's almost three. They should be showing up any minute.* A small column of dust appeared on a far hill, and soon he could see a long black car followed by a brown van speeding toward him. He slapped his knees, rose to his feet, and trudged down toward the road. *The time has come. . . .* Larson was dressed in a conservative blue business suit with a coordinated shirt and tie, hoping it would give him the image of a common man seeking an opportunity to become wealthy. He pulled his hat down to shade his eyes and stepped out onto the gravel. He took a deep breath and let it out slowly. *This will be a test of how well you think you've read the man,* he told himself. He forced a friendly smile on his face. *Let's just hope you're as smart as you think you are.*

The large black car slowed and stopped, with the van a short distance behind it. The driver stepped out, walked quickly around the car, and opened the back door.

Guido Salvatore stepped out, pulled on his hat, and smiled. "Roger, we finally meet," he said, proffering his hand.

Larson glanced at the van out of the corner of his eye, stepped forward, and grasped Salvatore's hand. "Guido, this is indeed a pleasure," he said, widening his smile. *Don't lay it on too thick, idiot.*

"It's a beautiful day, isn't it?" Salvatore asked, waving a hand at the countryside. "But those clouds rolling in look like rain, don't they?"

"Yes, they do, but we can always use the rain," Larson agreed. "Do you have my money?"

"A businessman," Salvatore said and smiled. "Do you have my gold? Is it up there in your truck?" he asked, pointing at the vehicle in the trees.

Before Larson could react, the driver stepped forward and patted him down for a weapon.

"Just force of habit for him," Salvatore assured Larson. "Nothing personal."

"I'd like to see the money," Larson said, nervously adjusting his suit coat.

"Of course," Salvatore agreed. He snapped his fingers above his shoulder.

The driver opened the front door, brought out a small leather suitcase, and laid it on the hood of the car. He turned aside, closed the door, and stood with his hands folded in front of him.

"Take a look, Roger," Salvatore said with a motion toward the case.

Larson stepped up, snapped the locks, opened the lid, and nodded. The case was tightly packed with bundles of paper money. He quickly riffled down through them, closed the lid, and snapped the locks closed. He nodded and smiled.

"Roger, there's something familiar about you. Are you sure

we've never met? I don't forget a face."

"No, we've never met," Larson answered. *God, don't tell me he remembers my face from the time he came storming out of Werner's office and almost knocked us down.*

"No matter," Salvatore said. "It'll come to me eventually where I've seen you. Now, is the gold up there in your truck?"

"No, as a matter of fact, the gold is through that gate and down the trail over there," Larson answered and motioned across the road.

Salvatore turned and looked where Larson had pointed. He raised his hand and two men dressed in black-and-white pin-striped suits and black hats opened their doors and stepped out of the van.

Larson drew back, fear showing on his face. "I . . . I . . . I thought we were going to do this the right way," he stammered, and loosened his tie. "I trusted you. All my friends trust you. I thought we were going to do business together."

"Be calm," Salvatore soothed. "These are my two gold experts. They'll be doing the assay work back there in the van."

Larson looked relieved. "I'm sorry. I'm just . . . This is all new to me."

"How do my men find the gold?" Salvatore asked.

"They'll go down the hill until they come to a small stone-front dugout. The key to the lock is hanging from a nail under the eaves to the right-hand side of the door."

"Did you men hear that?" Salvatore called.

"We heard, Mister Salvatore," one of them answered as they started across the road.

"So, Roger, tell me more about these establishments you and your friends are going to be opening," Salvatore instructed. "We can have a good talk while we're waiting."

Larson droned on about the luxurious clubs he had invented in his mind, watching and waiting for the men to come back to report on their find.

Suddenly, one of them came running into sight, waving a gold bar in his hand. "Mister Salvatore," he shouted. "Look at this, and that ain't all."

Salvatore turned and started across the road to meet the man.

The man handed Salvatore the bar of gold and fought to catch his breath.

Salvatore hefted the bar, looked at it and smiled broadly. "This is nice. Damned nice," he said, as he looked at the Iron Cross and the numbers stamped into the soft gold metal. It was exactly as Roger Tompkins had described. "Are there eighteen bars down there?" His mind was doing mental calculations as to the profit from the gold.

"I don't know, we didn't take the time to count 'em, but wait," the man panted. "The gold bars are stacked on cases of *whiskey!*"

CHAPTER FIFTY-NINE

Guido Salvatore's face became blank. "What?"

"That little stone place, dug into the side of the hill, is full of cases of whiskey, too."

Salvatore spun and glared at Larson. "What kind of shit is this?" he demanded.

Larson raised his hands and shrugged. "You got me. When I arranged to have a place for you to look at the gold, they didn't tell me anything about any whiskey."

Salvatore clawed open his coat, yanked his pistol free, and pointed it at Larson's face.

"You," he shouted at the driver. "You keep a gun on this bastard until I get back. If he tries anything smart, don't kill him, shoot him in the leg. I want him alive to talk to him after I check this out!"

The driver pulled out a large automatic pistol, cocked it, and pushed it into Larson's back. "I've got him."

"Let's go," Salvatore shouted, and motioned to the trail across the road. "And keep an eye on that damned money. Lock it in the trunk of the car."

Larson grabbed his stomach and began to cough, gag, and retch as the two men crossed the road and disappeared from sight. "I've got ulcers and there's some medicine in my truck," he moaned. "Can we go get it?"

"No way," the driver answered, shaking his head and waving his pistol. "You ain't going anywhere near that truck until Mister

Salvatore gets back and says it's okay."

"Can I at least go over there across the road and sit by that big rock until this shit in my gut calms down?" He folded, falling to his knees, coughing and gagging. "I know I'm gonna puke."

"We'll go over there," the man answered and grabbed the suitcase of money. "Stand in the middle of the road until I tell you to move." He moved to the back of the car, pulled out a ring, and selected a key. "Face over that way," he ordered.

Larson heard him open and close the trunk, then felt the barrel of the man's pistol poked into his back.

"Move it."

Larson staggered across the road to the rock and flopped down beside it, continuing to make sounds of pain.

Guido Salvatore slid on the steep grassy slope, but managed to catch his balance as he reached the front of the dugout. He pushed into the room and waited for his eyes to adjust to the darkness. The other two men crowded in behind him. "Get out of the damned door," he ordered. "I need some light in here."

The men stepped into the room and stood beside the door.

Salvatore stepped to the pile of gold bars, lifted one, and hefted it to feel the weight. He smiled, but the smile immediately left his face as he looked at the cases of whiskey.

"What in the hell is this asshole trying to pull on me!" he shouted, pointing the gold bar at the stacks of wooden cases along the wall. Each was stenciled SUPERIOR RYE.

Louie Bergavin lowered the binoculars from his eyes and put his hands on the wooden T-handled plunger of the detonator. "Seen enough *Mister* Salvatore?" he asked and shoved down the handle.

The detonation of the dynamite was so fast that Salvatore and the two men never saw or heard the flash of the explosion when it hurled them back, against, and through the sandstone wall.

The last thing burned into Guido Salvatore's mind was the gold bar in his hand and the stacked cases of his stolen whiskey.

Bergavin swung the binoculars back to his eyes in time to see the rock walls on the front of the dugout erupt with a roar of flame and smoke. The roof seemed to hang in the air and then suddenly drop down into the space where the walls had been. With a loud *poof* the whiskey began to burn as blue-and-white flames engulfed the wooden remains of the building.

"What the hell was that?" the driver asked at the sound and turned to see a cloud of smoke rolling up into the sky. "Something blew up down there!"

"No shit, now put that pistol on the ground," Larson ordered the man, whose eyes widened with fear when he turned to see a short-barreled shotgun pointed at his gut.

The man gaped at him with open-mouthed wonder. "What . . . ?"

"It's a simple decision. You put the pistol on the ground, or I'll cut you in half," Larson growled as he cocked the hammers on the shotgun.

The man hesitated as if trying to decide what to do.

"Don't be stupid," Larson warned, waving the barrels of the shotgun.

The man nodded and uncocked the pistol with a shaking hand and dropped it to the ground.

"That's better. Now, let's go back to the car."

The man lowered his hands, and then as he turned he yanked another smaller pistol from his coat pocket.

The flash of fire and the burst of lead from the barrels of the shotgun lifted him in the air with a spray of crimson and unceremoniously dropped his torn body in the grass.

Larson waved at the cloud of gun smoke as it passed back

over him. "I was right. He was a stupid son-of-a-bitch." He lowered the shotgun, leaned it against the rock, turned, and walked down the hill toward the smoking remains of the dugout. The smell of the explosives and the sweet aroma of whiskey were almost overpowering as he got closer to the smoke and flames marking the site of his grandfather's building.

Louie Bergavin came trudging down from a nearby hill, swinging the detonator by the handle. "Damn, it smells like a distillery around here, or at least what's left of one."

"Yeah, that good quality whiskey burns well, doesn't it?" Larson agreed.

"Do you suppose we'll be able to find any of those gold bars?" Bergavin asked, looking around the area that was littered with cut sandstones, splintered wooden whiskey cases and brown broken glass. The shredded, grossly misshapen bodies of the three dead men were hardly recognizable. The dynamite had been placed behind the cases of whiskey and the explosion shattered the glass bottles into thousands of minute, razor sharp flying missiles that had the effect of pulverizing and shredding human flesh.

"Yeah, at least some of them," Larson answered. "I'm sure they're scattered over there in the woods and in the valley. That explosion wouldn't hurt them, but it sure as hell probably threw them a long way. A case of dynamite puts out one hell of a blast."

"Should we go look for some of the gold bars now or get the hell out of here?" Bergavin asked.

"Let's go up and get the vehicles moved back into the trees. Someone might stop. We'll come back down to look for the gold after we get them moved, and then see what we can do about the fire."

Larson and Bergavin scurried to the top of the hill. Both were relieved to look both ways and see no sign of traffic.

Larson pointed at the driver's crumpled body. "Let me get this guy moved over on the other side of the rock so he can't be seen from the road." He grabbed the dead man's wrists and dragged him behind the boulder. "Now I've gotta find his car keys." He leaned the shotgun against the rock before kneeling and rifling through the man's pockets. "Here they are," he said, holding up a ring of keys and grabbing up the shotgun. "I'll drive the car up behind the trees. You take the van. I hope the keys are in it. When you get out, be sure to wipe down the steering wheel and anything else you touch. We can't afford to leave any fingerprints."

They trotted across the road to the vehicles. Bergavin opened the door of the van and held his thumb up before sliding in and starting the engine.

Larson opened the car, slid behind the wheel, and pulled the door shut. He studied the keys, selected the one for the ignition, and started the engine. He drove a wide circle into the ditch and up the slight incline to the grove of trees. He glanced in the mirror and saw the van close behind him. When he reached the far side of the grove, he turned under a tree, shut off the engine, climbed out, and walked to the rear of the car. He selected a key, unlocked the trunk, lifted out the case of money, slammed the lid, and meticulously wiped the handle with his jacket sleeve.

Bergavin pulled the van in, turned off the engine, and climbed out. He dug a handkerchief out of his pocket and rubbed down the steering wheel and the door handle before kneeing the door shut.

"I'll get my truck and bring it back here," Larson said. "I'll hide the money down by the road someplace, and we can pick it up when we leave."

"Wait a minute," Bergavin said. "I'll go with you and on down to the dugout to start looking for the gold while you move your truck back here."

A few minutes later Larson came running down the hill. "Hey, Louie, where are you? We've gotta do something about the fire. I could see smoke from up by the road."

Bergavin stepped out of the trees and triumphantly held up a glittering gold bar in each hand. "I've found six of them so far." He continued forward and finally stopped and looked down at one of the mangled bodies. His cheeks suddenly bulged; he tossed aside the gold bars and slapped his hand over his mouth as he dashed back toward the trees. He returned momentarily, wiping his mouth with a handkerchief and looking rather sheepish. "I'm sorry. . . . I've seen dead men before, but never quite so mangled as those."

"Don't worry about it, Louie. The first time I saw torn-up men I did the same thing. As a matter of fact, it happened a lot more times before I got used to it."

Suddenly thunder rolled, lightning cracked, and the air was filled with the smell of fresh rain.

"Looks like we're getting some help fighting the fire," Bergavin commented as the first fat rain drops began to slap down. "Want to take cover in the trees or make a run for the cars?"

"Let's search more here in the immediate area. The cops won't be going into the trees very far when they're investigating this, but I'd hate to have them find a bar anyway. They'd tear this place apart looking for more. We'll pick a place and stash these six and any more we find. We've got to bring that other dead man down here too. Then I'm gonna walk around in the rain and get good'n wet," Larson said. "I'm in need of a bath anyway."

CHAPTER SIXTY

Half an hour later, Andy Larson and Louie Bergavin, each with his own thoughts, trudged silently up the hill in the pouring rain. They had moved the dead man from beside the road down the hill and deposited him unceremoniously beside the remains of the others at the ruins of the dugout. After a brief search, they found and hid ten gold bars in the base of an old oak tree nearby. The rain had extinguished enough of the fire so they felt it was no longer a problem. They agreed that at the rate it was raining, the fire would be out within an hour.

"I left the wire strung for the dynamite back there," Bergavin said, swinging the detonator by his side. "Nobody'll be able to identify it."

"I've still got those two other shotguns hidden around here," Larson said.

"That was a good plan to have three of them. You should have been able to get your hands on at least one when you needed it."

"Yeah, one's right over by that bush, and one's in the tree where my truck was parked."

"How are you, or *we*, going to report this one?" Bergavin asked.

"I think it's best to just let it alone," Larson answered. "It could be months before anybody stumbles on this, if they ever do. The longer it takes, the better when it happens. I should be well established in Montana, and you'll be making sparks fly in your shop. Let's get to the truck."

Minutes later they were splashing down the road toward Mandan.

"What're you gonna do about the bullet holes in your truck doors?" Bergavin asked. "They come in that side and go out over here."

"Yeah, and the seats have a couple of rips from slugs."

"How badly is the hood shot up?"

"Three or four holes, but it's not a problem. I've already picked up a hood and two doors at O'Brian's junkyard. I figure we can replace them at your shop in a couple of hours. Luckily, the windshield didn't get hit," Larson answered. "God, do you realize how hard we've become? There's four mangled bodies lying back there in the rain, and we're talking about fixing bullet holes in a damned truck."

"How much money's in this case?" Bergavin asked, lifting it from his lap.

"There's supposed to be thirty-five thousand dollars in there."

Bergavin whistled. "Damn, now what?"

"I don't know about you, but I don't want any of it. To me it's blood money."

"I agree. I don't care to have anything to do with it either."

"I'd thought about giving some of it to Billy's mother, but we'd have to come up with some sort of a story about the money and how we got it. Then yesterday I found out old man Herman at the lumberyard isn't such a bad guy after all."

"How's that?"

"He had a life insurance policy on Billy, made out to his mother."

"Damn, I thought he was just a cheap-ass old slave driver."

"Billy earned his money working for him all right," Larson agreed. "Can you believe it was a five thousand dollar policy?

He took a buck out of Billy's paycheck every two weeks to pay for it."

"Well, that's good. We won't have to worry about her anymore."

Larson took a deep breath and let it out slowly. "This whole thing is gonna haunt me 'til the day I die, Louie. We were just gonna steal a truckload of whiskey from the wops. That's all it was supposed to be, steal a damned truckload of illegal whiskey. We were being criminals against the criminals. At the time it was almost like a prank. Now I've had three good friends killed. . . . Hell, I don't even know for sure how many others have died because of that damned truckload of booze."

"You're beating yourself up again, Andy," Bergavin interrupted. "We were all in on this. We all agreed to do it. It's that damned gold caused all the problems."

Larson glanced at Bergavin. "That's exactly what I said. That *fucking* gold is *cursed.*"

Chapter Sixty-One

The next morning Andy Larson and Louie Bergavin met for breakfast at Rosie's.

"Damn, you look rough," Bergavin teased. "I guess you don't get much sleep when you're still on your honeymoon."

Larson glared at him over the edge of his coffee cup. "Your day'll come, asshole. I've seen the way you get all calf-eyed around Jean. It's just a matter of time before you slip a ring on her finger and make her an honest woman."

Bergavin grinned foolishly and nodded. "Yeah, I suppose you're right."

"I was up most of the night planning what to do with the money and here's my plan."

"Well, let's hear it."

"The State Children's Home in Fargo can always use money."

"You mean the orphanage?"

Larson's face was suddenly creased by a large grin. "Give a little thought to what an extra thirty-five thousand dollars could do for those kids."

"I *like* that!" Bergavin exclaimed. "That is one hell of a good plan."

"We'll box it up and mail it to them with a phony return address. There's no way to trace it. We put a note in that says it's conscience money for liquor dealings."

Bergavin nodded and grinned. "Now we've still got that *cursed* gold to deal with. How many Saint-Gaudens are left?"

"Eight hundred and forty. About a bag and a half."

Bergavin glanced around the room to see if anyone was listening to them. "And they are where?"

Larson smiled. "I buried them before I set the dynamite in the dugout. As you face the building, they're buried about three feet down in the back left-hand corner, opposite the fireplace."

"So they're buried in the ruins of the dugout."

"And that explosion should have packed the dirt to the consistency of concrete."

Bergavin studied his coffee cup before he slowly raised it and took a drink. "There's a fortune out on that hillside, isn't there, Andy?"

Larson nodded as he took a deep breath and let it out slowly. "It's . . . it's . . . a lot of money for you, if you ever need it, Louie. I'll never touch the stuff myself."

"Did we ever figure out who the gold belonged to in the first place?" Bergavin asked.

"No, and I don't believe it belonged to Salvatore. It had to belong to someone higher up on the criminal ladder. I did some research on it while I was still working. Salvatore was a middleman who put on a big front, but I don't think he had that kind of hard cash. Most of his money was floating on the books. There's a man in Minneapolis known as Kidd Cann. His real name is Isadore Blumfeld. Possibly him. Maybe Dutch Schultz? Hell, you can go on up the ladder to the top. It could have belonged to Al Capone himself, who knows?"

Two months later in Wolf Point, Montana, Deputy Sheriff Andy Larson leaned forward and lifted the receiver from his phone. "Deputy Larson."

"Larson, this is Morton County, Sheriff Wenzel."

"Hello, Brad, how are things back there in Mandan?"

"Fine, Andy, how's life up in Wolf Point?"

"Cop work is cop work. What can I do for you?"

"I understand you own some land north of Mandan along the river, is that right?"

"Yeah, about fifty acres my grandpa left to me. It's about twenty miles north on the Blackstead Ranch road. You wanna buy it? It's too hilly to farm, but you can probably run some decent cattle on it."

"When was the last time you were there?"

"Oh, I'm not sure. Maybe . . . At least a year, maybe a little less? Why?"

"You know about a little stone dugout in a hill up there?"

"I sure do. Gramps was damned proud of that place. He'd built it when he first homesteaded before the turn of the century. It was a great place for playing cowboys and Indians, and we used to camp and sleep in there when we were kids."

"Did you go in it the last time you were there?" Wenzel asked.

"Sure, the key to the padlock is hanging from the eaves on the right side of the door."

"Was there anything unusual about it?"

"Where are you going with this line of questions, Brad? I'm a cop. Just come out and ask me what you want to know. Stop your damned dancing around."

"The place has been destroyed."

"Oh, no . . . Did somebody set fire to it? There wasn't a lot to burn."

"No, it was dynamited. Did you keep any dynamite in there?"

"No, there was a table and couple of chairs. A kerosene lamp or two. Bunk beds along the left wall. Some tin dishes, knives, forks and spoons on a shelf and a wash pan hanging under it. That's about all I can remember. A coffee pot hanging in the fireplace, but I'm damn sure there wasn't any dynamite. When did it happen?"

"Did you see any booze in there?"

"Booze?"

"Yeah, like forty or fifty cases."

"Okay, who put you up to this?" Larson demanded and began to chuckle. "You had me going for a while, but it's not funny anymore. Wouldn't I have noticed *forty* or *fifty* cases of liquor? Was it Torkelson? Who was it?"

"I'm serious about this, Larson. A couple of pheasant hunters found a fancy car and a van hidden in back of a grove of trees up there the other day. It looks like they'd been there for quite a while, and when they got to town they reported it. We went out and searched the area. That's when we found the remains of four men and the blown-up building. The place is littered with shattered glass and the remains of wooden whiskey cases."

"You are serious now."

"We've talked to some people who saw buzzards a while back, but they figured it was just a dead cow or something, so they didn't report it. Between the coyotes, the buzzards and other meat eaters, there wasn't a lot left for identification purposes, but we found out who it is. The fancy car gave us the main clue."

"So who is it?"

"A small time gangster and bootlegger from Minot, named Guido Salvatore. He's been missing for a couple of months, but in his business it's one of the risks he took. People in that line of work have tried to swim a river or a lake with more chain than they should try to carry. Sometimes they've even taken to wearing concrete overshoes."

"And a lot of times, they're never found," Larson interrupted. "You're preaching to the choir, Brad. I'm a cop, remember?"

"Yeah, I'm sorry," Wenzel apologized. "I got carried away. I wanted you to know about it. From the looks of it, it was some sort of a gang hit. What with the explosives and the liquor. The old dugout is pretty much gone."

"It's a damned shame. Gramps was always proud of that place. Thanks, Brad, I'll stop in to see you the next time I'm down there. I'd appreciate it if you'd keep me informed on anything new. Good-bye," Larson said, and hung up the phone. *He didn't mention anything about finding any gold, so I guess that's safe. I'd better call Louie.*

Andy Larson pushed into a phone booth and put some coins on the shelf under the phone. He flipped open a small book, dialed the operator, gave her the long-distance number, and waited for her to tell him how much money to deposit. After he dropped the coins in, he waited for the connection to be completed. "Louie, this is Andy. Here's the number in this phone booth. Go to a pay phone and call me back. I'll be waiting."

Minutes later the phone rang, and Larson lifted the receiver. "Hello, Louie, I just got a call from Sheriff Wenzel. They found the bodies of Salvatore and the others yesterday, but they don't have anything to go on. They're sure it's a gang hit, so I'd say we're in the clear. He didn't mention anything about any gold, so I guess it'll stay hidden."

"That's fine, Andy," Bergavin agreed. "It was in the papers this morning, and I was gonna call you tonight. I've gotta get back to work. Tell Becky hi from me. Bye."

Larson hung up the receiver and gave a sigh of relief. *That stupid idea of stealing a truckload of whiskey sure changed your life, Andy, old boy. It cost the lives of friends and enemies. I sure as hell hope you've learned some lessons and will be a better lawman because of it.* He scooped up his coins, dropped them in a pocket and pushed out of the phone booth to blink at the sun. *Time to go make life miserable for the bad guys.*

EPILOGUE

April 1983

Bismarck Tribune (AP). District Judge Clement Sands issued a ruling today on the gold bars found in Easter baskets left at ten small local churches last week. The pastors of the churches involved, each holding a gold bar, flanked the judge as he announced his decision. "I marvel at the brilliance of the gold bars found in the Easter baskets left at the altars of these churches," Sands began. "This is the kind of situation that makes me want to believe in the Easter Bunny," he joked. "My study of the ingots indicates the probability of them being war plunder from the First World War. Each of the bars has the indentation of a crude Iron Cross, the weight in kilograms and the number nineteen-eighteen, as a possible date, stamped into the soft metal. These things all point to the Great War. Sixty-five years is well over the statute of limitations and there is no real proof of ownership of the items. The bars weigh approximately ten pounds apiece, and the market value of gold today is three hundred and eighty dollars an ounce. That gives these bars a value of a little over forty-five thousand dollars each. I find no reason these bars of gold should not become the property of the churches where the baskets were bestowed, and therefore they may do with them as they deem fit. Whether you see this as a gift from God or the Easter Bunny, it is a thing of divine proportions. I'm sure the money will be put to good use."

Andy Larson's thick white hair ruffled in the light spring

breeze as he finished reading the newspaper story, folded the paper, and dropped it into a trash bin by the entrance to the Saint Mary's cemetery where he had been visiting his good friend, Louie Bergavin, and his own dear departed wife, Becky. He had a smile on his face that Becky had often referred to as that *you've-been-up-to-something-grin.* He wiped at the corner of an eye, knuckled his great, white walrus mustache, and dug his good luck piece from a pocket. "I think the curse of that gold has now been lifted," he said softly, as he pulled the cane from under his arm and limped off down the street, flipping high in the air and catching a well-worn Saint-Gaudens twenty-dollar gold piece. He began to whistle and then broke into song, *"Mademoiselle from Armentieres, parlez-vous? Mademoiselle from . . ."*

ABOUT THE AUTHOR

Mike Thompson is an award-winning photographer and writer. He retired from the government where he tested explosives and was curator of an Army museum. He is a Vietnam veteran (1966–67) with a military career spanning thirty-six years, including Air Force, Army, Army Reserves and National Guard. Mike, his wife, Ruthie, and cats, Rosie and Daisy, live on the Laughing Horse Ranch, Land and Cattle Company, San Angelo, Texas. He has owned several businesses, worked as an actor, carpenter, bartender, oil landman, raised horses and done many other things while trying to decide what he's going to be if he grows up. Today he writes, collects cowboy gear and owns a toy company, "The Legendary Texas Jackhorn."